Can't Help Loving You

Boulder Bodyguards Book 3

Nika Rhone

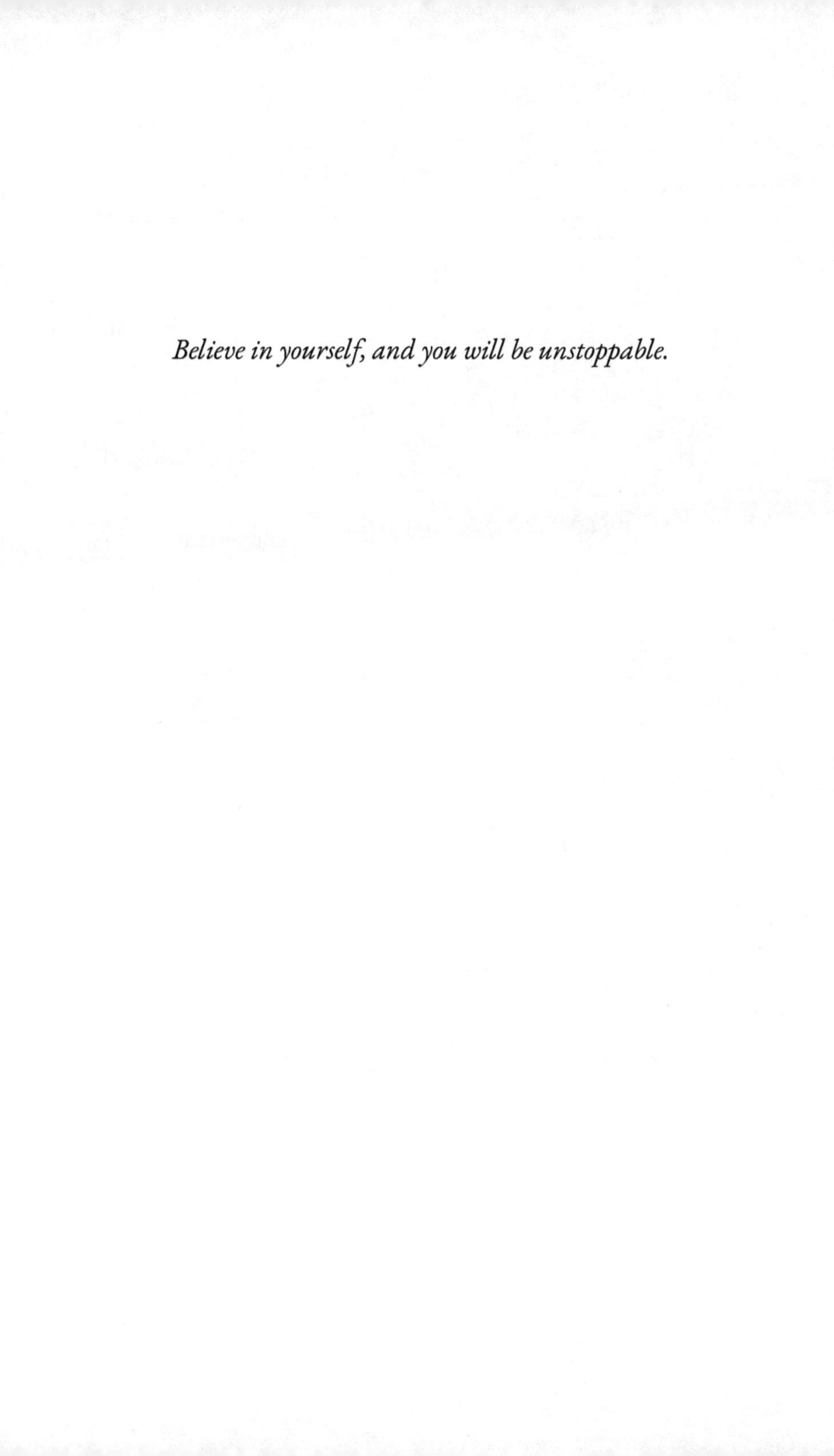

Believe in yourself, and you will be unstoppable.

Chapter 1

"Are you *freaking* kidding me?"

Lillian Beaumont stood in the parking lot and stared in utter disbelief. Tucked snug in its back corner space, her poor little turquoise Mini Cooper listed to one side like a drunken frat boy after an all-night kegger. She wanted to cry.

Or scream.

Parking in the very back corner of the lot behind the art gallery where she worked was supposed to keep her car safe from any more dings and scratches. And she ended up with a flat instead?

Fate, you're one twisted snarky bitch.

Hands clenched into fists, she walked to the driver's side for a closer look. It was a good thing there were no customers around, because the string of curses that popped out of her mouth was decidedly salty.

Not just one flat tire, but two. Front and rear.

"Great. Now I can't just get Peter to come over and change it for me."

Her twin didn't live too far away, and she could have guilted him into it, no problem. But she didn't need a fancy business degree to know two flats and one spare equaled totally screwed.

The urge to scream resurged.

She squelched it and pulled out her phone instead. Calling the garage that had done the bodywork on the Cooper the previous month, she crossed her fingers. Being late on a Saturday afternoon, there was a good chance they'd already closed for the day. She could feel her luck dripping away with every ring that went unanswered.

"Come on, *please* be there."

The gallery was in a good area of downtown Boulder, but she still didn't want to leave her car there all weekend. Not to mention Felix would bitch about her taking up a parking spot a customer could be using.

Relief sang through her when someone finally picked up.

After she explained the problem, Milo assured her one of his guys would come and get the car on a flatbed, but it might not be for an hour or more. Which would be after he closed.

"I'd stay late to get it done for you tonight if I could, but I don't have the right tires in stock. I can get them first thing Monday morning, though."

Which meant she'd be without her car until then.

Damn.

"That's fine. Thanks, Milo. I'll leave the key at the front desk of the gallery."

Cursing whatever bad karmic car juju she seemed to have manifested lately, Lillian slipped her phone back into her bag, then got into the car to push the driver's seat back. The Cooper was small enough to be almost perfect for her petite five-foot-two frame, but she still had to drive with the seat all the way forward. Anyone else would kneecap themselves on the steering column while getting in if she didn't adjust it back first.

A fun fact discovered the first time Peter had tried to drive it. Since he'd been making fun of her new "clown car" at the time, she hadn't been too upset to see him limping for a few days.

Checking the time, she pulled up the rideshare app on her phone and ordered herself a ride home. After making sure there was nothing in the car she needed to take with her, she locked it and trudged back into the gallery.

Bernice glanced up from behind the reception desk, customer-ready smile in place as Lillian pushed the etched glass door open. The smile eroded to a frown, her short bob of platinum hair with its signature chunk of purple swaying as she cocked her head in confusion.

"Forget something?"

"Oh, if only." She held out her key fob. "There's a tow truck coming, but it may be a while, so I told them I'd leave this with you."

"What's wrong with your car?"

"A double flat."

Bernice's mauve lips parted in an O of disbelief. "Shut up, no way!"

Lillian's smile felt tight on her face. "Only me, right?" She waggled the fob.

Bernice took it with a nod. "Oh, right. Sure, no problem at all, as long as they come before closing."

"They should, but if they don't, just text me and leave it in your desk. I'll have to swing back up and wait for them to get here." It wasn't until she said it that she remembered she wouldn't have a car to swing by with.

She suppressed a growl. This was really going to suck.

Depositing the key fob in the drawer, Bernice asked, "Want me to call you an Uber?" The phone that was like another appendage was already in her other hand.

"I have one coming, thanks."

She was about to take a seat and wait when it dawned on her this moment of supreme suckage might actually be a golden opportunity in disguise. There had been a small worm of suspicion digging into her brain for the past few weeks. Coming back to the gallery unexpectedly might just be her chance to see if she was imagining things or not.

Turning, she strode deeper into the gallery. "Be right back."

"Wait, where are you going?"

"I need to check something."

"But...what about your ride?"

"I'll only be a minute."

She liked Bernice, she really did. But she'd learned the hard way anything that went in the girl's ears was bound to come back out her mouth again at some point.

Usually to the wrong person.

Like the one time Lillian had vented her annoyance over the way a show for a local artist was handled, and she'd been called on the carpet by her boss a few days later about her "unprofessional attitude." As an assistant manager in his gallery, Felix had opined in his usual bombastic way, he expected more of her than that.

Fair enough. Too bad he didn't seem to "expect more" of his *other* assistant manager. The one whose mediocre efforts were the reason the show had done so poorly in the first place.

But there was something about Roman Reynolds that always caused Felix to turn a blind eye. Time and again he provided subpar performance, and time and again Felix just let it slide.

Roman wanted to half-ass doing his job? Fine. Felix wanted to ignore it? Also fine. He was the boss. But when said half-assness affected other people? Not fine by a mile. It only took one bad show to tank a newly emerging artist's career. Roman knew that.

He just didn't seem to care.

Frustrated didn't come close to how Lillian felt about it.

Taking a deep breath, she climbed the floating steel staircase to the hallway which hung like a catwalk above the open concept gallery. She loved everything about the airy, modern design of the space.

Except this one part.

Keeping her eyes focused straight ahead helped. But the small ball of anxiety that always settled in her chest as she made the climb to the offices appeared right on cue the minute her feet left solid ground. In the logical part of her brain, she knew the industrial metal stair, railing, and cable system wouldn't suddenly rip free of its moorings and collapse and kill her.

Her acrophobic lizard brain wasn't buying it.

Hugging the wall as much as possible along the catwalk, she opened the door to the office she shared with Roman with a sigh of relief. Which turned into a muffled squeak of surprise as she nearly walked straight into the man who was about to walk out.

Speak of the devil.

"Roman." Adopting the bland tone she used whenever they had to deal with one another, Lillian brushed past him. Her nose wrinkled at the sharp scent of his cologne.

"I thought you left."

Typical Roman. Normally he wore a thin veil of civility toward her in case there was someone around to notice. But since Felix wasn't in the building, and they were out of earshot of any customers and Bernice, he didn't even bother pretending.

Resisting the urge to say something snarky, she shrugged as she sat at her desk.

Without having to pull out the chair.

The one she knew she'd pushed in before she'd left a short time ago.

She gave him a direct look. "I forgot something."

Roman stared at her for a long minute, as though trying to intimidate her into saying more.

Pu-lease.

She had three brothers. She'd been winning staring contests since she was six. With men much more imposing than Roman and his carefully groomed almost-beard, tousled dark blond hair, and silly hipster glasses.

Some women might consider him attractive—it was obvious Bernice did—but the pretty package was no more than a thin veneer hiding the unpleasant person lurking inside. It just took some people longer to see through the mask than others.

As she'd known he would, Roman broke first.

"I have work to do." With a final glare, he left, leaving the door open on his way out.

Asshole.

She placed her fingertips on the top of her desk and studied it with a critical eye. Everything *looked* undisturbed, but...was the stack of invoices in the in-basket a little messier than she'd left them? Was the smell of his noxious cologne stronger here than it should have been if he'd been sitting at his own desk across the room?

Or was she just being paranoid?

Maybe she hadn't pushed her chair in all the way under the desk like she'd thought. She *had* been in a hurry to leave. And it wasn't as though there was anything to steal in her desk. Except maybe her client list, which was stored on her tablet, safe from prying, perfidious eyes with their trendy little glasses.

She shook her head in disgust. "He's making me nutso."

And yet...that worm of suspicion still twisted in her brain. She'd had an odd feeling about Roman since the first day he'd been hired. It was more than a simple clash of personalities or work ethics. There was something about him that was...off. Wrong. And it bugged the hell out of her.

When she opened the bottom drawer, her attention was immediately caught by the file folder not sitting flush with the rest, one corner jutting up. As though someone had shoved it back into place with haste.

Feeling the first whisper of true unease, she pulled it out. It was the file for an upcoming show she was handling. The artist they were showcasing was already something of a big deal in Aspen. It had been a bit of a coup for her to get him to sign with the Landis Gallery, since an equally prestigious gallery in Denver had also been vying for his work.

It only took flipping through a few pages to know she'd been right. She had a very specific order in which she kept things when she was planning a show. Always. Every time. An anal-retentive attention to detail which would have surprised the hell out of her friends, who considered her a bit of a loose cannon when it came to planning and follow-through.

And they weren't wrong. She did tend to hare off on one thing while still in the middle of another. Her squirrel brain—which often ran circles around her lizard brain—was always chasing the next shiny thing.

Which was why she was so meticulous about her work. If everything had a proper place, the less chance she had to screw up.

And things weren't in their proper place. Not so much that anyone besides her would notice the order of notes, contracts, and invoices had been changed. But she was certain. Someone had gone through the file.

Roman is a dead man.

Except...she had no proof of anything nefarious.

Sagging back in the chair, Lillian stared at the manila folder in frustration. If she went to Felix with her suspicions, he'd say that as an assistant manager, Roman had every right to refer to a file concerning a gallery event. And it was true.

If that was all he'd been doing.

She didn't believe that for a minute. The man was up to something, she could feel it. She didn't know what. But she would.

She checked her phone. Her ride would be there in like two minutes.

Fingers shaking with silent rage, she called the one person she not only knew she could share her suspicions with, but who might actually be able to help. Her best friend happened to be married to a man who knew a thing or two about investigating sneaky people.

Thea picked up on the third ring. "Hey, girl! What's up?"

"Hi, T," Lillian said, talking fast before she changed her mind. "I was wondering if maybe I could come over tonight and talk to you about something." Her fingers drummed on top of the file in front of her. "I think I might have a problem."

Houston, we have a problem.

Standing in front of the elevator doors, Rafael Delgado wanted to both curse and cheer as the woman he'd spent the last six months doing his best to avoid strode into the lobby of their apartment building. A petite little package of dynamite, with short, brown hair and dark chocolate eyes that were sexy as hell, he'd been drawn to Lillian Beaumont from the day he first met her. She probably didn't even remember it, but the moment had been carved into his brain with disturbing clarity.

It wasn't every day you got a boner the size of Pikes Peak when your friend introduced you to his sister. While standing in a room filled with her entire family. Including her three very large, very overprotective brothers. One of whom carried a gun.

Not one of his better days.

Almost two years later, he still had the same visceral reaction every time he saw her. Which was why he avoided it whenever possible. Not an easy task, since they now lived in the same building, but he made it work.

Mostly by having memorized her schedule.

A little stalkerish, maybe, but desperate times.

Since today was Saturday, she should have been home from her job at the snooty little gallery where she played at working almost an hour ago. So, what the hell was she doing strutting into the lobby now in that short little skirt and heels that stopped just shy of being fuck-me height, when she should be tucked away safe and snug in her top-floor apartment, out of his way?

Damn woman.

Lillian greeted him with a smile as she came to stand in front of the elevator beside him. "Hi, Rafe."

"Hey, Lillian." Two seconds in her presence, and his body was already sitting up to stretch and take notice. Too much longer, and they'd have liftoff.

He considered punching the call button again in the vain hope it would make the damn thing appear faster, but that would only make him look desperate. He shifted his stance to take the weight off his left leg, switching the bag of takeout from one arm to the other as he did.

Catching her noticing, he blurted out the first thing that came to mind to keep her from commenting. "Shouldn't you be home already?"

Oh, yeah. Real smooth, jackass.

Lillian quirked her little eyebrow at him. The one with the silver barbell through it that drove him wild, because it made him wonder what *else* on her body might also be pierced. Although the answer was probably nothing. She liked to play at being a rebel, the way she played at everything else in life. But beneath the wild child façade was nothing but wholesome heiress goodness.

That didn't stop him from fantasizing about it, though. Even when he reminded himself who she was and why he shouldn't be thinking about any of her body parts, pierced or not.

I am such a perv.

"I had car trouble." The small smile that had tipped her lips disappeared.

Just like that, his thoughts shifted from lascivious to concerned. "Everything okay?"

"Yeah, just a flat. I had to call the garage, and then, well, other stuff came up that took longer than I planned." She glanced at her watch.

"Late for a date?" Damn, why had he said that?

Pursing her ruby red lips, Lillian replied, "Maybe I am."

Oh, the dirty thoughts those luscious lips inspired.

Swallowing hard, he turned and glared at the still-closed elevator doors. "Why is this stupid thing taking so long?" Because if he didn't get away from her soon, there'd be no way he could hide his body's growing reaction to her.

She looked at the elevator, then at him, before reaching out, one finger extended, and very deliberately pushed the call button. There was an immediate *ding*, and the doors slid open.

Son of a bitch.

He could literally feel her waiting for him to say something.

Anything.

Finally, right before the doors started to close again, she stepped into the elevator, turned, and cocked her head in question.

Caught between being amused at his own expense and embarrassed as hell over being so distracted by her entrance he'd never pushed the damn button, Rafe joined her. He watched in silence as she ran her security card through the reader, then pushed the buttons for both of their floors.

As soon as the doors slid shut, he could smell her. The sweet and spicy scent that always seemed to follow her wrapped around him, intoxicating him, when all he should have been able to smell was the Chinese food in the sack he held.

This was worse than thinking about the piercings. Being enclosed in the small space with her, breathing her in. It wreaked havoc with his already questionable control. Even worse was knowing she was staring at him. Studying him. Not laughing at him, exactly, but he could sense her amusement even though she never said a word.

The rare occasions they bumped into each other were always like this. Him trying to play it cool, and doing something to make an utter ass out of himself instead.

It was high school and Debbie Waterhouse all over again.

At the third floor, the elevator stopped and opened. As he stepped out, the coward in him wanted to walk away without a word. The stupid in him made him say, "Enjoy your date."

Moron.

"I always do."

The suggestive tone in her voice made him look back as the doors were closing.

Which was probably her intent. She blew him a ruby-red kiss just before the silver doors met, blocking her from sight and leaving him staring at a distorted reflection of himself standing there like an idiot.

"Damn woman."

He pulled his keys from his pocket as he stomped down the beige-carpeted hallway. Why did she always have to affect him like that? And why did he let her? God knows he'd tried sticking her into a box labeled "off-limits" and forgetting about her, but that only worked when she wasn't around. As soon as they were face-to-face like that, *wham!* He lost twenty IQ points and his body started pumping out testosterone like it was prom night.

Every. Single. Time.

Maybe he should consider moving.

Even as he thought it, he knew that wasn't the answer. And not just because he still had six months left on his lease. He *liked* living here. The building, the apartment, the neighbors, the just-out-of-downtown location. It was a sweet set-up. With only four apartments on each of the four floors in the converted warehouse, it was quiet, comfortable, and best of all, affordable.

He wasn't about to let a pixie-sized troublemaker screw up his good thing.

Of course, she was the reason he had the good thing in the first place.

Buried under several layers of corporate holding companies, the actual owner of the building was Rupert Beaumont, Lillian's father. The millionaire investment wizard had quietly purchased it not long after she moved in a little over a year ago. Then he'd set about making security upgrades and other improvements to keep his little rebel both safe and happy.

Not that it was common knowledge who their landlord was. Rafe only found out because he'd been suspicious about the low rent when his friend Pete Beaumont had told him about the place. Pete had come clean about how his dad liked the idea of having a cop living in the building, and was willing to drastically drop the price to make it happen.

And what Rupert Beaumont wanted, he usually got.

Rafe wasn't one to trade favors. Especially when it came to his job. But since nothing was being asked of him except to live there, to be an extra, invisible layer of security for the building—which would be true no matter where he lived—it had seemed like a no-brainer.

What he hadn't taken into account was how hard it was going to be to occupy the same space as the object of his forbidden lust. Very, very hard.

Kind of like he was now.

"Damn woman," Rafe muttered again as he dropped his keys on the small table inside the apartment door.

"What woman?" On the couch, his brother Cristiano looked up from the book he'd had his face buried in all week, cramming for an upcoming test at culinary school. "And what took you so long? I'm starving."

Depositing the takeout bag on the kitchen table, Rafe went to the cabinet to get plates and napkins. "I had to wait for the elevator." Close enough to the truth.

Cris pulled the white cardboard containers out of the bag, sniffing each as he opened them with the appreciation of a true foodie.

"I notice you didn't answer the first question, so I'm gonna guess you're talking about the sexy lady from upstairs." He grinned at the dirty look Rafe shot him. "Come on, *hermano*. She's the only woman I know who can make you angry and horny at the same time." He broke apart one set of chopsticks, plucked out a piece of spicy chicken, and popped it into his mouth. A groan of approval rumbled from his throat.

Rafe set down the plates and grabbed his share of the food before his brother inhaled it all.

"Angry, yes."

Horny, also yes. How could he not be?

That skirt. Those heels. *Those lips.* Not to mention she'd been wearing another of those silky blouses she seemed to love so much. The kind that looked all slippery and soft as it hugged her perfect breasts, showing off a hint of cleavage. Just enough to get his motor revving.

Even when she wasn't even in the same room as him, it would seem.

He shifted, trying to adjust things that were suddenly pinching.

Yup. Definitely a perv.

"The only reason she gets you so angry is because you want her and you won't let yourself have her."

"I don't want her," Rafe gritted out as he stabbed at a dumpling.

Cris opened his eyes wide and innocent looking. "So, you wouldn't mind if I asked her out for drinks?"

The chopsticks paused halfway to Rafe's mouth. He stared at his baby brother, so similar to him in looks with his wavy black hair and piercing green eyes that people often mistook them for twins. "Try it and die."

"But you don't want her." Cris got up and went to the fridge. "Right."

"Her brother—"

"Spare me the 'she's my friend's sister' excuse." Cris thumped a bottle of beer down in front of Rafe. "What would you do if Pete wanted to date either Bria or Bella?"

"String him up by his balls." It would be the same no matter who was interested in their little sisters. No man was good enough for them.

"And after you got past that part?" When he didn't immediately reply, Cris sighed. "He wouldn't be your friend if he was a dick, and the girls have to be able to date *someone*, so why not someone you already know and like?"

"The girls" were nineteen and twenty-one, and both would have their brothers' nuts in a vise if they ever heard them discussing who they'd be "allowed" to date. But that didn't stop either Rafe or Cris, or their older brother Eduardo, from sticking their collective big brother noses where they weren't wanted.

It was what the Delgados did. Stuck together as a family, no matter what.

"Okay, fine. *Hypothetically*, I guess it wouldn't be too terrible if Pete dated one of them." After Rafe had laid down the law about how she was to be treated with the utmost respect, of course.

"So, hypothetically, he'd be okay with you dating his sister for the same reason."

Damn the little burst of excitement that shot straight from his chest to his groin at the thought. Not good. Without the protective layer of his friendship with Pete keeping Lillian in her little off-limits box, he might just be tempted to do something stupid.

"It's a moot point, anyway. She's not my type."

Cris's jaw almost hit the table. "Not your type? Not your *type*?" He shook his head. "I'm sorry, would that be the 'sexy, hot as hell' type, or the 'conveniently right upstairs whenever you want her' type?"

"Try the 'more money than God' type."

"Are you kidding me? That's the best you've got? She's rich, so she's not worth your time?"

"More like I'm not worth hers." He regretted the words the second they were out. "Look, I'll admit she's hot. I'm not blind." Or dead. Because only a dead man wouldn't react to the sensuality that seemed to roll off her in unrelenting waves. "Anyway, it's not about the money. It's about her using it to skim along life without making any serious commitments."

"She has a job, doesn't she?"

"Yeah, but according to her brother, she only took it to avoid getting a real job at their father's investment firm like she was supposed to." While spending the rest of her time going out to clubs and parties and basically living it up with the eclectic group of friends she always seemed to surround herself with.

Not that he was keeping tabs on her or anything.

"So? Not everyone wants to go into the family business."

Direct hit.

Everyone in the Delgado brood had found a place in their parents' successful Cuban-American restaurant. Everyone except Rafe. He'd spent a lot of time there growing up, but never felt the pull to cook and create the way his siblings did. His parents had been disappointed by his decision, but they'd supported him in it.

While he knew for a fact Lillian's family didn't.

No. I am not going to feel sorry for the poor little rich girl.

"You know, it doesn't even matter. I've got too much going on right now to think about getting involved with anyone, even if they weren't as high maintenance as Lillian Beaumont. I need to stay focused and on-goal." With that depressing reminder, Rafe swallowed the last of his beer.

He contemplated getting a second, but the dull ache in his leg dissuaded him. It was likely going to be one of those nights where he didn't get any sleep without the help of the pain meds he hated taking. So he got another beer for Cris and a bottle of water for himself instead.

A fact his nosy little brother was quick to pick up on.

Their sisters weren't the only ones with family getting all up in their business.

"You overdid it at physical therapy again."

"No pain, no gain." Rafe ignored the disgusted grunt his brother gave as commentary. "I know my limits."

"And you always have to push right past them."

True. But if he didn't work a little harder every time, he wasn't going to improve. And if he didn't improve, he wouldn't pass the mandatory physical to be reinstated to the department. And if he didn't pass the physical...

Then he didn't know what the hell would happen. Because if he wasn't allowed to go back to being a cop, he had no idea what—or who—he was supposed to be.

Chapter 2

"Don't you think you're overreacting just a little?"

Shock and disbelief body-slammed Lillian as she stared across the table at her supposed best friend in the world.

"Are you serious? Weren't you listening to what I said?"

"I was listening." Tucking her long chestnut curls behind one ear, Thea Fordham-Doyle leaned her chin on her hand as she looked back at Lillian. Sympathy shone from the deep blue eyes Lillian had always been jealous of. Depending on Thea's mood, the shade could range from warm tropic waters to frigid arctic ice, while her own brown eyes were always just...brown.

Boring.

And if there was one thing Lillian hated to be, it was boring.

She also hated not having her friend jump immediately to her defense after she'd outlined the many, *many* grievances she had against the jerk who was the bane of her professional existence.

The bane of her private existence was a matter she hadn't even started on yet. Not that Thea hadn't already heard her go on about her broody, too-sexy-for-anyone's-good neighbor a time or two.

Or ten.

"Then how can you say I'm overreacting? Roman Reynolds is a menace! He's lousy at his job, and he's out to make me look bad so he can look better by comparison. He went through my desk—"

"You think," Thea said.

"—and my files—"

"You think."

"—and *I think*"—she shot Thea a scowl—"I need to make sure he hasn't been doing anything else nefarious that could cause any problems. For me or the gallery."

"You see." Thea sat back in her seat and swiped her hand through the air. "That, right there. *That* would be the overreacting part. Nefarious, Lil? Seriously?"

She ran her finger around the rim of her wineglass and shrugged. "Nefarious. Devious. Sneaky, scheming, underhanded...pick a word. The point is, I don't trust him."

"Which sounds like a smart decision." Brennan Doyle, Thea's husband of a whole four and a half months, spoke for the first time since Lillian had launched into her recitation of her work woes.

To be honest, he'd been so still and quiet, she'd had almost forgotten he was there. It was all those years of fading into the background as a bodyguard. Doyle had put his time in the Marines to good use in the security career he'd transitioned into, and it was that expertise she was hoping to tap into now.

"See, Doyle believes me."

Thea bolted upright, outrage on her face. "I never said I didn't believe you! I just said you were being a little melodramatic about it. Which you were."

She was.

But after the day she'd had, Lillian was pretty sure she deserved to be a little over the top. Besides, that was kind of her thing. Her place in the trio of friends who had been together since middle school. The Royal Court, their security details had dubbed them, after their codenames. Three heiresses who shouldn't have clicked, but had.

Thea was the Lady, everyone's sounding board and voice of reason. Amelia Westlake was the quiet little Princess, the one they all did their best to protect from her dragon of a mother. And to Lillian had fallen the mantle of being their Queen Bee, the one who was always in motion, buzzing from one thought or plan to another and dragging the other two along in her wake, willing or not.

Growing up the lone girl in a houseful of big, loud, hell-raising brothers, she'd learned fast she needed to be just as loud and adventurous so as to not get lost in the crowd. And a lot more creative. Being the smallest didn't mean she couldn't take care of herself.

Something she still struggled to prove to her brothers, and father, to this day.

Which was why she needed to resolve her problems at work without asking for their help. Especially after what had happened last year. One small sign of trouble now, and they'd be hovering over her like a bunch of overprotective Neanderthals.

Again.

"If you're so certain Roman went through your files, then you should say something to your boss," Thea said.

Lillian sighed.

And yes, it was a dramatic one.

"I can't. Strictly speaking, Roman didn't do anything wrong, even if he did go through them. Which he did." She couldn't help but emphasize that fact. She knew what she knew. "They're about gallery clients and events, which means he has the right to look at them any time he wants, the same way I could look at any of the files in his desk. It's why the drawers aren't locked."

"Then why are you getting so upset?" Thea sounded confused.

How could she not get it?

"Because there was no *reason* for him to be looking at anything." And because she felt violated by someone poking through her things. Just like last time. Thea of all people should have figured that out.

"T, he *touched* my *stuff*." She hated that she couldn't keep the whine out of the words.

At last, understanding bloomed in her friend's expression. But it didn't give her the comfort she'd thought it would. It only made the sick feeling in the pit of her stomach cramp even tighter thanks to the pity accompanying the look.

Damn it, maybe she *was* overreacting. Maybe this had nothing to do with Roman, and everything to do with the other issues she clearly hadn't worked all the way through yet.

She knew which option her therapist would pick.

"Was anything missing from the file?" Doyle asked.

Lillian was pretty sure he was aware of everything that had happened at her parents' estate a year and a half ago. But unlike his wife, Doyle's demeanor held not one drop of pity. It was one-hundred percent professional, and helped drag her away from her downward spiral of doubt. She could kiss him.

"No, nothing."

"Added?"

"No."

"Had anything been altered?"

That one she had to think about. "I don't think so, but you can bet I'll be double checking first thing tomorrow."

"You said the file was for an upcoming event. What could go wrong that would make the evening a disaster for you?"

Lillian gave a half-hearted laugh. "What couldn't?" She gave it some thought. "Well, if nobody showed up, obviously. But we already sent out the invitations." She'd gone to the post office with them herself, not trusting them to the mail basket on Bernice's desk where Roman could get his sticky fingers on them.

Paranoid much, Lil?

"What else?" Doyle prompted.

"Well, there's a specific wine Felix always insists on serving. He considers it good luck because he was drinking it the night he met his current wife. It's been the only vintage served at the gallery ever since. Anything else would be..." She gave a theatrical shudder. "*Trés horrible.*"

Doyle's lips twitched. "Anything else?"

"Food, of course. If the food sucks, so will the sales."

"You're kidding."

"Nope. And without the free food, some people wouldn't even show up. Some art collectors can be a little strange and fickle, while others are just straight-up eccentric. I have one client who refuses to buy a painting with any red in it. She claims it's too angry, and disturbs the feng shui in her home. Do you know how hard it is to find paintings without a single drop of red anywhere?"

She caught the look on Doyle's face and waggled a finger at him.

"Don't go getting all judgey. You've got your own set of wackadoos in your line of work. What about the woman who insisted her bodyguard had to sleep in the same bed as her because she was afraid of being kidnapped in the middle of the night?"

Doyle shot an exasperated look at Thea, who smiled sweetly back without a hint of remorse.

Lillian repressed a snort. Yeah, like T wasn't going to share a juicy story like that with her friends. He had to know his wife better than that.

He looked skyward and sighed.

"Point taken. And for the record, we did *not* sign her as a client."

"I'm sure she was disappointed." Because she'd seen some of the bodyguards on Praetorian Security's payroll, and they were pretty yummylicious.

Doyle looked like he was going to say something, then shook his head and got his game face back on. "Did any of the pages you felt weren't in the order you left them have to do with the things that could make or break the showing?"

She closed her eyes and pictured the file as she'd been looking through it earlier. Her brain worked in a very visual way, so her hands moved in front of her, mimicking the motion of turning pages as she thought back to each and every invoice and contract she'd looked at. As she did, her suspicions Roman had been up to no good solidified into certainty.

Her eyes popped open. "Every one of them. The wine. The food. The rental company we use for the tables, chairs, plates. That slimy bastard is trying to sabotage my show!"

"Or to learn the right way to do it so he doesn't screw up the next time he puts one together." Thea gave an apologetic shrug when Lillian glared at her. "Playing devil's advocate here, but you have to admit it's a possibility, given the way you said he handled the last one he did."

That was Thea, always looking for the good in people.

But damn, she had a point. Roman *might* have realized he'd missed the bar when it came to his organizational skills. And he *might* have wanted to find a way to improve before Felix noticed his little pet wasn't all he pretended to be. And he *definitely* would want to do it in a way that didn't include needing to ask Lillian for help.

But in order for any of that to be true, it would mean Roman had to first admit he wasn't as good as he thought he was, and *that* Lillian didn't buy for a second. Roman sold himself so well because he believed his own hype.

In his mind, he was the consummate art dealer.

"I would check with all of your vendors." Unlike his wife, Doyle did *not* tend to think the best of people. "Make sure they know no one can change anything without your direct authorization. And by direct I mean they have to talk to you, or better yet, see you in person. No emailed instructions, no texts, nothing that can't be verified. It'll make things a little more complicated for you if you do need to change something, but it's the only way to be sure no one can screw around with your deliveries."

"No, it's perfect. Thanks, Doyle." After having called him by his surname for so many years, it was proving next to impossible to change and call him Brennan. Even Thea still called him Doyle most of the time. On the occasions when she did use his given name, there seemed such a sense of intimacy involved it made Lillian more than a little uncomfortable using it herself.

"Why don't we finish our wine in the den," Thea said. "I'll clear the dessert dishes later."

"Why don't I clear the table," Doyle said as they stood. "That way, the two of you can have your girl-time without me being in the way."

Thea smiled as she leaned over to kiss him. "Thanks, sweetie."

"You can thank me properly later," he murmured against her lips.

She probably wasn't supposed to hear that, so Lillian pretended she didn't. While also trying to ignore their little kiss as it turned into a lot of kiss, with some tongue and, if she wasn't mistaken, a small grope of Doyle's very fine ass.

She loved her friend, honest to God she did. But if the honeymoon phase lasted much longer for these two, she might just need to turn a hose on them.

Not that she was jealous.

Well, yeah, okay, maybe she was, a little. Not so much of the marriage, but of the fact Thea had fought for and won both of her dreams. She'd married the man she'd loved for years, and she was working for a prestigious interior design firm where she was already one of their most sought-after designers.

Despite having a family net worth larger than some countries' GDP, the Fordhams weren't the idle rich. Mr. Fordham had started his company from nothing, succeeding on merit and sheer determination. Thea was following in his footsteps. Not at his tech business, but along her own chosen career path. And he was totally cool with it.

If only *her* father could let go of the whole family dynasty thing as easily.

And of course, finding someone who looked at her the way Doyle did Thea wouldn't be a bad thing, either. She'd dated a lot of guys over the years. Most casual, some semi-serious. But she'd never once had that feeling deep in her gut that this was *the one*, the way Thea had known it about Doyle. Her brothers teased her she was too capricious to know how to have a stable, permanent relationship.

She was beginning to worry they might be right.

When was the last time she'd even been interested enough in someone to consider breaking the current drought her sex life was suffering from?

An image of her sexy downstairs neighbor with his piercing green eyes and yummy Latin looks pushed into her thoughts.

And she pushed it right back out again.

Sure, he got her motor purring, but he'd made it more than clear he wasn't interested. Hell, half the time she wasn't sure he even *liked* her. What little she knew about him she'd had to all but pry out of her brother, and even he didn't know a lot. And he was Rafe's friend.

It seemed Rafael Delgado was as stingy with information about himself as he was with his smiles. Which was a crying shame, because those smiles were of the highest panty-wetting caliber.

When God created that man, he hadn't skimped on the good stuff.

She peeked over at the lovebirds, who were now gazing at each other with nauseating adoration.

For crying out loud.

Lillian cleared her throat as she topped off both her wine and Thea's.

Taking the hint, Thea broke away from her husband, whose heated gaze promised later retribution for the butt-squeeze. She eyed the very full glasses. "Will you be okay to drive home after this?"

"Probably not. But since I'm not driving, I can walk a little on the wild side tonight." Not enough to get drunk, because going to work with a wine hangover would suck in oh-so many ways. But maybe enough to fuzz the edges of her very rotten day a little.

"Why aren't you...oh, no, not your car again!"

"Oh yes, my car. Again." Lillian took a healthy swallow of the mellow Merlot. How bad was it when everyone she talked to had the same reaction about her Cooper? "I had a flat. Two flats, actually. They towed it to the garage, but I won't be able to pick it up until Monday, so I took an Uber here."

"Oh Lil, that sucks."

"Yeah, it does. But silver lining, it was why I went back into the gallery. If I hadn't, Roman wouldn't have had to put the file back so fast without fixing it, and I never would have known what he was up to."

The timing of his fast exit from the office suddenly clicked.

"Bernice must have buzzed up and told him I was coming. That traitor!" Outrage and hurt swelled in her chest.

Doyle paused in collecting the dishes from the table. "This isn't the first problem you've had with your car?"

"No, some jerk keyed it a couple of weeks ago. And then I got backed into. That's why I've been parking all the way in the back corner since I got it back from the shop."

None of which mattered in the face of this unexpected betrayal and the conspiracy it represented. "I can't believe that two-faced bitch acted all concerned about my car when I came back in, when all she was doing was trying to delay me so Roman wouldn't get caught."

And she'd totally bought into it.

How stupid did that make her?

"What garage did you have it towed to?"

"I treated her to a day at the spa for her birthday last month."

"Lillian—"

"I mean, where's the loyalty?"

"Lil!" Thea's sharp tone cut into her escalating rant where Doyle's calmer attempts had failed.

"What?"

"What garage?" Doyle repeated.

"Oh. Um, Milo's, on Pine." She watched in bemusement as Doyle nodded and walked out of the dining room with the stack of dirty dishes in one hand and the remains of the chocolate cake they'd half demolished in the other. "That was weird."

Thea was also staring after her husband, but it probably had more to do with admiring his ass again. She hummed a small agreement to Lillian's observation, then led the way to the comfortable den at the back of the house.

Lillian snagged the bottle of wine and followed.

Just in case.

While Thea curled up in one of the oversized upholstered chairs that could fit a whole other person in it with her, Lillian prowled the room, too filled with aggravated energy to sit still.

Why did it bother her so much Bernice might be in cahoots with Roman? They'd hung out together a few times outside of work, but they weren't actually *friends*. Not yet, anyway.

And now probably not ever.

Still, the betrayal stung. Not to mention, it meant she now had more than one direction she needed to watch her back from at work.

"Is it me?" she asked, trying to swallow the hurt swamping her along with more of the wine.

"Is what you?"

"Am I just being a bitch about this thing with Roman because I don't like him? Should I let it go?"

"Absolutely not," Thea said, with utmost certainty. "What does your gut tell you?"

"That he's a two-bit con man up to no good and I need to take him down like the mangy dog he is." She bit her lip to hide a grin. "Too melodramatic?"

Thea pinched her thumb and forefinger together with a laugh. "Just a little."

Lillian sat on the couch as she laughed with her, but there wasn't a whole lot of humor in it. She loved her job at the gallery. No, she *needed* her job at the gallery.

Not for the money, of course. The stock she owned in her father's company kept her bank accounts fat and happy without the mediocre paycheck she got from Felix. No, she needed it because without it, she'd have no cover for what she was actually doing.

Something her father would no doubt disapprove of should he find out.

Rupert Beaumont was a tolerant man, but he had some very entrenched ideas. He'd expected all of his children to take up their places in the investment firm he'd built from modest success into a Fortune 500 listing. In his vision for the future, the four of them would take over and run things when he retired, creating a grand Beaumont family legacy.

Richard and Theo had complied without a whimper of protest.

It was his younger offspring who had balked at toeing the legacy line.

First Peter had chosen to join the Boulder police department, which had just about thrown their mother into hysterics. Then Lillian had taken her shiny new business degree and gone to work at a series of random jobs: retail, receptionist, even a short stint as a bartender. Anything that would keep her from accepting the job her father kept dangling in front of her like a toxic carrot.

As it always did, the mere thought of being chained to an office, no matter how plush and executive, gripped her lungs with claustrophobic tightness. She swallowed a large gulp of wine to try and loosen the vise.

She just couldn't do it, no matter how much she wanted to please her father. Oh, she could fake her way through the job for a while. She was good at that. But eventually, being trapped in such a structured, stifling environment would kill something inside of her.

No, she just had to resist the endless prodding and cajoling for a little while longer. She was almost ready to put everything into motion. Which was why her position at the gallery was so important, and why she wasn't about to let Roman freaking Reynolds screw it up for her. Whatever he was up to, she was going to figure it out and stop him.

Somehow.

"I heard from Mellie earlier today," Thea said, dragging Lillian's thoughts away from murder and mayhem and onto the absent member of their trio. "She said she'd call you tomorrow."

Lillian's mood immediately lightened. "How's she doing up there in Hayseed?"

"Hayden," Thea said with a roll of her eyes, "and she's loving it. She spent almost as long talking about the kids in her class as she did about Daryl, which was already pretty long. Now I know how I must have sounded to you guys when I was going on and on about Doyle," she added with a rueful grin.

"Yeah, you were pretty nauseating." Lillian's agreement earned her a mock scowl. "Is she still stringing Daryl along, or is she finally going to make an honest man out of him?"

"Hard to believe, but she's still leading him on a merry chase. He keeps asking her to marry him, and she keeps saying not yet. But I think he's wearing her down."

"Well, my money's on Daryl."

Lillian would have never pictured their friend falling in love with the strong, silent cowboy who had once been one of Thea's bodyguards. But seeing the two of them together at Thea's wedding convinced her they were perfect for each other. Moving to the small town in South Dakota where Daryl's family owned a horse ranch to take a job teaching first grade was a pretty good indication Amelia was serious about their relationship.

"He knows what he's up against. She's just a little gun-shy after last time."

"Last time" being the engagement from hell to the biggest loser on the face of the planet, Charles I'm-a-douche Davenport. Amelia had escaped marriage to that jackass by the skin of her teeth. Unfortunately, it was taking her a while to regain her confidence in her own judgment. But Lillian didn't doubt for a minute she'd end up with her hunky cowboy and get the same happy-ever ending Thea had gotten.

Not that Lillian begrudged her friends their happiness. Not at all.

She was beyond thrilled they'd each found the perfect someone who was their other half. It was just that she was feeling somehow...left behind. Forgotten.

Alone.

"Pathetic," Lillian muttered into her glass, draining the last of the wine.

"What?"

"I said I'm pathetic."

Whoops.

She hadn't meant to say that out loud.

"And a little drunk, maybe." Which could be a dangerous thing, given that alcohol tended to erode her filters, which were ridiculously thin to begin with. She set the empty glass down with careful precision and stood, waiting while her head caught up with the rest of her body.

Yup. Definitely buzzed.

"I think maybe I should call for a ride and head home."

"Don't be silly." Thea uncurled her long legs and got up. "I'll drive you."

"I'll be taking you home," Doyle said from the arched opening between den and dining room. "But first, we need to talk about something."

Buzzed she might be, but Lillian recognized Doyle's work-face when she saw it. Feeling a warning clench in her stomach, she sank back down onto the couch. "Okay. About what?"

"All the vandalism to your car. I just got off the phone with the mechanic."

It was way after closing time at the garage. But Lillian didn't doubt for a second Doyle had used some of his Praetorian connections to get poor Milo's personal number. "Well, the keying was vandalism for sure, but the bashed-in taillight was just a careless driver who didn't bother to leave a note."

Wasn't it?

The very serious look on Doyle's face had her beginning to question that assumption. "What's going on, Doyle?"

"Bren?" Thea asked when he didn't answer right away.

Looking grim, he replied, "Your tires weren't just flat. They were slashed."

Lillian stared at him, the words not making any sense. "Slashed?" She shook her head even as Doyle nodded, making the room wobble. "But, why? What does that mean?"

"It means your problem with Roman Reynolds just got a whole lot more serious."

Chapter 3

*P*ain.

It tore through his body, stealing his breath, coiling through his gut until he wanted to scream for somebody, anybody, to make it stop.

Hot, burning knives piercing his skin.

He flailed out to knock away the hands that were doing this to him, that were *killing* him. Instead, he found himself tied down, unable to defend himself as the pain went on, and on, and on.

Agony.

He wrenched himself away, and suddenly he was falling, dropping through the sky toward a ground that never seemed to come.

With a hard gasp, Rafe bolted upright in his bed. The sticky strands of the too-familiar dream clung to him for a few long seconds before reality reasserted itself. Breathing hard, he shuddered as the sweat coating his body met the cool air of his bedroom, the covers he'd gone to sleep under now a tangled knot on the floor.

There were no hands. No restraints. No one trying to kill him. It had all been a dream. Bits and pieces of disjointed reality swirled together in his brain, made worse by the damn painkiller he'd taken before bed despite his better judgment. Twisted remnants of what had happened over a year ago, when he'd made the biggest mistake of his career and cost a woman her life.

And almost his own.

But the pain…

The pain was real. It shot in hot, angry pulses from his leg, radiating into his hip and all the way down to his foot in undulating waves of fire.

With a curse, Rafe pressed his thumbs into the thick scar tissue on his left thigh, trying to massage out the cramp that wanted to twist his leg right off his body. So much for the meds helping him sleep. He hated taking the fucking things, but Cris had been right, he'd overdone it at physical therapy. Instead of speeding up his recovery, he'd probably set himself back at least a week.

Fucking wonderful.

The sensation of having a red-hot poker shoved into his leg wasn't any fun, but it also wasn't anything new. From the moment he woke up in the hospital after surgery, he'd been in pain. Sometimes he had trouble remembering a time when he hadn't been.

It ebbed and flowed, throbbed or stabbed, but no matter how good a day he was having, it was always there. A constant background ache that had become an enemy he couldn't seem to defeat, no matter how hard he tried.

One of them, anyway.

Standing under a pounding hot shower might help ease the cramp quicker, but at—he squinted at the clock on his nightstand—three o'clock in the ever-fucking morning, the sound might wake up Cris, whose bedroom was on the other side of the bathroom between them. Sometimes Rafe missed the privacy of living alone he'd enjoyed before.

Before the accident.

Before he wondered if he'd be able to walk normally again.

Before his entire existence as a police officer had been thrown into question.

But he couldn't be sorry about having Cris around, either. He was used to always going and doing. Keeping busy. Sitting around while he worked through physical therapy and waited for the department to decide he was fit enough to return to even light duty was a slow road to insanity.

His little brother might get on his last nerve sometimes, but being alone in this apartment with nothing but his own rotten temper for company would have been a hundred times worse.

Rafe snorted as he hobbled down the hall to the bathroom. True as that might be, even if Cris hadn't jumped at the chance to move in with him like a man granted parole, being alone still would have been better than recuperating in his parents' house for another day.

His brother hadn't been the only one feeling the need for freedom.

By the time Pete had told him about the apartment, Rafe had been ready to gnaw his own leg off to escape his family's tender loving care. Between his mother and his sisters, he'd been coddled, pampered, and waited on to within an inch of his sanity.

Which was why he hadn't fully thought through what it would be like to live in the same building as the tempting woman sleeping ten feet above his head. Desperation sometimes made for strange bedfellows.

He let out a low groan as the regrettable turn of phrase conjured up an image of Lillian laying sprawled on a big bed, wearing something made of that slippery silk she loved so much. Knowing he was in the bedroom right below hers always had the horny little fucker in his head working overtime, coming up with all sorts of inappropriate thoughts like that.

If it had been anyone else, he would have enjoyed the mental peep-show fantasy. Maybe even given himself a happy ending to finish the job. But using Lillian Beaumont as wank material was a low he would *not* allow himself to sink to.

No matter what his frustrated dick wanted.

Grabbing the heating pad from under the bathroom sink, Rafe continued his slow, limping journey to the living room, where he plugged it in and lowered himself onto the couch with a sound that was half-relief, half-pain. After wrapping the pad around his thigh, it only took a minute for the heat to start working its magic. Tight muscles eased, and he drew his first breath not through clenched teeth since he'd been pulled out of the nightmare.

His head fell back against the cushion.

I fucking hate this.

Hated not having control over his body.

And worse, not knowing if he ever would again.

The shattered femur wasn't the problem. It had been patched back together with enough titanium rods and screws to make him light up the precinct metal detector like a Christmas tree every time he went through. It wasn't pretty, but it was solid.

It was the damage to the muscles, tendons, and nerves that left his future on more precarious ground. If they didn't heal right, it would be worse than just being left with a permanent impairment. It would be the end of his career.

Not going to happen.

He didn't care how many specialists he had to see, or how hard he had to work. He wasn't giving up until he was back on the job doing what he loved. Protecting the city and the people in it. Making a difference.

He was getting his life back, and no one would tell him different.

The sound of a key at the front door snapped his attention from his inner cheerleading back outward with a jolt. His hand twitched for the gun that was locked away in the safe bolted under his bed. Not that he needed it. He could tell from the exaggerated attempts to enter quietly the intruder was more than a little inebriated.

Since most criminals didn't burgle drunk, that left one other person it could be.

"Cris."

Eyes already adjusted to the lack of light, it was easy for Rafe to see the way his brother froze at the unexpected voice. Coming into the dark apartment from the lighted hallway, Cris's night vision would have been compromised, which meant he probably hadn't seen Rafe sitting there. Or expected him to be awake at such a ridiculous hour.

Wanting to keep that advantage, Rafe didn't bother to turn on a light.

"I thought you went to a study group meeting." One he'd assumed Cris had returned from hours ago.

So much for not wanting to wake him up.

"Hey, Rafe!" His brother's voice held the too-bright tone of a drunk who knew he was caught, but still hoped to jolly his way out of trouble. "Whatcha doin' up so late? It's..." He brought his watch up to his face despite the darkness, then dropped his arm as though it were too heavy to hold up. "It's late."

"Yeah, it is. Where were you?"

"I, uh...I had study group."

"After that."

"After?" Cris managed a credible amount of confusion.

"Yeah, after."

"Oh, well, uh, a few of us, uh, went out for a beer. You know, to, uh, blow off a little steam."

"Sounds like it was more than a little."

Cris spat out a curse, his drunken bonhomie turning to hostility in less than a heartbeat. "What the hell's wrong with having a little fun sometimes?"

"There's a little fun, and there's a little too much fun." Not that he expected his brother to appreciate the difference right now. He'd dealt with enough drunks over the past few years to know they all believed they were in perfect control.

He'd scraped enough parts of them off the pavement to prove they weren't.

Cris sneered. "A little too much for who? Just because you've turned into a fucking old man doesn't mean I can't go out and have a good time with my friends on the one Saturday night I don't have to be at the restaurant."

Old man?

He only had five years on his brother. Was it just the booze talking, or did Cris really see him that way?

"I didn't say not to have a good time. All I'm saying is to dial it back a little."

"You're not *papa*, bro, so get the hell off my back about what I do or don't do."

That stung. He wasn't trying to be their father. He was just hardwired to try and protect everyone around him. Even if they were currently being a drunken dickhead.

"Fair enough. You're a big boy. You should be able to make your own decisions." No matter how wrong or stupid they might be.

"Damn right," came the cocky reply.

But Rafe wasn't done quite yet.

"Just tell me you didn't drive home like this, did you?" Because if so, he'd have to go light a candle that his idiot brother had gotten home in one piece.

And then chew him a new asshole in the morning.

"No." The single word managed to sound both guilty and sullen. "Paula drove me home."

Thank God for small miracles.

Rafe sighed. "Go to bed, Cris."

"S'what I was trying to do when you stopped me," he muttered as he staggered into motion.

Listening to his brother bump along the wall all the way to his bedroom, Rafe shook his head and prayed the wild streak Cris had shown ever since he'd gotten out from under their mother's watchful eye would blow over soon. He was acting more like he was eighteen than twenty-three.

So far, his schooling hadn't been affected. Neither had his work at Bayamo. Until either of those things happened, Rafe didn't have a real reason to tank his brother's fun.

Despite the hangover the size of a bus he'd wake up with later.

Suitable penance for being stupid, all things considered. But that didn't stop Rafe from grabbing a bottle of water and a couple of aspirin to bring to his brother, who'd only managed to get one leg of his skinny jeans off before falling face-first across the bed. He'd stacked his arms under his head like he planned to sleep right there.

"Serve you right if I took a picture of you like this and sent it to *Mami*." Rafe bit back a laugh at the horrified look of panic Cris gave him. He helped his brother strip down to his shorts and poured him under the covers.

"Here." Rafe handed him the water and aspirin. "Drink the whole thing before you pass out. Trust me, you'll feel better when you wake up if you do."

"*Gracias, hermano.*"

Rafe waved away the slurred thanks and turned to leave.

"You don't always have to take care of everybody's problems, you know," Cris said. "You're not responsible for the world."

Rafe pulled the door shut behind him. Maybe not the whole world. But he was responsible for his little slice of it, and for keeping everyone there safe and well.

Even when they needed to be protected from themselves.

Chapter 4

"**I**'m coming, I'm coming. Hold your freaking horses."

Lillian dragged her robe on over the skimpy shorts and tank-top pajamas as she stumbled to answer the demanding knock threatening to take down her apartment door. She was halfway there when the very impatient person started a long, slow knock she recognized all too well.

"Oh, damn."

Why me?

Much as she'd rather not face him, she didn't have a choice.

After shutting off the alarm system, she turned the deadbolt with an irritated snap. Muttering one more curse under her breath, she yanked the door open to glare at the man in the intimidating black police uniform standing there. "What?"

"That's how you answer the door when you don't know who's on the other side?"

"No, that's how I open it when I know my very annoying little brother is on the other side." Reluctantly, she opened the door wider to let him in, no matter how tempting it was to close it in his face instead. He'd just stand out there pounding until she opened it again.

"How could you know it was me? You didn't even check through the peephole."

"And you know that how?"

"Because I had my finger over it." Peter walked past her and stopped, crossing his arms as he stared down at her wearing his best cop-face. "And stop calling me your little brother. You were born a whole ten minutes before me."

"Which still makes me your big sister." She smirked as she closed the door, knowing how much it bothered her twin to have been born second, thereby cementing him forever in the role of baby of the family.

If he was going to show up at this ungodly hour, he deserved some grief in return.

"*Big* sister?" Peter scoffed. "Older, maybe, but big? Not hardly."

Used to the digs about her small stature in comparison to her brother's six-foot-plus muscular build, Lillian didn't bite. Instead, she pushed past him and headed toward the kitchen, leaving him to follow or not. "If you're staying, I need coffee."

To her disappointment but not surprise, he followed.

"Good idea." He paused. "Why are you still in your pajamas?"

"Because I just woke up. Thanks for that, by the way."

Actual sleep had eluded her for the longest time, but she'd managed to doze off sometime after two a.m. She could make do with five hours, but one more would have been nice. Especially considering the day she knew she was going to have.

Peter was just the beginning of the nightmare that was to come.

"It's after seven."

"Yeah, well, I don't have to be at work till eleven-thirty."

Popping a pod into the coffeemaker, she stared at it as though she could make it brew faster through sheer willpower. The fact Peter was here bright and early in full official regalia meant Milo hadn't wasted any time filing the police report Doyle insisted on the night before.

Deep down, she'd almost sort of thought that when she woke up this morning, it would have all been a bad dream. Or a mistake. Or *something*. Peter's presence crushed that weak hope like a bug.

Almost before the machine was done dripping, she grabbed the fire engine red ceramic mug and inhaled the intoxicating hazelnut mocha aroma before she took a long, satisfying sip.

Nirvana.

"So, I assume you're here for a reason and not just to mooch my coffee?"

Peter settled onto one of the stools along the dark granite island as she dropped a new pod into the machine. "You know why I'm here."

She sighed. "Yeah. Doyle told me he ordered Milo to file a report first thing this morning."

"Ah, that's how you guessed it was me at the door."

"No. It was the stupid knock thing you do." She imitated it on the counter. "Do you have any idea how annoying that is?"

Peter grinned.

"Of course you do," Lillian muttered, pulling down another oversized mug from the glass-fronted cabinet. "Why else would you do it?" They might both be twenty-four, but she swore she was the only one who acted their age sometimes. "Plus, there was the fact you didn't need to be buzzed into the building, or up the elevator, so it had to be either one of my neighbors or someone who has a guest pass."

Her building didn't have a doorman, but it was loaded with other fancy security features which made it almost as secure as if it did. Not to mention the extra add-ons to her apartment her father had insisted on.

She might have balked when Hans, the head of her father's security team, had them installed, but she actually did sleep a little better knowing they were there. Just in case.

Not that she'd ever admit it.

"Do me a favor." Peter accepted the forest green mug with an audible rumble of approval at the chocolaty scent. "Don't assume next time. Use the peephole first, *before* you turn off the alarm or unlock the door."

"Fine."

She hated using the peephole. She had to drag the little stepstool she kept in the entryway over so she could stand on it to look out. It made her feel like she was six. Hans had tried putting in a door with a lower peephole to accommodate her height, or lack thereof, but all she'd been able to see was her visitors' chests.

Not helpful.

Lillian watched with exasperated amusement as her brother not-so-casually looked around the kitchen as he sipped his coffee. "If you're looking for donuts, I don't have any."

"Blatant stereotyping, sis. Donuts aren't the only thing cops eat." He gave another look around. "Coffee cake or sticky buns would be just as good."

"Well, sorry, I'm all out of sweets." She avoided looking at him as she said it. It was a big, fat lie, and her brother had always been a walking lie-detector when it came to her, even before he joined the police department.

"Lil..."

"Okay, fine." With great reluctance, she retrieved the leftover chocolate cake from the fridge. "Didn't you have breakfast this morning?"

"Yeah, but that was hours ago." Eyes lighting up when he saw the cake, he reached for it, then yelped when she slapped his hand. "Hey!"

"Pretend you have manners and wait a second." She retrieved a plate and fork, pulled a knife from the wooden block on the counter, and sliced off a hunk. Thea had generously parted with her favorite dessert because in her mind, there wasn't anything chocolate couldn't make better.

Most of the time, Lillian agreed.

After last night's revelations, however, she didn't think there was enough chocolate in the state to make up for the disaster her life had suddenly become.

But what the hell, it wouldn't hurt to try.

Grabbing another plate and fork, she cut herself a much smaller slice and sat next to her brother at the kitchen island, where they both worshiped at the altar of gooey chocolate goodness. As with many twins, they shared a lot of the same likes and habits. An abiding love of sweets was one of them.

A desire to forge their own paths was another.

Which was why Pete, of all people, would understand what you're doing.

She shooed away the pesky little voice in her head. The one that always got her into trouble. She hadn't told anyone her secret, not even Thea. The urge to confide in *someone* gnawed at her sometimes, but every time she was going to, the words seemed to stick in her throat.

Once she said them out loud, put it out into the universe, that was it. It would be real. And then she'd be morally obligated to follow through or look like a failure.

Again.

That was her biggest problem. Had been her entire life. She always had big dreams, big plans, big ideas. But her follow-through often left a lot to be desired. Which was why when her father had caved to her desire to attend art school, he'd countered with a deal that she get a business degree, too. As something to fall back on, "just in case" she ever needed it.

What he'd really meant was *when* she needed it.

She knew her dad would never hurt her intentionally. And that part of his purpose had been to entice her closer to the family fold. But his lack of faith in her, his belief she'd lose interest like she always did and just move on to the next shiny thing was like a needle that kept poking her over and over again.

Partly because deep down, she kind of worried about the same thing.

Could she stick to her plan to the bitter end?

Felix certainly wasn't making it easy for her. And now all this

Roman/Bernice nonsense she had to worry about would be another distraction. Maybe what she needed was something to make sure she stayed on track. Something to hold her accountable to the follow-through.

Or someone.

She peeked over at her brother, who was shoveling the last of his cake into his mouth with a happy grin. What if she told him? No, what if she *showed* him? Her studio, the recent canvas she'd spent so many hours slaving over, the others stacked against the walls drying. Explained her plan to him. Got an unbiased opinion about the whole crazy scheme.

Granted, Peter wouldn't know a Picasso from a Pollock, but he was surprisingly supportive of her art. He'd even retrieved several of her early works from the garbage bin and hung them in his apartment, much to her embarrassed pleasure.

But he'd also tell her if he thought she was headed down a one-way street into oncoming traffic. For all he loved to tease her, he'd go out of his way to protect her from any potential harm. Even the self-inflicted kind.

Okay. I'm doing this.

She put her fork down, squared her shoulders, and swiveled her stool to face him. This was it. She was going to—

"So, about your tires."

—chicken out and wait for a better time. Again.

I am such a wussy coward.

Peter scraped a glob of frosting from the plate and licked the tines of the fork clean, then pulled out his notepad. Just like that, he wasn't her brother anymore, he was a cop. "Have you had any problems with anyone at the gallery lately? Any disgruntled customers? Have you fired or disciplined any employees?"

"No, nothing like that." Although she wouldn't mind having a discussion with Bernice about the dangers of pissing off one boss to suck up to another. "But there is someone you might want to look into." She told him all about what had happened the previous day with Roman. He didn't write down much, but he looked thoughtful by the time she was done.

"And this guy, he's trying for the same manager's position that you want, right?"

"Yes." She was hoping she wouldn't need it, but it was her one safety net in case her other plans crashed and burned. At least she'd be able to stay in the art world. Otherwise, her father would swoop in over her still smoking remains and drag her off into nine-to-five hell.

"And he's been at the gallery, what?" He referred to his notes. "About four months now?"

"Something like that. Felix hired him right after Kevin left."

A loss that had been devastating for her. The gallery's former manager, Kevin had been the one to champion her to Felix, to get him to take a chance on her despite her spotty work history. He'd seen her passion for the art, and become not only her mentor, but a friend.

His move back to New York had hurt on both a professional and a personal level.

And if Roman was promoted to his old position instead of her, it would be an insult to the high standards Kevin had set.

"When did the damage to your car start?"

"Um..." She thought back to the night she'd come out of work to find the ugly gash carved into the custom turquoise paint all the way down the driver's side. It still hurt to think of her sweet little Cooper being violated like that. "About six weeks ago, give or take."

Peter's lips hardened as he jotted something down.

"Has this Roman guy done anything besides snoop through your desk to make you think he could be responsible for what happened to your car yesterday? Any aggressive body language or flashes of temper? Anything that might have made you feel threatened?"

Roman, threatening?

She almost laughed. He *so* wasn't.

Tall, lanky, with manicured hands and more product in his hair than her and Bernice combined, he was the least imposing man Lillian knew. He was annoying, arrogant, nosy, and if her suspicions about Bernice were correct, manipulative as hell.

But try as she might, she couldn't picture him skulking around the parking lot with a knife going all stabby on her tires.

"No, nothing." Which was too bad. Roman as the bad guy in all of this would have made her life a lot easier. "He's a jerk, but he's a harmless jerk. Physically, anyway."

Professionally, he was a damn snake in the grass.

"Don't discount him just because he doesn't seem the type. Not everyone shows their true colors to the world. Not until it's too late."

The reminder sent a shiver of unease through her, making her clutch the mug tighter with both hands. Thea had once been the target of a stalker who'd turned out to be someone nobody had suspected because he'd been so...average.

So not the type.

And, of course, there was Sean. Not even Hans had been suspicious of him.

Sobered by the memory of how easily anyone could be fooled, and the potential consequences, she nodded her agreement.

"I mean it, Lil. I want you to be extra careful whenever you're anywhere near this guy. Don't be alone with him, don't get in a car with him, don't—"

"Okay, okay, I get it." She shot him an exasperated glare. "We do work together, remember? I can't avoid him entirely. Mostly we just see each other coming and going, but sometimes our schedules overlap when there's a show, or if there's a shipment Felix isn't available to handle." Which was rare. Felix was the ultimate control freak when it came to his gallery.

Which made his attitude toward Roman's shortcomings all the more perplexing.

"Just promise me you'll be careful."

The honest concern in her brother's tone helped temper the bossiness.

"I promise."

Lillian made them each another cup of coffee as Peter questioned her about everyone else she'd come into contact with in the past few months—there were a lot—and discussed which of them might be a potential suspect—none. At least to her mind.

Peter kept his thoughts to himself as he tucked his little notebook away and stood.

"If anything else happens," he said, draping his arm over her shoulders as they walked toward the door, "anything at all suspicious, you let me know. Immediately. Okay? Even if you don't think it has anything to do with the case."

Great. She was a case.

She bit her lip as they stopped at the door, dreading the next question but she had to ask.

"You're not going to tell Dad about this, are you?" The incredulous look she got back was answer enough. Of course he was.

Hell, he probably already had.

"Someone's targeting you, Lil. You might treat your safety like it's a joke, but I sure as hell don't, and neither does Dad."

"I do not!" The unfair accusation made her bristle.

"Oh yeah?" Peter crossed his arms, his biceps straining the sleeves of his uniform. "Is that why you refused to let him assign you a bodyguard when you moved out?"

Lillian crossed her own arms, but it didn't have the same effect.

"I refused because I'm perfectly safe here. I agreed to the alarm system, didn't I? And all the other things Dad insisted on. I don't need a bodyguard too. You don't have one."

"I'm a cop." The exaggerated patience of the reply emphasized how little he thought of her reasoning. "I don't need a bodyguard. I carry my own gun."

"I could get a gun."

"God help us all," Peter muttered.

Since she didn't want a gun anyway, she abandoned that argument. "Theo and Richard don't have bodyguards."

"They have *staff*."

Which, from the way he said it, translated to *people with guns*.

"I'm perfectly safe."

"Your car might disagree."

"Then get a bodyguard for my car."

Okay, yes, she was being a brat. But this was what always happened whenever she tried to have a rational discussion with one of her brothers. They'd state their position, she'd state hers, and then they'd ignore everything she said and bulldoze right over her.

It was infuriating as hell.

Especially when Peter knew the reason she didn't want a bodyguard lurking around. Even just talking about it was giving her hives.

The muscle along his jawline bunched and flexed, a sure sign he was grinding his teeth. Then he sighed and leaned down to press a kiss to her forehead.

"Just be careful, squirt. Mom wouldn't be able to handle it if anything happened to you."

Hell.

She squeezed her eyes shut as his words punched a hole through her shield of stubborn defiance. "Damn, you play dirty."

"Only when I have to."

Closing the door behind him, she turned the deadbolt, knowing full well he was on the other side, waiting to hear the lock slide home. Sure enough, he gave an acknowledging double-tap on the door. She rolled her eyes, but still smiled as she walked back to the kitchen.

Her brother might be a major pain in the ass, but he meant well.

After rinsing the mugs and plates and putting them in the dishwasher, she dried her hands on the bright yellow dishtowel.

Peter's little dig about their mother had found the soft spot in her armor of independence.

She might tease him about being the baby of the family, but the truth was, between her being the only girl and having the stature of a Keebler elf, her mother always worried about Lillian far more than she did any of her sons. Of course, that might have also had something to do with the harebrained stunts she'd pulled as a kid, trying to keep up with them.

Her mother often lamented she didn't know how she wasn't completely gray.

Or bald.

Lillian tossed the towel aside and shuffled down the hallway to her bedroom. She couldn't be mad about her mother's overprotective instincts. She worried because she cared. And because what happened with Sean had freaked her out almost as much as it had Lillian.

A chill chased through her.

This wasn't the same thing. Not at all.

But was her mother going to see it that way?

A groan escaped her.

No. No, she wasn't.

"Damn it."

It had taken her *months* to get her mom to stop coming by to check up on her after she'd moved into the apartment. And even longer to end the daily phone calls to "just say hi." She loved her mom to pieces, but all that helicoptering had made her feel about twelve instead of twenty-four.

Once she got wind of this new problem—which Lillian *still* hadn't quite wrapped her head around as actually being something real enough to worry about—her mom was going to go right back to her hovering ways. Privacy and personal space were going to be a distant memory.

In fact, she wouldn't be surprised if both of her parents were knocking down her door the minute she got home from work, demanding she move back to the estate for a little while. Just until things got straightened out.

That so wasn't going to happen.

Not that it wouldn't be an uphill battle. Resisting the combined might of her parents' powers of persuasion would be tough. Lucky for her, she'd inherited that same skill from them. It was one of the reasons she'd always been able to get Thea and Amelia to go along with her harebrained schemes.

For a hot second, she considered calling Thea to see if she wanted to go out to dinner after the gallery closed, then discarded it as the coward's way out. It would also just be delaying the inevitable.

No, she needed to face her parents as she meant to go on. Firm. Determined. Strong. She could do this. Everything would be fine.

She flopped down onto the rumpled bed she'd crawled out of less than an hour ago with another groan, this one more heartfelt than the last.

It wouldn't be fine. It was going to suck.

Could this day possibly get any worse?

Chapter 5

"**Y**ou want me to do *what?*"

Rafe stared at the man sitting across his kitchen table, sipping coffee as though he hadn't just said the most asinine thing he'd ever heard in his life.

"You heard me."

"You want me to spy on your sister?"

The fingers of Pete Beaumont's free hand tapped a rapid staccato on the table. "Not spy. Keep an eye on."

"I don't see a difference."

"The difference is one is creepy, and the other is—"

"Also creepy." With a scowl, Rafe took a long swallow of his coffee, hating the small jump his pulse gave. He really was a perv, if the mere thought of following Lillian around got his motor humming.

"You did it once before and didn't have a problem with it."

Of course, Pete would remind him of that one slight lapse in judgment.

"That was different. The guy had a bad driving record." Which was why he'd allowed himself to be talked into following Lillian and her date in his police cruiser. A subtle warning to keep the guy from doing anything stupid while he had Lillian in the car. It had nothing at all to do with the fact it wasn't long after he'd first met her and had that unfortunate bout of insta-lust.

Riiight.

"And it worked."

Pete sounded smug, but he was right. It *had* worked. No speeding, no drinking and driving. In fact, the guy had dropped Lillian back at home nice and early, and was never heard from again. Of course, Lillian had been furious at her brother for his obvious involvement, but to this day she still had no idea of Rafe's complicity in that night's little adventure.

And he planned to keep it that way.

He shook his head. "That may be. But what you're talking about now is something else entirely."

"So, you don't think the vandalism to her car is anything to worry about?"

Hell yeah, he did.

"That's not what I'm saying. I'm saying that if you want someone to keep an eye on your sister, your family has a whole slew of security people who get paid to do exactly that." It was easy to forget sometimes Pete was loaded, but facts were facts, no matter how down-to-earth his friend was. The Beaumonts were Richie Rich rich.

"True, but she knows all of them."

"She knows me too."

"Yeah, but she *likes* you."

Good thing his mug was almost empty, or Rafe would have been wearing some second-degree burns in his lap when he jolted in surprise. "She *what*?"

"You're her neighbor, and my friend. She brought you cookies when you first moved in, didn't she?"

He was still stuck back on the "she likes you" comment. "Yeah, so?"

"So, my sister doesn't bake for just anyone. If she brought you cookies, then she's accepted you as one of her flock."

Rafe's lip curled at the unflattering term. He definitely didn't want to be included in the eclectic group of people Lillian surrounded herself with. The woman was always in motion, going somewhere, doing something, dating someone. And where she went, so did her little entourage.

Pete had once likened her to the Pied Piper, and Rafe had to admit, he wasn't wrong. Like her brothers, Lillian had a natural charisma that made her a born leader. Too bad the only place she seemed capable of leading anyone was to parties, dance clubs, and trouble.

"She's not stupid. Why don't you explain it to her?"

"I just wasted thirty minutes of my morning doing exactly that," Pete replied with disgust. "And no, she's not stupid. But she is stubborn as hell, and she's got her head set against having any security assigned to keep her safe, even now."

His fingers beat a faster staccato. "Look, I can't tell you everything without breaking confidences, but there was...an incident before she moved in here, and it made her skittish about letting anyone get too much into her personal space. Which is why if she sees any of dad's staff hanging around, she'll go ballistic. But if she notices you..."

"Then she'll think I'm her weird neighbor who keeps following her around town. Hell, she'd probably pepper spray my ass. No thanks."

He might not have a shot at ever getting together with her, much as that fantasy might pop into his brain at the most inopportune times. It didn't mean he wanted her to think he was some sleezoid asshole, either.

And what the *fuck* was that about an incident making her skittish?

Before he could ask, Pete said, "Look, I'm not asking you to do full-on surveillance or anything. Just swing by the gallery once in a while when she's working and look at some art. Maybe, I don't know, show up at the same place when she goes out to eat, or to one of her clubs."

"So, you want me to date your sister?" Rafe almost laughed at the growl that left his friend's throat.

"I'm talking about keeping an eye on her, not dating her."

"Dinner. Dancing. Sure sounds like a date to me." He hid his grin behind his coffee mug. Pete was as easy to bait as his own brothers.

"It's just for a couple of days," Pete said, ignoring the taunt, "until either we catch a break in the case and make an arrest, or my father gets her to change her mind about the security detail. They're going over her car today to look for any potential evidence."

As if it would be that easy.

Rafe knew as well as Pete the chances of catching the person responsible for the vandalism to Lillian's tiny toy car were slim at best. Finding trace evidence was a long shot. With no cameras on the gallery parking lot and no obvious motive for anyone to have committed the acts, the police wouldn't get very far.

That left getting Lillian to change her mind. And while Rupert Beaumont might be one badass business tycoon who made his competitors quake in their fancy Ferragamos, when it came to his little girl, *she* called the shots, not him.

Look what happened when she'd rejected the penthouse in the uber-secure building he'd picked out for her and moved in here instead. Daddy had caved, then purchased the building on the sly so he could install all the extra security he wanted without Lillian's feathers getting ruffled.

That was when it clicked.

Of course, Rupert wouldn't just give up if he couldn't convince his daughter to allow a bodyguard to shadow her. He'd work around her refusal and put his people in place anyhow, but in a way she wouldn't notice. Asking Rafe to keep an eye on her was a stop-gap measure until the senior Beaumont and his scary-as-hell security chief got their pieces into place on the game board.

Which made Rafe nothing more than a pawn.

The realization should have pissed him off. But since the end game was all about protecting the Queen—the ridiculous call sign Lillian's security detail had stuck her with years ago—Rafe was actually okay with it.

What he wasn't okay with was the idea of cozying up to Lillian under false pretenses. If he started spending time with her out of the blue, asking her to go places or even tagging along as one of her flock—he grimaced in distaste—she might get the wrong idea. Hell, if he spent that much time with her, *he* might start to get the wrong idea.

Especially if she aimed any more of those ruby kisses his way.

Fuck.

Just thinking about those pouty lips had Rafe shifting to ease the sudden discomfort in his jeans. Thankfully, Pete remained too focused on making his case to notice.

"If nothing else, it'll get you out of this apartment more. Weren't you bitching the other day about being bored out of your skull?" Raising a mocking brow, he leaned back in his chair. "It's not like you've got anything better to do at the moment, right?"

Rafe glared as the barb hit home. "You're a real fuckhead, you know that?"

"But I'm not wrong."

No, he wasn't.

He *had* been complaining when they'd gone out for a beer last weekend. He was sick to death of his own company and of sitting around doing nothing. Hell, he'd even joked he might just chain himself to the police station's front doors until they agreed to let him back on active duty. Even crossing guard duty would be better than this ongoing limbo of uselessness.

Oh, he helped out at the restaurant, or tinkered with his truck, or went to the gym until he was sore and hurting. But none of it lessened the unrelenting boredom of just marking time. As much as he hated to admit it, following Lillian around for a few days just might be the break in his monotonous routine he'd been craving.

But it was a craving he couldn't allow himself to indulge.

She was a craving he couldn't indulge.

"I don't think it would work."

Mug thumping to the table, Pete leaned forward, his tone urgent and pleading. "She's my sister, Rafe. I just want to keep her safe."

Fucking fuck.

"Fine. I'll think about it."

"Thanks, man." Getting up from the table, he slapped Rafe on the shoulder as he walked by. "I knew I could count on you."

"I said I'd think about it," Rafe called after him. The only answer he got was the apartment door slamming. "Asshole."

It really was too bad Pete hadn't gone into the family business. Clearly, he'd inherited the same negotiation and manipulation skills which made the rest of the Beaumonts so damned successful.

That didn't mean he was going to be railroaded into agreeing to this sketchy plan, despite what Pete thought. As much as he didn't want anything bad to happen to Lillian, he still wasn't convinced he was the best person to play babysitter.

For a lot of reasons.

The biggest being that if he found himself in prolonged close contact with the enticing little pixie, he wasn't sure he'd be able to keep his mind on the job. No matter his intentions to remain professional about it, he just knew he'd end up distracted.

Just like the last time he'd tried to protect someone, and it had all gone horribly wrong.

He didn't need another heaping of guilt added to his conscience.

Glancing at the clock on the microwave, he drank the last dregs of his coffee. After putting both mugs in the sink, he headed to his bedroom to finish getting dressed, massaging the dull leftover ache in his leg as he went. The doc would have his balls in a sling if he was late again.

Not that they weren't halfway there already.

In addition to the surgeons and physical therapists who'd helped put all his pieces back together again, the department in all its infinite wisdom had decided he needed to start seeing a shrink, too. To work through the trauma, they said. To make sure he was really okay.

And while he'd love to tell them where to shove the idea, he had a sick feeling that if he didn't hit all his marks with Dr. Wong, he could kiss his career goodbye.

⸻ ◆ ⸻

The doctor's office was on the other side of town. Since this was his third session with her, he knew exactly how the next hour would go before he even stepped into her muted pastel inner sanctum.

How do you feel about what happened? Are you still having the dreams? If you could go back and change one thing about that day, what would it be?

The answers were easy. *Hate it. Yes.* And *I'd shoot the fucker.*

Not that those were the answers he gave out loud.

He wasn't that stupid.

No, he gave the answers he figured the doc wanted to hear. The ones that didn't scream *Psycho cop, take his gun away!* The ones that said instead *Yes, I have my shit together and can be trusted to go back to work without endangering anyone, including myself.*

By the conclusion of another frustrating and pointless session of having his thoughts and feelings poked and prodded until they were raw and bleeding, his mood was foul. The drive home was made on full autopilot as he played and replayed the last fifty minutes in his head, questioning every expression, every gesture the doc had made in response to his answers.

He wasn't as certain she was buying his *nothing wrong with me* routine as he had been when he'd walked in her door.

Especially when he wasn't sure he believed it himself some days.

He'd made a choice that had fucked not just his own life, but the lives of so many innocent people. One split-second. That was all he'd had to make a decision. And it had been the wrong one.

Did he even have the right to be put back into such a position of

58

trust again?

Idling at a red light, he noticed for the first time where his absent-minded driving had taken him. Not home, but right into the heart of the mall district. In fact, he was only a block or so away from the gallery where Lillian worked.

Well, hell. Even his subconscious seemed to be working against him today. He still hadn't made up his mind about agreeing to Pete's request, damn it.

Part of him wanted nothing to do with getting in the middle of what seemed to be some kind of family power struggle. But another part of him knew that if for any reason his own sisters were in need of protection, from dangers real or imagined, he'd hope his friends would help if he asked them to.

Fuck me sideways.

Switching lanes before he could think any harder about it, he made a right turn and took a slow cruise in front of the gallery. There was a fair amount of foot traffic on the sidewalk. It seemed the pleasant spring weather had encouraged everyone to take advantage of the sunny Sunday afternoon to do some shopping.

A lot of those shoppers slowed or even stopped to look into the gallery's large front window. As he passed, a young couple went inside, the woman looking a lot more enthusiastic about it than her male companion.

I feel ya, pal.

Art wasn't something he was much good at. It was one of those "know it when you see it" kind of things for him. Styles and trends meant nothing. He simply knew what appealed to him, and it wasn't paintings of people who looked like they had three eyes and a melting cat sitting on their head.

Driving past the place gave him no answers. Making a few quick turns, he came back down the block again and pulled into the small parking lot across from the gallery. He lucked into a street-facing spot as another car backed out, squeezing his truck in just ahead of the gray Toyota headed for the same space.

He got a long bleat of the horn and a hand gesture, both of which he ignored.

You snooze, you lose.

Weekend parking downtown was problematic even before the prime tourist season started. Once that happened, it turned into the freaking Wild West. Rafe would end up being called to at least one or two incidents every day as tempers flared and people lost their minds.

He'd even seen CCTV footage of one woman using her beefy SUV to shove a smaller car out of the parking spot she thought she'd been robbed of. Then she'd walked away as casual as you please to go do her shopping.

People got nuts over the stupidest things.

But it didn't feel right to write off the damage to Lillian's car as simple parking lot vigilante justice. The keying, maybe. But to take a knife to someone's tires in broad daylight? That said someone with a very specific purpose to him, not bored kids looking to cause trouble or someone pissed about her taking up a prime parking space for eight hours.

Try as he might, he couldn't ignore the possible danger it represented.

Or the knot he got in his stomach about what might happen if the knife-wielding vandal decided to make their next strike a more personal one.

That was the possibility that tipped the scales for him.

"Fuck it. I'm in."

Drumming his fingers on the steering wheel, Rafe watched the flow of people in front of the gallery. He might be in, but hell if he knew what it was he could actually *do*. He wasn't going to just sit in the truck and stare at the building all day.

Besides, inside the gallery was the second safest place Lillian could be after her own apartment. It was when she left work and was out in the open that she'd become vulnerable. That was when he needed to be close.

He just wasn't sure how to make it happen.

As he sat mulling it over, the couple from before exited the gallery, a small, well-wrapped canvas tucked under the man's arm. That sparked an idea.

Rafe crossed the street and mingled into the lunchtime crowd, making his way to the display window of the gallery. Which was when he saw the painting making everybody stop and take a second look.

It wasn't a huge canvas. Only about two feet wide and maybe three high. It was covered with a splash of pastels in undulating waves all around the central figure of the piece. The woman had been painted from behind, her blonde hair scooped away from her neck with both hands, exposing the long, elegant back bared by the blue gown she wore. She stood still, but there was a feeling of movement that imbued the overall design, making it both soft and vibrant at the same time.

Even to his plebeian appraisal, it was breathtaking.

Jostled by the passing crowd, he tore his eyes from the painting to go in. The front door was itself a piece of art, with detailed etching done to the large glass panels at top and bottom. A heavy band of silver ran across the center with the name of the gallery on it.

When he stepped inside, the heavy door shushed closed, muffling the street noise. The cool and quiet should have given the large space a cavern-like quality, but the strategic lighting and high ceilings helped keep it feeling open and airy.

"Welcome to the Landis Gallery. How can I help you today?"

Rafe turned at the voice. A young woman with short, bleached-out hair with a wild shock of purple in it was smiling at him from behind a small reception desk to the right of the entrance. He figured her to be in her twenties, maybe around the same age as Lillian, or even a little younger. It was hard to tell with all the makeup.

"I was just going to look around a bit, if that's okay."

"Absolutely." Her smile widened, making the double gold barbells bisecting her left eyebrow glint in the overhead light. Unlike the one Lillian wore, though, these didn't tempt him to wicked thoughts. "Let me know if you have any questions, or if you need anything. Anything at all."

"Ah, I will. Thanks."

He had the uncomfortable feeling she was staring at his ass as he made his way to the painting visible through the front window. It was just as captivating up close. Even more so, without the layer of UV-tinted glass to detract from the vibrancy of the colors. The small card attached gave it the title *Lady Dreaming*, but it didn't list the artist, or the price.

Crap. In art-speak, that probably meant it would be way out of his price range. But the more he looked at it, the more he knew he wanted it.

"I see you're enjoying our...oh!"

Turning at the familiar voice, Rafe couldn't hide his grin at Lillian's adorable look of confusion. "Hi."

"Hi, yourself." She visibly shook herself out of her surprise and smiled. "Sorry, it's just that you're so out of place here." She winced. "That's not what I meant. I mean, I wasn't expecting to see you. Here. Where I work. I'm used to seeing you at home, in the lobby, or the elevator or something. Never...here. Wow, that sounded stupid even to me." She gave an embarrassed laugh.

"It's okay. I know what you meant."

Lillian was always so cool and in control. It was the first time he'd ever seen her appear flustered. He kind of liked it.

He also liked the deep red dress she was wearing today. Silk again, like the blouse she had on the day before, and it cupped her body just as faithfully. It took all of his willpower not to take advantage of his greater height to sneak a peek down her enticing cleavage.

Thankfully oblivious to where his thoughts—and eyes—had

strayed, Lillian's smile bloomed and she laughed again, this time a more natural, happy sound that went straight to his groin. Cursing the unfortunate reaction, he locked it down before he could embarrass them both.

"So, are you looking for anything in particular?"

Rafe went with a half-truth.

"I've been in my place for a few months now, so I figured it wouldn't hurt if I found something to make it look a little more like I live there." He and his brother had all the necessities, but aside from the few things he'd kept from his old apartment, decorating had pretty much fallen into the bachelor style. Which meant a huge TV and gaming system, but very little else.

"Do you have any stylistic preferences? Landscape, portrait...dogs playing poker?" Her tone was all business, but her dark eyes were still laughing.

"I hadn't thought too much about it." Another truth, since he hadn't planned on coming into the gallery until about five minutes ago. "I was going to look around, but then I saw this piece." He gestured to the painting.

"Ah, *Dreaming*." Lillian nodded. "She's been catching a lot of eyes since we put her in the window."

Hell. If no one had bought the painting yet, it meant the price had to be something outrageous. Still, he had to ask. "How much would something like this go for?"

She looked surprised, then pleased, then flustered. "Oh, I'm sorry, it's not for sale. It's on temporary loan to the gallery from the artist."

"Oh, okay." That didn't sound right, though. Wasn't the whole purpose of putting a painting in a gallery to sell it?

Seeming to read his confusion, she said, "It's a bit of a litmus test. Sometimes newer artists have to prove they can draw an audience before the gallery will agree to give them their own showing. If the painting creates enough buzz by drawing customers inside, then odds are good their work will sell well enough to make it worth the gallery's while. Which," she added with a shake of her head, "is probably more than you wanted to know."

"No, no. Paying dues. I get it." Not unlike the free food his parents had doled out that first year while trying to attract attention to the newest *Cubano* restaurant in downtown Boulder. It had taken years before they'd built up their clientele to where there was now a waiting list to get a table most weekends.

"So, if the artist gets the showing, does that mean the painting will be for sale then?" Rafe didn't know why, but he *really* wanted it.

"Possibly. Probably." Lillian shrugged. The movement drew the red silk of her dress tight across her breasts, making him lose his breath for a second. "I can't say for sure. Artists sometimes get sentimental about certain pieces and don't want to let them go at any price."

"Well, it's a moot point, anyway. I doubt I could afford it."

"Oh, I don't know about that." Lillian looped her arm through his and led him away from the painting and deeper into the gallery, the soft cinnamon scent of her perfume wrapping around him in a heady cloud. "New artists don't command the big bucks. But in the meantime, let's see if we can't find you something else you like just as much and can take home with you today."

Rafe allowed her to lead him away, even though he knew the only thing he was going home with today was her. All he had to do was figure out how to make that happen without her realizing it.

Chapter 6

"**O**h. My. God." Bernice stared after Rafe as the heavy glass door closed behind him. "He was *hawt*." She emphasized her assessment by fanning herself with one of the brochures on her little desk.

"Bernice…" It was an unprofessional thing to say, but really, how could Lillian blame her? Rafe was much too good looking for any woman's peace of mind. Dressed in dark-washed jeans with a white collared shirt, sleeves rolled back to show off his tan, muscular forearms, he wasn't just hot, he was *smoking* hot.

Not that she'd noticed or anything.

"Do you know him? Tell me you know him."

"He's my neighbor."

Bernice let out a small squeal. "You lucky duck!"

"Bernice…"

Undeterred, she said, "Please tell me he's coming back because I forgot to tell him I want to have his babies."

Rolling her eyes, Lillian walked to the painting in the front window that was catching so many eyes. A small thrill ran through her. It had been a hard sell to Felix, to let her place a painting by some no-name artist in such a prominent spot. Display windows were prime real estate, designed to drive foot traffic and reserved for the big names that commanded even bigger price tags.

She'd wanted to prove the painting could attract interest based on its artistic merit alone, with no name attached, big or otherwise.

It had only been a few days, but so far *Dreaming* had done its job.

In general, people always slowed and looked to see what was visible through the large display window as they walked past, but not many came inside. Art wasn't the same kind of impulse buy as shoes or even a piece of jewelry. But it seemed to her off-the-street walk-ins had been on the rise, and all of them had asked about the painting in the window.

Suck on that, Felix.

Fussing with the angle of the easel even though it was already perfect, she stole a quick look outside, hoping for one last glimpse of the man who had thrown her day into utter chaos. It was just as well he was already out of sight. One more look at that fine ass might have done her in entirely.

Bumping into him at home was at least something she could deal with because it was expected. Seeing him here? It had been so *un*expected she'd lost all grip on the cool, poised façade she was able to wear around him the rest of the time. She'd come off sounding like a total idiot.

No, worse, like an *insulting* idiot. She'd meant to convey her surprise at seeing him, not imply she thought he didn't have a refined enough taste to appreciate art. Or that as a cop he couldn't afford it.

Open mouth, insert both size five feet.

Either it hadn't come off sounding as bad as she'd thought, or Rafe had a good sense of humor. He hadn't seemed offended by her unfortunate inability to string a coherent thought together.

In fact, he'd been so not offended, he'd asked if she wanted to get something to eat after she got off of work. And she'd said no. *No!* To the hottest man she'd ever known, or probably ever would.

She was officially a moron.

It wasn't like she hadn't gone out with other men who were attractive, or even who got her hormones purring. But Rafe was more than that. Something much more dangerous.

He was exactly the kind of guy she could fall for.

It wasn't just his looks, incredible as they were. It was the entire package. He was nice, considerate, and patient as any saint that ever lived, as proven almost every week by Mrs. Gabreski in 1B. Who, knowing he was a policeman, called him up at all hours of the night to come investigate any suspicious noises she heard from outside, insisting there were peeping Toms trying to see into her bedroom.

Since Mrs. G was in her eighties and looked a little like a blue-haired Yoda, the likelihood of that was pretty slim. But Rafe went and looked for her anyway, every time. She knew, because Mrs. G made a point of telling her every week when she took her grocery shopping.

And if all that wasn't enough, he was also a hero.

She knew he didn't like it when people brought it up, but it was no secret he'd been injured while saving a woman from the husband who was trying to beat her to death. The limp he'd had when he first moved into the building might be gone, but the fact he was still on medical leave after so many months told her his injuries had been pretty severe.

Looks. Heart. Courage. Yup, Rafe was the whole package all right.

Which was why she needed to stay far, far away from him.

Her plan was so close to falling into place. She couldn't risk being distracted, not even by him. *Especially* not by him.

She needed to focus on her goals first. *Then* she could think about maybe finding someone to settle into some kind of semi-normal relationship with. She knew herself well enough to accept she wasn't like Thea or Amelia. She couldn't split her attention between a full-time career and a full-time man in her life. She needed to pick one and put all of her concentration into doing it right.

Both were far too important to give less than her best.

So, as yummy as Rafael Delgado was, she was going to chalk up the dinner invitation to a friendly gesture from a neighbor and leave it at that.

Of course, that meant she'd have to stop teasing him whenever they ran into each other. Which was kind of a bummer. Watching such a gorgeous man get flustered over her had been a guilty pleasure of hers for the past few months. It would be a hard habit to break.

One which got even harder when she stepped out onto the sidewalk at a quarter past seven and found not the Uber she'd called at the curb, but the vintage dark-green and black truck she'd seen in Rafe's parking spot. It always caught her eye because while most guys went for the bigger, newer models with all the bells and whistles, his truck was a throwback to a different time. With its huge chrome grill and thick, white sidewall tires, it was almost as much a piece of art as it was a vehicle.

Proof he did have good taste, his interest in *Dreaming* notwithstanding.

Damn.

The reminder of her earlier gaff only made it harder for her to handle his second unexpected appearance of the day. She took a few seconds longer than necessary to lock the gallery's door, using the time to find her Zen and decide how she was going to play it. Cool and aloof? Annoyed and standoffish?

Hot and bothered?

By the time she turned back around, deciding on friendly but firm, Rafe had gotten out of the truck and was standing on the sidewalk near the passenger door.

"We meet again," Lillian said, tucking the key ring into her purse. She let her question of why that was seep into her tone.

Rafe had the grace to look uncomfortable.

"Yeah, I know you said no to dinner, but, uh, I figured since I was still in the area, I could at least swing by and give you a ride home."

"Oh."

"A little too creepy?"

Lillian smiled, relaxing at his rueful tone. "Just a little."

"Told him so," Rafe muttered.

"Told who what?"

"Uh, nothing." Rafe gestured toward the truck. "The offer stands. Or I can wait with you while you call for another ride if you want."

Meaning he'd sent the first one away. She should be annoyed at his highhanded gesture, but it was tough to work up any real steam when he was giving her that *I know I screwed up but don't hold it against me* look.

He'd probably gotten away with bloody murder as a kid turning that on his mother. Young, old, related or not, it was doubtful any female on the planet was immune to that woebegone expression.

It was the eyes, she decided as she allowed him to open the door and usher her into the front seat. They were a crystalline green flecked with gold, ringed by lashes so thick and dark that on another man she'd suspect there was mascara involved. Those eyes conveyed more emotion than any words ever could.

She was an absolute sucker for eyes, and his were to die for.

Her fingers twitched for a pencil as she watched him circle around the front of the truck and wait for traffic to clear before continuing to his door and climbing in. What she wouldn't give to have him sit for her, just once. She couldn't ask him to, though. Not now. It would be a little too awkward for them both.

Pity.

As she shifted on the unfamiliar flatness of the bench seat to put on her seatbelt, Rafe started the engine, which fired up with a throaty rumble. She grinned. While the truck had been meticulously restored, it had clearly gotten a few modern upgrades as well. With two older brothers who were both self-admitted car whores, she got the allure of the almighty big engine to guys. She didn't understand it, but she got it.

"Thank you for the ride," she said after a minute, breaking the silence filled only by the soft music coming from the radio. "You went out of your way for me, and I wasn't very nice about it. So, thank you."

"My pleasure."

An image of Rafe's gorgeous eyes filled with a different kind of pleasure flashed through her mind, courtesy of her inner hussy who clearly hadn't gotten the 'hands-off' memo.

Why should I, when hands on would be so much more fun?

Biting her lip, she stared out the side window, willing away the blush she could feel hitting her cheeks. Thank God she didn't have Amelia's lily-white complexion, which showed every little hint of color whenever she got embarrassed. That didn't mean someone trained to observe people's reactions wouldn't still notice.

Hoping to distract them both, she stroked her hand over the dashboard. It was so devoid of all the instruments and add-ons from modern cars, it almost looked unfinished. But at the same time, there was something about the simplicity of the clean lines that appealed to her.

"You did a really nice job restoring this."

There was the briefest hesitation.

"Thanks. It took a lot of hours hunting online for parts and even longer piecing them all together, but I'm happy with the way it came out." Pride was evident in his words.

"I'm surprised you risk driving it around every day. Aren't you worried about it getting damaged or stolen?"

"I didn't restore it so I could park it in a garage somewhere and admire it. It's just a truck. It's meant to be used."

"That doesn't mean you wouldn't care if something happened to it, though. My little Cooper is just a car, and it bugs the heck out of me someone…" Her words trailed off as a thought struck her.

"Someone what?"

"How did you know I needed a ride?"

"Uh…what?"

"How did you know I needed a ride?" She turned in her seat to face him. The better to see his sneaky, lying face as he visibly scrambled for an answer to what should have been a very simple question.

"You…must have mentioned it when you were turning me down

for dinner."

"Yeah, no. It never came up."

"Well, you told me yesterday you were having car trouble, and I didn't see it parked outside the gallery today, so I assumed—"

"Strike two." Her temper rose like a boiling teakettle as her worst suspicions were confirmed. "Care to try again?"

Rafe flinched at the caustic bite in her tone. He shot her a quick look before focusing on making the turn into the garage entrance under their building. He leaned out of the window and punched in his code, waited for the gate to lift, and started driving inside before he finally answered.

"Your brother told me about your car."

The small satisfaction that he'd told the truth this time was far outweighed by the crushing sense of betrayal as the entire afternoon was suddenly rescripted in her mind. Rafe hadn't wandered by the gallery and been drawn inside by the painting. Hadn't asked her to dinner because he'd succumbed to the desire to take her on a date. Hell, he hadn't even "just happened to be in the area" so he could give her a ride.

Staged and planned, every last bit of it.

Peter is so dead when I get my hands on him.

They pulled into Rafe's parking spot. When he cut the engine, the silence was deafening.

"He only said something because he was worried about you."

"Right," Lillian said with a bitter laugh. "What did he do, run downstairs and knock on your door the minute he left my place this morning to ask you to babysit me?"

She'd meant to be sarcastic, but the silence from the other side of the truck was telling. The knife of betrayal plunged a little deeper. "Oh my God, he did, didn't he?"

"He just asked me to keep an eye on you for a few days."

"It's the same thing!" Fumbling with her seatbelt, she wrenched the door open and all but fell out of the truck in her haste to get away. Good thing she was already too humiliated to be embarrassed by her clumsy retreat.

"It is not the…damn it, Lillian, will you stop?"

Stalking around the back of the truck, she saw from the corner of her eye Rafe's door pop open. She picked up her pace, heels clicking in time to her growing fury against the concrete floor. "Leave me alone, Rafe. I mean it."

"No. I'm sorry, but I can't. Not while you're all bent up about this."

She didn't reply, because really, didn't she have a right to be pissed about having her life managed for her? Peter had broken through the protective netting that had ringed them since birth and forged his own way. Why couldn't he let her do the same?

And Rafe. That jab of hurt stabbed into her chest all over again.

How could he treat her like this? Act all interested and gallant and into her, when it was all about doing her brother a favor?

Bastard.

Determined footsteps started coming up behind her. Lillian put on another burst of speed and made it to the elevator first. Stepping inside, she ran her keycard through the reader and stabbed the "close door" button.

"You never asked why I told him I'd do it," were the last words she heard as the elevator doors slid shut. They pinged around in her head as her finger hovered over the fourth-floor button without pressing it.

Why *had* Rafe agreed to play babysitter? Did it really matter? The fact was, he'd lied to her. Okay, maybe he hadn't lied outright, but a lie of omission was still a lie. Wasn't it? She had the moral high ground here. Nothing Rafe could say would change that.

Could it?

With a sigh of defeat, her finger dropped to the "open door" button and gave it one long push. The silver doors parted. Rafe stood in front of them, hands tucked into his jeans back pockets, face tipped toward the ceiling as though he'd been asking for divine intervention.

His head snapped back down, and his eyes locked onto hers. There was surprise in those crystalline depths. And a little bit of wariness.

Smart man.

"Okay, why did you say yes to my brother's stupid request?" She kept her finger on the button to keep the doors open, making it clear that if she didn't like his answer, they were shutting again. This time for good.

"Because he told me he wanted to keep his sister safe. And I knew how I'd feel if someone was messing with one of my sisters." The look on his face said that someone would be a very sorry person indeed once he got his hands on them.

The righteous anger that had been building started to leak away.

Damn him and his good answer.

"Fine." With a huff, she moved to the side, allowing him into the elevator.

"I told him you'd be pissed."

"Yeah, well, you were right." Pressing the buttons for the third and fourth floors, she leaned against the side railing, arms crossed as she stared at the opposite wall, refusing to look at Rafe and be suckered in by "the look" again. He was too good at it, and she needed to stay angry. If she didn't, she would almost certainly start crying.

And she'd had quite enough humiliation for one day, thank you very much.

"Can I ask a question?"

She considered refusing, then shrugged. "Sure, knock yourself out."

"Why are you so dead set against allowing yourself to be protected?"

"Because everyone is blowing the whole thing way out of proportion. Someone keyed my car and vandalized my tires. That doesn't warrant a SWAT team following me around twenty-four-seven."

"It's a lot more serious than that, and you know it."

She did. But she wasn't prepared to lose this battle just yet. The very thought of having someone getting close to her again, into her space, watching her...

She shuddered. Nope. Couldn't do it. Never again.

Not that she was prepared to explain the why of it to Rafe, now or ever.

"I'm just so sick of people thinking I can't take care of myself. I'm not an idiot."

"No, you're not." There was a *ding* as the elevator doors slid open. Rafe stepped up to them, putting a hand on one side to keep it from sliding shut again as he looked at her, trying to catch her eye. "Which is why you know it's foolish to play with your safety when you have the means at hand to ensure it."

It wasn't until he stepped out into the hallway that she finally allowed herself to look at him.

Their eyes met.

"Don't be stupid. Take the security detail." The doors closed on the command like a very firm period.

Lillian's head thunked back against the wall.

Damn it.

Part of her knew he was one-hundred percent right. The rest of her was still squirming away from the very thought like it was a cockroach trying to crawl up her leg. She had a feeling she was going to have to reconcile those two very opposing reactions sooner rather than later, if the way everyone in her life was ganging up on her was any indication.

The need to choose arrived even sooner than expected.

When she opened her apartment door, the one person she had any chance in hell of swaying to her way of thinking in all of this was sitting on her couch, sipping a glass of wine as she leafed through a magazine. She looked up and smiled.

Lillian's heart dropped. She recognized that particular smile. It meant her one potential ally had already gone over to the dark side.

"Hi, Mom."

Chapter 7

"I was expecting Dad to come with you to do the guilt thing." Lillian slid her oversized purse over the back of one of the kitchen island stools before going to give her mother a kiss on the cheek. The familiar floral scent of the L'Eau Bleue she wore was always a reminder of love and safety. It made her want to curl up on the cushion beside her mother and put her head on her lap like she'd done as a child.

Instead, she poured herself a glass of the wine her mother had opened and collapsed into the chair opposite the couch, kicking off her shoes with a long sigh of relief.

"I don't know how you wear those," her mother commented, looking at the ridiculously high heels.

Lillian shrugged. "You get used to them." That didn't mean her feet didn't start to whimper by the end of the day.

"The things women will do for beauty." Her mother shook her head before taking another sip of wine.

In truth, her vast collection of high heels had a more practical purpose than just making her legs look great. They allowed her to hold a conversation with someone without talking to their bellybutton.

Her short stature wasn't so much a problem in her personal life. However, she'd found that when talking to customers at the gallery, the extra few inches the heels provided gave a boost to her confidence as well as her height. But she didn't correct her mother's assumption.

She wouldn't understand, anyway. At a statuesque five-foot-nine, Patricia Beaumont had never needed a stepstool to see out her own front door.

Then again, the front door of the Beaumont mansion didn't exactly have a peephole. It had a camera system and a team of live security personnel. A fact that until last year had made Lillian feel safe and well cared for. Now, just the thought of all of those eyes watching her every move, all the time, made her skin crawl.

Taking a large slug of wine, she popped to her feet.

"I'm going to get out of this dress before I spill something on it. Be right back." Scooping up her heels in one hand, she cradled the glass in the other and escaped down the hallway to her bedroom. There, she shed the silk wrap dress and traded it for a pair of comfy sweats and a cotton top.

After pulling on thick socks to ward off the chill from the hardwood floors, she downed the last swallow of wine left in her glass, took a deep breath to brace for the battle to come, and reluctantly abandoned the sanctuary of the bedroom.

Her mother was still on the couch, magazine forgotten. Waiting.

Lillian looked at the bottle of wine with deep longing as she retook her seat, but resisted the urge to pour herself more. Her head was already a little swimmy from the glass she'd sucked down. On an empty stomach, and on top of the three glasses she'd imbibed at Thea's the night before, her tolerance to alcohol was at a perilous low.

She waited, knowing her mother wouldn't take long to get right to it.

"I want you to move back home."

And there it was. Not even bothering to warm up, her mother had gone right to the big guns.

Damn.

"Mom, I appreciate your concern, but don't you think you're overreacting a little bit?" The fact that her words echoed Thea's from the night before wasn't lost on her.

"It's not overreacting to want to keep you safe."

"I'm perfectly safe right where I am. Dad made sure of it." She couldn't tell from her mother's guarded expression whether or not she grasped Lillian was aware of the open secret as to the identity of her landlord.

It had ticked her off at the time, knowing her father had gone behind her back after he made such a point of "allowing" her the freedom to choose where she wanted to live. But in the end, she'd accepted that as long as he didn't actively try to involve his security people in her day-to-day life, she could live with his other meddling.

Especially since she wasn't the only one who benefited from the security upgrades to the building. Knowing her neighbors were safer, too, seemed like a fair tradeoff for her father's underhanded sneakiness.

Most of the time.

At the moment, it was feeling more like a huge mistake. She'd given her parents a key to the apartment for emergencies, but she hadn't given them the code for the alarm system. The fact her mother had been able to turn it off when she'd let herself in meant Lillian's much-valued privacy was more of an illusion than she'd thought.

"At least come back while the police investigate. A few days at most. It wouldn't be *that* bad, would it?"

Yes. Yes, it would.

And not just for the reasons her mom thought.

"There's no reason for everyone to be so upset over some random vandalism." If only people would take her suspicions about Roman and his snoopfest half as seriously.

Her mother's lips pinched in displeasure. "You're not going to change your mind about this, are you?"

As much as she wanted to calm her mother's worries, she just couldn't do it.

"Sorry, but no."

With a sigh, her mother nodded. "All right, then. We'll do it your way."

Surprised and a little suspicious at how easily she'd given up, Lillian asked, "We will?"

"Yes." Leaning forward, her mother poured a small amount of wine into her glass, then into Lillian's. "I'll move in tomorrow."

"You'll…wait, what? Whoa!" Lillian shot to the edge of her seat, throwing both hands up like a cop trying to stop traffic. "What do you mean, you'll move in?"

Taking a small sip, her mother relaxed back into the plush couch. "You don't want to move back home, and since I know you won't agree to having a security detail move in with you…" She cocked a questioning brow.

"God, no." Lillian shuddered.

Her mother nodded. "So, me moving in is the only logical compromise."

"Compromise? How is that a compromise?"

In what universe was that a compromise?

"Sweetheart, I know *you* don't think this incident with your car is anything to worry about. But I have to tell you, I couldn't sleep at all last night, knowing you were here in this apartment all alone. If you won't move back to the estate, I won't be able to rest easy, not knowing if you're safe."

"Then I'll call you every night when I get home from work, and again before I go to bed." The first pinpricks of desperation tingled at her mother's implacable expression. "And first thing in the morning. Lunchtime too, if it would make you feel better."

"The only thing that would make me feel better would be knowing you're not alone." Her mom shook her head. "There's nothing else for me to do but to move in until they get this taken care of."

"You can't!"

She didn't realize she'd almost shouted the words until her mother blinked at her in surprise, glass halfway to her mouth.

"Whyever not?"

"Because...because you know how much you hate to sleep apart from Dad. That's why you always go with him when he has to travel for business."

"I go with him to make sure he eats and sleeps while he's gone. You know how hyper-focused on business your father can get."

"I thought that's what Lyle was for."

"Do you honestly see Lyle telling your father to put his files away and go to bed?"

Picturing the slightly built, balding man who had been Rupert Beaumont's right hand for as long as Lillian could remember, she had to admit she couldn't. She also didn't want to think about how, exactly, her mother convinced her business-minded husband to abandon work for the bedroom. Lillian shuddered inside.

There were some things about your parents better left unthought.

"Well, then, what about..." She floundered, seeking something. Anything. Then she remembered the huge Mardi Gras-themed event her mother was spearheading to help raise money for the local literacy fund.

"The charity ball! You have to be hip-deep in the final preparations for it right now. I wouldn't want your project to suffer because you were twiddling your thumbs sitting here keeping me company instead of taking care of all the stuff you need to take care of."

She didn't know the inner mechanics of running a huge event like the ball, but she did know it involved a ton of time, and a crap-ton of meetings. And that her mother was just as hands-on obsessed about her projects as Felix was with his gallery.

The line between her eyebrows puckering, her mother tapped the platinum band of her wedding ring against her glass, a sure sign she was agitated. A small shaft of guilt ran through Lillian. But it wasn't nearly strong enough to overtake the sheer panic the thought of having her mother for a roommate caused.

"You may be right," her mother said finally. "With all the final details left to be taken care of, it would be wrong of me to not give it my full attention."

Relief whooshed over Lillian.

Crisis averted.

"So I suppose I'll just have to turn the reins over to someone who can."

Wait, *what*?

"Mom, no. This event has been your baby. You can't give it up!"

"Sweetheart, *you're* my baby. The ball is just one event in dozens that the foundation puts on every year. You tell me which should take precedence." She sat back, everything about her saying her mind was made up.

Damn, damn, damn.

As much as she didn't want her mother invading her space, she didn't want her giving up the ball, either. As head of the Everbrite Foundation, the philanthropic arm of the Beaumont investment firm, her mother had found her true calling.

She put a lot of hard work into making each event something unique and special, but it had been clear from the start this one was a little nearer and dearer to her heart. The Mardi Gras theme was a direct nod to her husband's Cajun roots. For her to step back before she got to see it to fruition would be all kinds of wrong.

"I'll bring a bag or two over tomorrow morning and get settled in," her mother went on as though everything had been decided. "Don't worry, you won't even know I'm here." She smiled. "Who knows? It might even end up being fun."

"No."

The smile dimmed. "No, it won't be fun?"

"No, you can't move in."

"And why not?"

"Because..." Lillian floundered again, trying to come up with the one argument that would keep her mother both happy and far, far away. "Because you only want to move in because you think I'm all alone at night, and...well...I'm not. Alone. You know, at night." She shoved her glass to her lips to stop the words spilling from them in such gleeful abandon.

She wasn't alone at night? What the hell?

"Oh?" Her mother's head cocked to the side in that way she did when she'd heard something she either didn't understand or didn't like.

Lillian would bet right now it was a little of both.

"I, um, I'm sort of seeing someone, and, well, he sometimes spends the night. Most nights, actually." Lillian stumbled on with the lie. "I mean, he stays here on the nights I don't stay at his place."

"You didn't tell me you were seeing anyone special." There was a hint of suspicion in her mother's tone which matched the sharp look in her all-knowing mom eyes.

Crap.

"It's still kind of new, and, well, I didn't want to jinx it by saying anything too soon."

Lies upon lies. She was so going to hell.

"Really?" Her mother's flat tone said she wasn't buying it.

"Really." She forced herself to meet her mother's gaze, the brown eyes so like her own narrowing. "Why would I lie?"

"Hmm." The ring tapped against the glass again in a quick, sharp staccato. "So, who is this mystery man you're all but living with, but haven't seen fit to introduce to your parents yet?"

<hr>

"I need you to move in with me."

Rafe looked down at Lillian's flushed face and wondered what rabbit hole he'd fallen into today. Less than an hour had passed since she'd all but slammed a door in his face, both figuratively and literally, and pretty much told him to go to hell. Now here she was, standing outside his apartment, looking just a little bit drunk, and asking him to move in with her.

No, correction. *Telling* him to move in with her.

Let the weirdness games begin.

"Come again?" Maybe he'd heard her wrong. It was the only logical explanation.

"I need you to move in with me."

Huh.

Playing along to see where the weird went, he leaned one shoulder against the doorjamb and casually crossed his arms. "Wow, this is so sudden. Are you sure we're not moving too fast? We wouldn't want to do anything we'd regret."

"What?"

"I mean, we hardly know each other, and living together is such a big step."

"What?"

It might have been the wine he could smell sweetening her breath, or maybe something else that had her all flustered and out of sorts. But it was obvious his teasing was sailing right over her head. Lillian was definitely off her usual game.

He, on the other hand, was enjoying the hell out of himself.

The little minx had been tormenting him for months. Sexy winks. Blowing kisses. Chipping away at the control he forced himself to cling to whenever she was around, leaving him always off-balanced and frustrated.

It felt good to have the tables turned, even if he didn't have a clue what was going on.

"What are you talking about?" Lillian shook her head. "Never mind. We don't have time. We have to go."

"Go where?"

"To my apartment." She gave him a look of immense frustration. "Haven't you been listening to anything I've said?"

"Yes, but damned if I understood any of it." He was pretty sure she gave a little growl at that and had to bite back a grin. "Why don't you start at the beginning and explain why you feel the sudden urge to shack up?"

"I don't have time to explain it all, but my mother is upstairs, right this second, and if I don't produce you in the next few minutes, she's going to think I was lying and first thing tomorrow she's going to show up with her bags because she thinks I'm all alone, and I love my mother, I swear I do, but I can't have her move in with me, it would be a complete and utter disaster, so I need you to come with me now to make sure that doesn't happen."

This time he was the one to say, "What?"

He'd heard rambling explanations before, but Lillian could give an auctioneer a run for his money in the say-it-all-in-one-breath department.

"Please, Rafe." She stepped closer and placed her hands on his crossed forearms as she looked up at him. "I need your help."

The heat of her hands burned against his bare skin. It traveled up his arms, then shot straight south, causing an immediate and unwelcome problem that made him glad she was too focused on his face to notice.

Hopefully.

He straightened from the doorjamb, expecting it would make her drop her hands, but she tightened her grip instead, as though afraid he was going to get away.

"*Please.*"

He still wasn't sure what she was asking him to do, but when she looked at him with those melted-chocolate eyes and pleaded in that low, throaty voice, it was impossible to say no. This was different from Pete tapping into his protective instincts by playing the brother card. This was pure, unconscious sex appeal.

She had him by the balls and didn't even know it.

"Okay, I'll help."

Lillian sagged in relief. "Thank you." Recovering, she tugged at his arm. "Come on, we have to hurry."

"Okay, okay, wait a second." After turning off the oven he'd been about to throw one of his mother's care-package-slash-guilt-trip heat-and-eat meals into for dinner, he grabbed his keys and locked the apartment.

"Come *on*." She practically danced in the hallway as he double-checked the door out of habit.

"You know, when you do that, you look a lot like my little cousin when she has to pee." He accepted the swat she gave his arm as due justice for the jibe. "I'll need a little more information before we get up there," he said as she dragged him toward the elevator.

He spent the brief ride up to the fourth floor listening to Lillian's semi-coherent explanation—again—for why they needed to convince her mother the two of them were all but living together. Parts of it even made sense. But he got the distinct impression she hadn't thought things all the way through before she wove her little web of lies.

Based on the way his day had been going, one of those sticky strands was probably going to pull loose at the most inopportune time and strangle them both.

His steps slowed as they walked toward her door so he could study her without her knowing it. She was wearing a pair of slouchy sweatpants and a plain baby-blue t-shirt that covered her impressive cleavage right up to her neck. It was so the opposite of what he was used to seeing her wear, it was almost jarring.

It also made him wonder what else was different about her in private than the very flamboyant face she showed the world.

She paused at the door and looked back at him, hands on hips, and tapped her foot.

Tapped. Her. Foot.

He almost burst out laughing. She was so freaking adorable.

It was then he noticed she was wearing nothing but socks on her feet. It had to be the first time he'd ever seen her without a pair of those killer heels she ran around in. Minus the added height, she barely came up to his collarbone.

"You know what to say, right?" she asked.

Not a clue.

"I'll follow your lead."

That seemed to satisfy her. Visibly steeling herself, Lillian unlocked the door and went inside. He followed, closing the door and, assuming his role, placed his hand lightly on her back as they walked. She jumped in surprise.

Judging by the way she pursed her lips as she rose from the couch, he had a bad feeling Lillian's mother had noticed. Or maybe she just wasn't thrilled to be coming face-to-face with the man who was sleeping with her daughter.

Supposedly sleeping with her daughter.

"Mom, you remember Rafael Delgado, don't you?"

"Of course." Patricia smiled and offered her hand. "Peter's friend from the police force. How nice to see you again, Rafael."

"It's nice to see you too, Mrs. Beaumont." He shook her cool, smooth hand with a careful grip. "And just Rafe is fine."

He noticed she didn't invite him to call her Patricia.

Rather than retake her previous spot, she moved to one of the chairs, leaving the couch for himself and Lillian. Once more placing his hand on Lillian's back as they moved around the coffee table to sit, he could feel her heart racing like a hunted doe.

At least this time, she didn't flinch.

"I have to admit, I was a bit surprised when my daughter told me about the two of you," Patricia said, settling back into the cushy chair for what was certain to be a long, uncomfortable interrogation.

Not as surprised as I was.

Rafe had always liked Patricia Beaumont. She'd been very kind and welcoming to him whenever Pete had invited him to family functions over the past few years.

Somewhere in her early fifties, she was one of those rare women who looked her age and didn't seem to mind one bit. Her light brown hair showed a few touches of silver at the temples, and the laugh lines around her eyes hadn't been erased by injections or a scalpel. She had an understated elegance that blended well with the maternal warmth she normally exuded.

A warmth which was noticeably absent as she waited for him to explain himself.

"And why is that?" he asked.

"Well, for one thing, she hasn't mentioned she was seeing anyone special."

"Does she always tell you who she's dating?"

A small frown formed. "Well, no. But this is a little different, wouldn't you say? Since according to her, you're practically living together."

"That might be overstating it a bit," he said, picking his words with care. "But I'd say the amount of time we spend in each other's company and what we do with it is our private business, wouldn't you?"

"Not when my daughter's safety is at issue."

To Patricia's credit, she wasn't just being a nosy, overbearing mom. She was clearly concerned about Lillian's wellbeing. Which made it a lot harder for him to be okay with lying to her like this.

Damn.

This was what happened when he let his hormones do his talking.

"Mrs. Beaumont, I promise you that your daughter's safety is of the utmost importance to me as well. It wouldn't matter if we were dating or not. I'd still do whatever it took to keep her safe."

That, at least, was the absolute truth.

Patricia was just beginning to look appeased when he made the mistake of reaching over and putting his hand on top of Lillian's where it lay on her leg. As she had before, she started at his touch before recovering and giving him a weak smile.

But the damage was done. The hint of suspicion was back in Patricia's eyes, the small bit of trust he'd built with her gone with one quick twitch.

They needed to fix this, fast.

He grasped Lillian's hand and stood. "Would you excuse us for a second, please?" Not waiting for an answer, he tugged Lillian to her feet and all but dragged her toward the kitchen. That was too open to the living room, offering no privacy, so he continued down the hall to the first bedroom and pulled her inside.

"She's not buying it," Lillian moaned.

"Of course not, when you keep acting like I've hit you with a Taser when I touch you."

"I don't!"

"You do. But I think we can fix that. We just need to get this out of the way." Before he could think too much and talk himself out of it, he tugged her closer and pressed his mouth to hers.

Her lips were soft and passive, but her whole body went stiff with shock. And yet, she didn't pull away. Encouraged, he moved his lips over hers with gentle pressure, keeping the kiss easy and nonthreatening. Finally, he lifted his head, ending the kiss with a soft sigh.

Opening eyes she'd closed at some point during the kiss, Lillian looked up at him with a mixture of shock and, if he wasn't deluding himself, a smoldering spark of sexual interest.

"Why did you do that?" she whispered.

"So you'd relax and be more comfortable when I touch you."

"Oh."

"And," he added, needing to be honest, "because I wanted to."

"*Oh.*"

Before he could ask if he should apologize, Lillian slid her arms up over his shoulders and around his neck.

"What if I want to, too? That's only fair, right?" Without waiting for an answer, she put her lips to his. For a second, the kiss was as chaste as the first. A pleasant press of lips and nothing else.

And then it was so much more.

Heat flashed through his body as her lips parted. Her teeth tugged on his lower lip until he let her in, her tongue darting in to tease at his, encouraging him to play. With a groan, Rafe answered the call. He pulled her tight against him, the feel of her body against his stoking the flames of passion higher and faster.

Too high and too fast, some rational part of him cautioned.

But months, no *years* of wanting and not having her had pushed him far beyond the point of good sense. He sank into the kiss with every unfulfilled desire leading the charge, and was greedily satisfied when the response he got from her was just as wild and unrestrained.

He was calculating how to get them both to the bed without breaking the kiss when the sound of a throat being cleared sliced through the haze of lust like a bucket of ice water.

Lillian must not have heard it. When he lifted his mouth from hers, she made a sound of dissatisfaction and chased him, landing another quick kiss before she caught on to Rafe's attempt to hold her off. Her breath hitched as she figured out what he already knew.

"Mom," she choked out weakly.

Angry with himself for letting what was supposed to be a simple kiss get so out of control, he struggled to collect himself as he turned to face Patricia, who was hovering in the open doorway behind them.

"Mrs. Beaumont, I'm sorry. We were..."

Yeah, there was no good way to finish that sentence.

To his surprise, Patricia waved a hand and smiled.

Smiled.

"Don't worry about it, Rafe. And please, call me Patricia."

"Uh, all right."

"Good." Her smile widened. "Well, I think I've found out everything I needed to know here. I'll just see myself out."

"Let me walk you to the door," Lillian said.

Patricia's smile turned a bit wicked. "No need to interrupt what you're doing. I know the way." She looked at Rafe, her gaze sharp. "Take care of my baby."

"I plan to." It was a promise he intended to keep.

As her mother disappeared from the doorway, Lillian collapsed against his chest with a mortified groan. "Oh, my God." The muffled words were followed by a small snort of laughter. "That was…"

"Embarrassing?"

Because there was still something humiliating about being caught necking by a parent, no matter how old you were, and whether they were yours or not.

"To like the millionth degree." She picked her head up and looked at him. "I am *so* sorry I dragged you into this."

"I'm not." Did she even realized how sexy she looked at that minute? With her breasts pressing against him, and her face tipped up with those reddened lips practically begging for another kiss?

Or ten.

Fuck.

He needed to leave before he crossed a line he'd regret come morning.

"Now that your mother's gone, I should probably head home, too."

But he didn't move. Couldn't. Not yet. Not when this was all he was ever going to have of her. He wanted to soak up the heady experience of touching Lillian Beaumont like this for just one more greedy minute.

"Do you have to?"

"Yeah. I think I do." He swallowed hard and reached for her arms to set her away.

"What if I don't want you to?"

Chapter 8

Rafe froze at her words before he rasped out his answer.

"Then I *know* I have to go."

That wasn't what she wanted to hear.

How could he say such a thing, when she could damn well feel how much he wanted to stay pressing into her belly?

Then he surprised her by catching the lower lip she'd started to push out in a pout with his teeth and giving it a nip. The sensation shot straight to her core, sensitizing her breasts, and making her gasp in surprise and delight.

"Ask me again tomorrow when you're not hopped up on adrenaline and merlot, and I guarantee you'll get a different answer." Rafe's voice was so filled with dark promise she couldn't control the shiver of anticipation that shuddered through her. She knew he felt it, because his smile was both knowing and satisfied.

She would have liked to argue with his suggestion her actions were being influenced by the stress of the situation she'd placed them both in this evening. But she had to admit as he led her by the hand to her front door, her head *was* a teensy bit muddy. He was wrong, though. It wasn't from the wine, or the adrenaline.

It was him.

He muddled her thinking. Destroyed her control. Made her want to explore where she'd only just reminded herself that morning she dared not go. Sex with this man wouldn't be simple or casual. It would be dark, and wild, and involve far too much emotion for what she was willing to give to a relationship right now.

If she was smart, she'd accept the gift he'd given her of time and distance, and, come tomorrow, they'd go back to the way they'd been before. Friendly neighbors and acquaintances. Nothing more.

Except…she really didn't want to be smart.

And she really, *really* wanted there to be more.

Stopping at the door, Rafe turned and skimmed the backs of his fingers down her cheek in a gentle caress, his gaze still hot but his voice neutral when he said, "We'll talk tomorrow."

"Okay."

She thought he might kiss her again, but instead he stepped back and opened the door. "Make sure you lock up and set your alarm."

"Okay."

The struggle in him was almost palpable as he hovered in the doorway. He ran his thumb down her cheek again and pressed his forehead to hers. "I'm going to take my time driving you wet and wild when I finally get you naked under me," he whispered.

"Definitely okay," she whispered back, grinning when he groaned and wrenched himself away. He stalked out of the apartment and stopped to wait in the hallway, hands fisted at his sides, chest rising and falling with rapid breaths.

Just like the previous day on the elevator, she waited until the door was almost closed before blowing him a kiss. She was rewarded by a muffled spat of Spanish that was no doubt a few curses aimed her way.

Biting her lip, she sagged against the door. The sensation reignited the sensual spark from when Rafe had used his teeth to do the same thing, making her body heat up again. If he weren't out there waiting to hear the beep of the alarm being set, she would have groaned out loud.

Smart?

Oh, no. There wasn't a chance in hell she'd end up being smart about her attraction to the five-alarm hotness that was Rafael Delgado. No woman on the planet had that much willpower.

Which meant she had to be careful instead, and focus on not losing sight of her ultimate goal. As long as she didn't let herself get too invested in whatever came of their physical relationship, she should be fine.

Probably.

After she set the alarm and dragged the stepstool over to check through the peephole Rafe was gone, Lillian collected the wine bottle and glasses and brought them to the kitchen. A little trickle of guilt invaded her hormone high. She didn't enjoy lying to her mother, but what choice had she left her?

It was all so stupid. Everyone was making way too much of the whole thing with her car. Was it a little unnerving someone had slashed her tires? Of course it was. She wasn't stupid. But she also wasn't helpless, and she refused to upheave her entire life because of someone else's anger management issues.

Since she hadn't been able to grocery shop without her car, her dinner options were slim. When she looked in the fridge, though, she was pleasantly surprised to find two wrapped chicken Caesar salads that hadn't been there this morning.

The trickle of guilt increased to a gush. Her mother must have brought them. Probably planning to use the time it took for them to have dinner together to plead her case about Lillian moving back home.

Sorry, no. Not gonna happen.

Her mother knew why. Both her parents did.

But what neither of them seemed to grasp was that simply removing the person who created the issue in the first place didn't make it disappear. Sean had stripped away every ounce of comfort and safety her family home used to represent. Spending one night there would be an uncomfortable feat. Any longer would be more like a vacation in hell.

Covered in fire ants.

And honey.

Having her mother stay at her apartment would have been less painful, but no less uncomfortable. In the year she'd lived on her own, Lillian had gotten used to having her personal space. Her own little schedules and daily rituals. Having someone, anyone, stay with her, even the mother she loved and adored, would disrupt her entire life.

That would affect her ability to create.

And that was unacceptable. Especially now.

Time was not her friend.

Taking one of the salads and a fork, Lillian went down the hallway to the bedroom at the end, which was considered the main bedroom because it was larger. Lucky for her Rafe had pulled her into the other bedroom and not this one, or she would have had some explaining to do.

Rafe.

Thank God he'd gone along with her crazy scheme. And it was crazy, she could admit it. She hadn't had time to think it through. Her mother's announcement took her by surprise, and she'd gone with the first thing that came to mind.

And the first person.

Which was only because she'd just been with him. And that he lived right downstairs and was the only person she could produce on the spot. It had nothing to do with the way she'd fantasized over his denim-clad ass. Or the random dreams of him that sometimes left her achy and wanting.

Settling onto her stool, she speared a piece of delicately seasoned chicken. It didn't matter. She'd told the lie, Rafe backed her up, and her mother had bought it.

Because of that kiss, a little voice reminded her.

Oh, sweet baby Jesus, that kiss.

In her twenty-four years, she'd been kissed, she'd made out, and she'd had sex.

That kiss had been like all three wrapped up in one by those two very talented lips. Rafe had gotten her hotter faster than any man in her life.

Ever.

Lillian shook her head. She needed to stop thinking about her shagalicious neighbor and get down to work. With a critical eye, she studied the canvas on the easel in front of her. The colors were a delicate mix of pastels, the central figure a seated woman wearing a flowing blue dress, her head turned away as she leaned into the cello she held.

It was almost done. Yet it didn't call to her tonight the way her paintings usually did when they were so close to completion. Instead, another urge rode her, and she knew her muse well enough to follow where it would lead, rather than the other way around.

Replacing the canvas with a fresh one, already primed and ready for paint, she turned on the radio and set up her paints as she ate the rest of her salad. By the time she was done with both, she still didn't know what she was going to be painting.

But as she always did, she trusted in her instincts and began.

Lost in the thrall of her art, she didn't register the passing of time until her fingers started to cramp. She worked through the pain for a brief span, but finally bowed to the knowledge that if she pushed much longer, it would affect the quality of her work.

Cleaning up by rote, she refused to look at the partially finished piece until she'd put everything back in its place. Then, she took a deep breath and turned to see it for the first time as a whole, rather than the individual parts that had emerged as her brush labored over the images her mind was creating.

The breath left her again in a hard rush.

This was so different from her other work that for a second it felt as though it wasn't even her own. All of her paintings were soft, pastel, alive and vibrant, but at the same time subdued and quiet. It wasn't a style she'd chosen. It was just how her paintings always seemed to come out of her hands.

But this one...this was bold. Strong.

Sensual.

She studied the long sweep of spine, tight with muscles. The curve of taut, naked buttocks. The powerful legs. It was far from finished, but where it usually took several sessions to block in the basics of the form she was laying down, this time it was almost whole the first time out. If she could, she'd keep going, still feeling the creative twitch in her hands, but she knew better than to overdo.

Taking one last look at the painting before she switched off the light, her breath caught when she realized *who* she'd just spent the evening painting.

Even though his face was turned away, there was enough of a hint in the jaw and the cheekbone that it was impossible to deny. Her nude bore more than a passing resemblance to the sexy white knight from downstairs. It was there in his profile, in his dark hair, in his dusky brown skin tone. All of that was Rafe. Everything else was entirely imagination, of course, since she'd never even seen him without a shirt on.

Suddenly, her creative urge was replaced by a new one.

To find out firsthand just how close her imagination had come to the real thing.

━━━◆○◆━━━

"I brought coffee."

Lillian blinked groggily up at the man who stood outside her door and waited for her brain to process the words. It was slow going. While her neurons fired up, she took in the deliciously edible picture he made.

Faded, ripped jeans and sneakers. A Boulder PD baseball jersey snug enough to show off his lean, muscled chest. And a morning scruff that said he hadn't acquainted himself with his razor yet today.

Yum.

"You know, you're the second cop in two days to wake me up by pounding on my door at the crack of dawn." She tore her gaze from his deliciousness to zero in on the cardboard tray he carried in one hand. "At least you're smart enough to bring me caffeine as a bribe."

She didn't waste any time removing one of the large to-go cups and taking a swallow. "Nectar of the gods," she murmured as she took another sip, ignoring the smile Rafe was trying to hide.

"The coffee is a peace offering." He lifted the white paper bag in his other hand. "The pastries are the bribe."

Her mouth watered at the familiar logo from the bakery down the block. She opened the door wider. "Okay, you've redeemed yourself for the unreasonable hour."

"You know, it *is* after seven." He passed her and headed toward the kitchen.

Lillian groaned as she followed. "Please don't tell me you're one of *them.*"

"One of who?"

"A morning person." She didn't think she could take another one of those in her life. Both Thea and Amelia were. So was her mother, and most of her family, with the sole exception of Peter, who'd been known to hibernate for twelve hours straight if given the opportunity.

As always seemed the case, she was the odd one out. She preferred late-night hours and sleeping in. It was just the way her body clock ran.

"By nature, no. But by necessity for work, yes." Rafe looked around. "Plates?"

Going to the cabinet, she grabbed two hex-shaped plates glazed in deep indigo and brought them to the island. The fist-sized danishes Rafe took from the bag made her mouth water almost as much as the man himself did.

Focusing her attention on only one thing that was bad for her at a time, she took a huge bite of the pastry and closed her eyes as the flavors exploded over her tongue. It might not be the breakfast of champions, but it was a lot tastier than the bowl of bland nutritious cereal she would have poured for herself if Rafe hadn't shown up bearing tasty gifts.

Which now that her brain had been jolted awake by the double whammy of caffeine and sugar, she started to wonder why, exactly, he had.

"Not that I don't appreciate it," she said after she swallowed, "but I have to wonder why you felt the need to bring a bribe. Or a peace offering, for that matter."

"The peace offering was because I wasn't sure if I needed to apologize or not."

"Apologize? For what? If anyone should be apologizing, it's me, for dragging you up here last night like I did." Something she still couldn't quite believe she'd done. She wouldn't have thought twice about involving Thea or Des in one of her little schemes, but they were close friends. Rafe wasn't. He was barely more than a casual acquaintance, really.

More than that, after that kiss, her naughty inner imp reminded her.

Oh, that kiss.

She'd had a long, restless night thanks to its residual effects. Every time she closed her eyes, she'd felt the softness of his lips against hers, the hardness of the rest of him, and the heat that had her close to imploding with frustrated desire.

Self-satisfaction had been a poor substitute.

"You'd better not be trying to apologize for kissing me," she said, suddenly certain that was why he'd come. Why were men so stupid sometimes? "That was right up there in the category of one of the best kisses ever, and I don't want you ruining it by getting all stupid and remorseful and saying it never should have happened, or I was drunk and you took advantage. You kissed me. You can't take it back." She tilted her chin up and crossed her arms, daring him to apologize now.

Rafe was silent for a few seconds, studying her face. His lips twitched, but he got them back under control. Which was a good thing, because if he laughed, she'd have to hurt him.

"One of the best kisses ever, huh?"

She sniffed, refusing to let her embarrassment show. "It was up there. Could still use some work, though."

"Duly noted," he replied with a nod. His lips twitched again.

"If you laugh at me, I swear..."

All hint of amusement faded from his expression. "I have no intention of laughing at you. Just like I have no intention of apologizing for kissing you."

Lillian blinked. "You don't?"

"No. Did you have a little too much to drink last night? Maybe. But you weren't drunk, and you were in total control of your faculties. And if anyone could be accused of taking advantage of anyone else, let me remind you that *you* kissed *me* the second time." He sounded a little too pleased about that.

Lillian cleared her throat. She'd sort of forgotten that tiny detail in all the lusty aftermath. "Well, I'm not apologizing either."

He grinned. "Good to know."

"So?"

"So...what I wanted to apologize for was for what I said right before I left. I might have been a little out of line. And if I was, I'm sorry."

Sorry he was out of line, not sorry he'd said it.

Interesting distinction.

She needed to knock Rafe off balance the way he had her with that little reminder she'd been the one to practically jump him the second time. Lillian cocked her head and made a confused face. "What you said before you left?"

"Yes."

"I don't think I remember." Total lie. She remembered each word like it was seared into her brain. "Maybe you could refresh my memory. What was it you said, exactly?"

She gloated in satisfaction as his calm, amused demeanor slipped into deer-in-headlights territory. But then, just as fast, a gleam that should have worried her entered those green-gold jaguar eyes of his. That *would* have worried her if she didn't on some level *want* the result she was about to get.

Rafe wiped his fingers on his napkin with slow, methodical movements, his gaze locked on hers. "I believe it was something along the lines of a promise. That I was going to drive you wet and wild. Slowly, and without mercy, until you were screaming from the sheer pleasure of it." He cocked his head in imitation of hers. "Sounding familiar now?"

The pulse in her neck started to throb in the same rapid rhythm as the one between her legs. "Maybe a little." Her voice was a breathy whisper. She cleared her throat. "Although I don't seem to recall the part about the screaming."

"An oversight on my part." He leaned in closer. "Trust me. There will be screaming."

"The good kind, I hope."

He leaned closer still. "Only the very best kind, *te lo prometo.*"

I promise you.

Thank you, high school Spanish.

"Well, then, I guess there's no apology needed." Lillian bridged the last gap and feathered her lips across his. "Is there?"

"*Dios mio.*" Rafe groaned against her mouth, taking it in a hard, hungry kiss before he broke away with another harsh curse. "You taste so good."

She ran her tongue over her lips. "Maybe it's the danish," she teased, enjoying the way his gaze zeroed in on her mouth.

"Maybe we'll have to test that theory." He brought his hands up to cup her face. "What time do you have to be at work?"

The feel of his hands on her skin made her shiver despite the heat threatening to melt her from the inside out. "I don't. I have the day off."

"Better and better." His fingers skimmed her cheeks once, twice, turning the shivers into shudders of anticipation. "Why don't we—" He broke off with an annoyed growl when the phone rang from a few feet away on the kitchen counter.

Lillian seconded the sentiment.

But there were very few people who had the number to the landline her father insisted she have installed. Ignoring it was out of the question. Movements stiff with regret and thwarted passion, she leaned back enough on the stool to look over and see the caller ID screen. She missed the warmth of Rafe's fingers the second his hands slid away.

"Let it ring," he urged, his displaced hands now caressing her legs.

The skimpy cotton shorts she wore were no protection from the tantalizing press of his warm hands. "I have to answer," she groaned. "It's my mother."

His hands stilled. Then, with a low, rumbling laugh dark with frustration, he let them slide away. "Tell her that her timing sucks."

"Seriously," Lillian muttered, as she got up to grab the handset. "Mom, hi. Is everything okay?"

"Of course it is, dear." Her mother sounded disgustingly chipper.

Stupid morning people.

"I just called to say good morning, and, well, I wanted to say I was sorry for any...well, awkwardness which might have resulted from my rather unfortunate interruption."

Which one?

Lillian dared a glance over at Rafe, who was devouring the rest of his pastry. Lord, what she would give to be that danish. With great difficulty, she dragged her mind back to the conversation. "It's fine,

Mom. No problem at all."

"Oh good, I'm so glad."

She narrowed her eyes. Her mother sounded a little *too* glad. "Why?"

"Well, I wouldn't want Rafe to feel awkward around the family because of it, that's all."

A bad feeling started. "Mom..."

"You *will* be bringing him with you to your brother's party tonight, won't you?"

Crap.

Her brother's birthday. The reason she'd taken the day off.

She squeezed her eyes shut, all plans of spending a lazy day exploring the possibilities of a naked Rafe in her bed vanishing. The lie she'd fashioned was beginning to feel more like a noose.

"Lillian?" Her mother's voice broke the silence. "Is everything all right?"

"Yeah. Yes, Mom, everything's fine. It's just..." She scrambled for an excuse that wouldn't sound like one. "I don't think he can make it." As soon as she said it, Lillian felt Rafe's attention focus on her, but she refused to meet his gaze.

"Well, whyever not?"

"Because..." She floundered. She wasn't a liar by nature. Every embellishment she made only provided more chances to trip herself up. Maybe she needed to just throw in the towel and come clean. Suck it up and let her mother move in for a few days.

How bad could it be?

"Lillian?" Her mother's voice jarred her out of her pinwheeling thoughts of confession.

"Um..."

"Let me talk to him."

"What?"

"Let me talk to him," her mother repeated. When Lillian didn't answer right away, she said, "Is there a problem with me speaking with him?"

There it was. The perfect opportunity to come clean. Lillian opened her mouth...

And couldn't do it.

Panic cramped her stomach as she looked over at Rafe, who was watching her with an intense look on his face. "Um, no, but..." She mouthed *she wants to talk to you*.

To her surprise, he reached out for the phone. Unsure if it was the right thing or not, she gave it to him.

"Good morning, Mrs. Beaumont." Rafe's gaze stayed locked with Lillian's as he listened. "Okay, right. Patricia," he said, with a soft chuckle, "and no, you didn't wake us. We were just having breakfast."

Lillian groaned to herself at the not-so-subtle subtext.

"Yes, I've learned she's not much of a morning person. Yes, I know." Rafe listened some more, nodding as he did. Lillian strained to hear what her mother was saying, but it was impossible. Rafe's expression gave nothing away, and neither did his occasional "uh huhs" and "rights."

"No, you're right," he said, finally, giving Lillian a smile. "I agree. No, it's not a problem at all. Right. Okay, then, we'll see you tonight. Goodbye."

Staring in disbelief as he thumbed the phone off, Lillian said in a strangled voice, "You agreed to come to the party?"

"Yes." Calm as you please, he picked up his coffee and took a sip. Like he hadn't just tossed them both into the lion pit.

"Why would you do that?" Didn't he understand the enormous problem he'd created?

"Because it was the only way your mother would continue to believe we're a couple. She was already having her doubts."

"No, she wasn't." Not after seeing that kiss.

Rafe gave her a "come on" look.

"Why else would she have called this early in the morning? And on the landline, rather than on your cell? You said it yourself. You're not a morning person."

"Because..." Because he was right. She was checking up on them. Lillian's eyes widened as another realization hit her. "You knew she'd call."

"I thought she might."

"That's the reason you came over." Like a Greek bearing gifts. The rat.

"One of them, but not the only one."

"Oh, really?"

"Yes, really." He leaned in closer until their noses almost touched. "You never asked me what the bribe was for."

"Um, what?" Being this close to him was playing merry havoc with her hormones.

"Ask me what the bribe is for."

"Um...what's the bribe for?"

Rafe leaned in even closer, his mouth brushing her cheek on its way to her ear, where he whispered, "To make sure you didn't say no when I told you I really am moving in."

Chapter 9

He probably could have handled that better.

Rafe accepted that fact a few hours later as he negotiated his truck through the afternoon traffic on US-36 on their way back from Denver. *Asking* would have been a much better choice than *telling* Lillian he planned to move in with her for the duration. But he was of the school of thought it was better to seek forgiveness than permission.

Of course, that school didn't have a class on dealing with an irate pixie who was not at all fond of being told what to do.

Lucky for him, he'd already been in the apartment, which made it harder for her to get rid of him until she heard him out. Not that she'd done a lot of listening. First had been incredulous laughter, followed by some angry foot stomping when she realized he wasn't kidding. She'd concluded with a long monologue peppered with more than a few interesting adjectives that he'd tuned out of about halfway through. The gist of it had been he was out of his mind if he thought she would allow him to bully his way into her home.

Having two sisters of equally dramatic bent, Rafe let her go until she wound herself down. The worst part was, she hadn't been wrong about a lot of what she said. He *was* planning to make her agree to his plan. Somehow.

He just had to find the right approach.

The fact it was for her own safety didn't seem to make one bit of difference to her, which frustrated the hell out of him. Not that he thought she was in any immediate danger. The vandal was probably someone acting out in an isolated fit of anger. A disgruntled artist Lillian wouldn't give a show to. Or maybe an ex-lover who hadn't wanted to be an ex.

That last possibility bothered him a lot more than it should have.

Grave danger or not, though, he'd made a promise. He hadn't come out and told Patricia Beaumont he was spending his nights with her daughter, but he'd implied it. And he'd told her nothing but the absolute truth when he said he'd do whatever it took to keep Lillian safe. So, he wasn't backing down on this no matter how loud or long Lillian argued about it.

It was just taking a little longer than he'd expected for her to give in.

The matter had been tabled—if you could call it that—when Lillian walked out of the living room in the middle of him talking. She came out of her bedroom twenty minutes later dressed in tight jeans, high-heeled boots, and a top that resembled a corset more than it did a blouse. Slinging the suitcase she called a purse over one delicate shoulder as she headed for the front door, she'd announced she was going out to pick up her brother's birthday present.

He hadn't bothered to argue. Like the good little bodyguard he was planning to be for the next few days, he fell into step behind her and followed her down to the garage, where she led the way to her car.

Or, rather, the empty slot where her car was supposed to be. By the slump to her otherwise rigid shoulders, it was clear she'd forgotten the police hadn't yet returned the little toy she drove. She turned and walked back toward his truck.

That little sign of defeat just about killed him.

The only thing Rafe had going for him was that Lillian seemed incapable of staying quiet for long. About halfway through their thirty-five-minute drive down to Denver, she'd broken the tense silence by asking if he knew when her car would be returned. She looked so depressed when he said no, he almost felt bad for calling Pete while she was getting dressed and asking him to delay the car's release as long as possible.

Almost.

But not enough to give her back the means to evade him at will. Keeping her safe meant keeping her close, not zipping around town from party to party.

By the time they arrived at the Pepsi Center, they'd reached what amounted to détente. But Rafe knew the war was far from over. What he was still a little confused about, though, was why they were fighting about this in the first place.

He hadn't imagined the interest in Lillian's eyes. Or in the rest of her, for that matter. They were going to end up in bed at some point in the near—very near—future. Those tight little nipples that pressed up against him this morning, and the way she'd all but melted in his arms, had ended any questions he'd had about *that*.

Rafe swallowed a groan. *Dios*, she'd been like the sweetest candy he'd ever tasted. If the phone hadn't interrupted, he doubted he would have stopped until he'd sampled every last delectable inch of her.

And maybe gone back for seconds.

Not thoughts he should have while driving, when there wasn't any polite way to adjust himself and relieve the sudden pressure in his jeans.

Kissing Lillian last night had been a tactical error on his part. He'd known all along that if he ever touched her, his resolve would crumble like an overbaked taco shell. It was why he'd worked so hard to keep the barrier of distance between them all these months. And yet he'd been stupid enough to think he could handle kissing her, just once, without paying the price.

What had he been thinking?

Oh, right. That they needed to convince her mother they were a couple. And tonight, they would have to sell the same lie to her entire family. Wouldn't that be a fucking fun evening.

He was either going to lose his ever-loving mind trying to hide the way his body reacted whenever he got close to Lillian, or her brothers were going to put him out of his misery and kill him outright.

If their father didn't beat them to it.

Détente lasted until they got back to Lillian's apartment. She had no choice but to let him in, since he was carrying the heavy package they'd gone all the way down to Denver to collect. He wasn't much of a hockey fan, but he'd been duly impressed with the framed and mounted jersey signed by the entire 2001 Colorado Avalanche Stanley Cup winning team.

Theo, Lillian had gloated, was going to shit kittens over it.

Rafe didn't know about that. But he figured it was a damn nice gift, even for a man who could buy himself just about anything he wanted. Including the entire hockey team *and* their arena.

"Thank you for carrying that up, and for driving me to get it," Lillian said as he leaned the box against the couch. She stayed right beside the door, making no move to close it. "I'm sure you had much better things to do with your day."

As hints went, it was a pretty poor one.

He smiled and dropped into one of the chairs. "No problem at all. I'm entirely at your disposal."

Lillian scowled at him a long moment before swinging the door shut on a sigh. "Why are you being so stubborn about this?" She sat in the other chair with a dramatic flop.

"Why are you?"

"Because I don't need protecting! I keep telling everyone they're overreacting. People's cars get vandalized in parking lots all the time. It doesn't make it personal."

It might have sounded like she was trying to make him believe that, but he could tell it was herself she was working so hard to convince. The slashed tires had rattled her more than she was admitting, and *still* she resisted the help everyone offered. He needed to know why.

But first, he needed to clear something else up.

"You do know that me staying here is in no way contingent on you sleeping with me, right?" If it hadn't been such a serious subject, he might have been amused by the way her mouth fell open.

But it was serious. He needed to make sure she understood what he'd meant, and not what he'd finally realized she might have *thought* he meant.

"When I told you I was moving in, I should have made it clear that it was into the spare bedroom, not yours. I'm sorry if it sounded like I was taking our sleeping together for granted, or like I was expecting anything in exchange for my offer to protect you."

"What? Why would you...I never thought—" She jumped to her feet and planted her fists on her hips. "Rafael Delgado, what a horrible thing to say! I never once, for a single second, thought you were trying to get into my bed."

She bit her lip when he quirked an eyebrow at her. "Well, okay, yes, you were. But that's an entirely different matter. This"—she waved her hand between them—"has nothing to do with that, and everything to do with you being an overprotective Neanderthal, just like my brothers."

Rafe stood. "Actually, this"—he mimicked her gesture—"is about the lie *you* told to your mother and asked *me* to go along with."

"For one night!"

"Oh? And what about that phone call this morning?" He advanced on her a step, which she matched in retreat.

"That was a...a fluke. A one-time thing. She won't be checking up on us again."

"You don't really believe that, do you?"

Another step.

Another retreat.

"I, uh...of course I do."

He grinned. "You're a terrible liar."

Jamming her fists onto her hips again, Lillian glared at him. "I am not." Realizing what she'd said, she made a sound of pure frustration. "God, you're so annoying!"

"Because I'm right?"

"No, because you're a man."

Rafe felt his blood warm as he continued to stalk her, one step at a time, until her back hit the edge of the kitchen island. Before his prey could slip away, he placed both hands on the cool granite, caging her between them as he leaned his body close to hers. Close, but not touching.

That decision needed to be hers alone.

"And you're a woman." He dipped his face toward her neck and inhaled the spicy scent that was uniquely hers. "God, I want you." He was rewarded by a hitch in her breath and the rapid dilation of her pupils.

"This might not be a good idea," she whispered.

"It's definitely not a good idea." He touched his lips oh-so softly to the corner of her mouth. "But I can't seem to remember why anymore."

And he couldn't. Months, *years* of resistance had been erased with one kiss, and try as he might, there wasn't any reason compelling enough to make him step back from her now. Not when he finally had her right where he'd fantasized about so many times.

Right or wrong, he was going to take whatever she was willing to offer and deal with the consequences later.

"So, what do you want to do?" He pressed another feather-light kiss to the other corner of her mouth.

Teasing.

Enticing.

Asking.

Lillian looked up at him, her dark-chocolate eyes sheened with arousal, and moistened her lips. "What do I want?"

"Tell me."

She met his gaze almost defiantly and said, "I want you to make me scream."

◆

The look of pure, primal lust stamped onto Rafe's expression sent a rush of moisture between her thighs and eased the discomfort saying those provocative words had caused.

Shy, she wasn't. But asking—no, telling a man you wanted him to make you scream in pleasure wasn't part of her usual repertoire. It didn't matter he'd promised to do that very thing just a few short hours ago. The fact she was giving him permission to do it was a big deal.

The fact she *wanted* him to do it was even bigger.

Pushing away the dark memories that threatened to intrude and ruin the moment, Lillian licked her lips again and was rewarded when Rafe's nostrils flared. Good. She didn't want him thinking too hard about anything, either. She wanted them both to enjoy this, because she couldn't be certain it would ever happen again.

"So, Rafe." She slipped her arms around his neck, fingers sifting through the short hair at his nape. "Think you're *up* for it?" Leaving no room for doubt about her intent, she pressed herself against him. And *holy hell*, was he ever up.

A thrill of anticipation tingled through her body.

Rafe growled—actually *growled*—as he caught her up against him and lifted her as though she weighed nothing to sit on the edge of the island. His fingers tugged at the laces on the side of the corset-inspired top her friend Des had designed for his spring line, growling again when the laces fought back.

Lillian seconded the sentiment. She was about to suggest he just cut the stupid things when the rigid constriction loosened. Not wasting a moment, Rafe freed her breasts, his tongue finding one tight nipple and giving it an enthusiastic hello.

The warmth of his mouth contrasted with the cool air as he shifted his attention to the other neglected nipple, where he feasted like a man starved. Which was ridiculous, because a man like Rafael Delgado had to be dripping in hot, willing women every day of the week.

But for today, at least, he was hers, and she wasn't about to miss a minute of her chance to see if her imagination had done him justice. With a light tug on his hair, she got him to abandon his prize and shift his attention to her mouth.

At first, the kiss was hard and punishing, almost bruising. But then he seemed to rein himself in and gentled the connection to a series of light, teasing kisses and licks.

Oh, *hell* no.

This time, the tug she gave on his hair wasn't nearly as gentle.

When his uncertain gaze met hers, she said very clearly, "Don't hold back from me. I won't break." She gave him a wicked grin and nipped his chin. Hard. "Promise."

She didn't understand the words he muttered in reply, but he seemed to know exactly what she wanted. His mouth attacked hers, his tongue driving inside and conquering every inch of it with ruthless greed. She groaned into the kiss, her fingers clutching his shoulders as her body hummed into overdrive under the sensual onslaught.

She didn't know why this flipped her switch the way it did, but she'd learned not to worry about it. Everyone had their kinks. Having her partner go all alpha male just happened to get her motor running.

Having *Rafe* be that alpha male damn near made her purr.

Gasping out a hard breath, he pressed his mouth to her neck before leaning his forehead on her shoulder. "Christ, woman, I always knew you'd be the death of me." Before she could reply, he slid his hands under her ass and lifted, surprising a gasp out of her. "Wrap your legs around me."

Any other time, the harsh order would have put her hackles up and had her looking to do the exact opposite. But right here, right now, she couldn't move fast enough to do as he said.

As Rafe took her mouth again, she was only vaguely aware of him moving. She was too caught up in the carnal web he was weaving to think about where he was taking her until he deposited her in the middle of the bed.

She looked up at him from her boneless sprawl, breathing hard.

So was he. "I hope to fuck you have rubbers, because I don't think I could make it down to my place and back without hurting something."

Her gaze dropped to where he was pressing his hand against—she swallowed—the impressive erection straining his jeans.

"In the nightstand." It was only as he yanked the drawer open she remembered what else she kept in there.

Oh shit.

A dark grin creased Rafe's face. "Well, well, well." He reached in and came out with a pair of pink, fuzzy handcuffs dangling from one finger. "Having cops and robbers fantasies, *querida*?"

The cuffs had been a gag prize from a bachelorette party she'd attended. But that didn't explain why she kept them. Or why they played such a prominent role in some of her naughtier dreams about her sexy downstairs neighbor.

Not that she'd give Rafe the satisfaction of either admission. Or the chance to examine what other personal-care items she had stored at her bedside.

Or herself time to get twitchy about him touching any of it.

She batted her eyes. "Only about you, Officer Delgado." Her reward was a loud *thunk* when Rafe dropped the cuffs back into the drawer.

"You are so fucking killing me."

Pulling out a strip of condoms from the box he unearthed, he tossed them on top of the nightstand. As he turned his attention back to Lillian, one hand loosened the button and zipper on his jeans. He let out a low moan of relief as the material parted.

So did she.

This is really happening.

Watching Rafe strip off the snug baseball jersey and toss it to the floor, her hormones stood up and cheered. She'd been so busy the past few months focusing on her plan, she hadn't done much more than go dancing at Blaze a few times when her friends harassed her into leaving her studio. Her bed had been cold and lonely for far too long, and Rafe was far too enticing.

The combination could lead to disaster if she wasn't careful.

"You have way too many clothes on for what I have planned for you." The rough velvet of his voice sent a shiver through her body.

"Then maybe you need to take them off me."

It was probably foolish to taunt him like that, but she couldn't regret it. Not when he scooped up first one foot, then the other, quickly divesting each one of the high-heeled boots that pinched her toes but made her ass look amazing in jeans. Which were the next thing to go, removed with the efficiency of a magician whisking away a tablecloth and leaving the place setting behind.

Or in this case, the tiny black thong.

The corset top had only stayed on because it had been pressed between them on the trip from the living room. Now it hung loose, her breasts spilling over the top. It was the last major barrier to being naked, and for the briefest second, she hesitated to have it gone.

But then it was, and the heat and hunger shining from Rafe's eyes chased away the chill of self-doubt beginning to creep in.

"*Dios mio*, just look at you." The whispered words were heavy with lust.

"I'd rather be looking at you." She gave a pointed look at his jeans, which were riding low on his lean hips but blocked what was sure to be a spectacular view.

She didn't imagine the hesitation in Rafe's hands before they went to the waistband of his pants. Or the way he shifted his body to the side when he kicked off his sneakers and jerked his jeans down his long legs. Or the way he flinched ever-so-slightly as she sucked in a breath at the sight of the scar that marred his left thigh almost from hip to knee.

She'd known he'd been hurt on the job. Bad enough that he wasn't back to work even close to a year later. But seeing the tangible evidence was still a shock.

One that had the potential of ruining everything wonderful that had been building between them if she didn't fix the mistake of her reaction.

Fast.

She slipped from the bed to her knees in front of him and placed a hand on each of his thighs for balance, ignoring the way his left leg twitched at her touch as though he wanted to pull away. Instead, she pressed a reverent kiss on the damaged flesh before focusing all her attention on the enticing bulge that stretched the material of his dark blue boxer-briefs to its limits.

With gentle care, she put her teeth to the bulge and bit down, just a little, her eyes on him to judge his reaction. Some guys were too nervous about teeth near their jewels to enjoy the tiny dark pleasure.

If she had to guess by the wild look on Rafe's face, though, he wasn't one of them.

Smiling, she released him from her teeth and slid her hands up to the band of his briefs. With a slowness meant to torment, she pulled the material down over his erection until it finally sprang free, the dark, swollen head bobbing back to slap against Rafe's taut belly.

Unable to resist, she leaned in and ran her tongue up the firm length, curling it under the crest before finishing with a kiss on top. "Mmmm." She rolled her eyes back up at him and very deliberately licked her lips. "Yummy."

Proving he'd forgotten all about his scarred leg, Rafe growled out something guttural and filthy and scooped her up from the floor.

He collapsed onto the bed with her, his mouth on hers in another punishing kiss.

Lillian reveled in the dominance of it. The way he took and demanded. Her hands were just as greedy as they ran along the bare skin of his back, down to his tight ass, pulling him even closer as his erection ground against her throbbing mound.

The flimsy cloth of her thong was a barrier she wanted gone.

Now.

But she also didn't want him to stop the pressure against her clit that sent wave after wave of sensation pulsing through her entire body.

She couldn't have both. So she grabbed his ass even tighter and held on as the waves turned to a tsunami and flooded her with so many incredible sensations she was surprised she didn't just shatter into a million pieces from the sheer pleasure.

Only when her body had been wrung dry was she able to focus back on Rafe's face, still suspended above her as he waited for her to come back to her senses. Somehow, she managed a grin.

"Well, you certainly know how to keep a promise." Because she knew for certain she'd shouted when she hit her peak.

"Oh, I'm just getting started."

She thought he was kidding.

He wasn't.

Two more incredible orgasms later, and she was pretty sure she'd need to be squeegeed up off the bed like one giant puddle of satiated woman. True to his word, Rafe had made her scream again, longer and louder each time. She only hoped the neighbors she shared a wall with weren't home, or there'd be a very uncomfortable hallway encounter in her future.

Not that Walter and Andrew didn't make some noise of their own sometimes, but still.

Awk-ward.

"Uncle," she said with a small gasp for breath. "You win. I can't take any more."

Wrong thing to say.

Rafe sat back on his ankles and fisted his erection, the tip glistening and so engorged it had to be almost painful. "You can't?" He stroked himself again. "Not even this?"

Lillian groaned, caught between the need to feel him inside her and the certain knowledge she was already so sensitive her next orgasm would kill her dead.

But oh, what a glorious way to go.

She watched with hungry eyes as he sheathed himself in a condom before coming over her body, his eyes so dark and intent she couldn't look away. Especially not when he started to press into her. His blunt tip burrowed deeper with each stroke through her swollen tissue, drawing sounds from her throat she couldn't have stopped if she tried.

Once he was fully seated, Rafe captured her hands and held them over her head, their fingers interlaced. Then he started to move with purpose.

It was too much. Too intimate. Too...everything.

But still she couldn't tear her gaze from his as their bodies strained against one another, hot and slick, until she couldn't hold it off any longer. With a hoarse cry, the orgasm overtook her and swept her away.

She was barely aware of Rafe's guttural shout at his own release. Or the loss of his heat when he left her and came back, pulling the blanket over the both of them before cradling her to his chest. Warm, content, and completely done in, she drifted beneath the darkness of sleep with the comforting thump of Rafe's strong heart beating against her ear.

Chapter 10

"So...handcuffs, huh?"

After a short doze that recharged them both, Lillian lay wrapped in Rafe's arms, running her fingers along his broad chest and enjoying the afterglow of some seriously epic sex. Rafe's teasing question nudged her out of her happy zone and back into reality.

Would it have been too much to ask for him to pretend he'd never looked in that drawer?

Burrowing her face into his shoulder, she let out a half-groan, half-laugh. "Not gonna give me a pass on that one, huh?"

"Are you kidding? Would you, if you were me?"

This time, it was a full laugh that popped out. "Hell, no." It didn't make it any less embarrassing, though. "They're from a bachelorette party. Brand new, never used," she added, peeking up at him.

Rafe gave her a considering look. "But you've thought about it."

Why lie?

"Once or twice." As much as the idea might intrigue her inner kink, though, there hadn't been a single man in her bed she'd felt like taking the cuffs for a test drive with since they took up residence in her drawer.

Until now.

She swatted the naughty imp out of her head.

Still giving her that look, like he was trying to peel back her skull and see inside, Rafe stroked a fingertip along her cheek. "You're the most fascinating tangle of contradictions."

"Nah, I'm pretty much in-your-face straightforward."

Sometimes too much so, if you listened to some people.

"Oh?" Rafe's thumb rubbed a small circle over her shoulder. "Then tell me, why are you using this bedroom, which is smaller and has a fire escape ruining the view, when I know you've got bigger windows and a gorgeous view in the other room, because I have the same one?"

She didn't even bother to ask how he knew this was her room. There were enough of her clothes and other belongings scattered around for anyone to figure it out, much less a man trained to observe.

Hell, he probably figured it out when they'd been in here the night before, having their...discussion. She hadn't even questioned it when he carried her in here before. She'd just thought it was because it was the nearest bed.

Stupid, stupid, stupid.

Rather than answer, she pressed her head to his shoulder again, giving herself time to think without him looking at her like that. Like he was willing to wait as long as it took for her to spill her secrets.

Did she dare? Could she risk trusting him that much?

The small, circular strokes continued on her shoulder, the touch an odd mixture of comforting and sensual. "You can tell me anything, *mi pequeña duendecilla*," he murmured against her hair. The tenderness in his voice made her shiver. "What are you hiding behind door number one?"

Impetuous decisions were one of her greatest failings. They got her into trouble all the time. She could just never seem to stop herself when the urge hit.

Like now.

Before she could find a good reason to talk herself out of it, she pressed a kiss to Rafe's neck and bounced out of bed. She snatched up his discarded baseball jersey and tugged it over her head, the bottom hem reaching all the way to her still-rubbery thighs.

That well-loved sensation, along with the slight prickle of beard-burn across her breasts, kept her feeling like a freshly tumbled woman rather than a little kid in the oversized shirt.

When Rafe didn't move to follow, she tossed his jeans onto the bed. He put a hand on them, his expression closed and measured. "Kicking me out of your bed already?"

She rolled her eyes. "As if I were that stupid."

His lips twitched. "Then what?"

Now or never.

"I thought you wanted to know what was in the other room?"

Not waiting for an answer, she spun and left, walking the short distance to the door at the end of the hall that safeguarded her biggest secret. Her breath hitched, like it did at the start of one of her mini panic-attacks. But the warm hand that touched her back eased the knot in her chest before it could fully form.

Taking strength from that connection, Lillian swung the door open and stepped inside, Rafe right beside her. She bit her lip, watching him as his curious gaze ranged over everything from the easel to the canvases stacked against the wall. From his expression, it was impossible to tell what he was thinking, and it was killing her.

Needing to fill the silence, she said, "You were right about the window in the other bedroom. The light in here is much better, so I ended up switching things around and making this my studio." More silence. "But you were wrong about this room being bigger, since they ate into the square footage when they built the panic room my father insisted on before I moved in. They're both around the same size now." Still nothing. "Well?"

Rafe did a second slow perusal of the canvases. His gaze seemed to linger first on the almost finished piece of the cello player she'd put aside, and then on the male nude still sitting on the easel, waiting for her to come back and breathe life into the incomplete image. She wondered if he saw the truth in either.

She bounced on her bare toes, feeling like she was going to explode out of her skin. "*Well*? What do you think?"

"What do I think?" He turned to look at her. "I think you're one hell of an artist."

The words were said with such simple acceptance, she had to blink back the silly moisture that came to her eyes.

"Why would you hide something like this? These are incredible." He walked over to study the almost finished picture which was a companion to the one in the gallery window before giving her a chiding look. "A no-name artist paying their dues, huh?"

"I *am* a no-name artist. And I *do* have to pay my dues." She grimaced. "Felix has a strict anti-nepotism policy. No free rides just because he knows you."

"Or because you work for him."

"Exactly. He likes what he's seen, but he's not sold on giving me my own showing yet. *Lady Dreaming* is my way of proving I deserve a shot."

"He's crazy if he doesn't give it to you."

On that, they agreed.

But much as she didn't want to, she also understood the situation from Felix's point of view. "He has to consider the gallery's reputation."

And then there was Kevin. When the previous gallery manager defected to a big-name SoHo gallery back in New York, Felix's displeasure had spilled over onto Lillian since she'd been Kevin's protégé.

Felix wasn't above cutting off his nose to spite his snooty face if his ego was involved.

Just like he'd never admit hiring Roman had been a mistake of ever-increasing proportions.

Rafe walked back to her and asked one of his earlier questions again. "Why are you keeping this a secret? I'd think you'd want to show this off to the world."

"I will. When the time is right."

And the idea didn't make her want to throw up.

He gave her a long look before shaking his head. "I don't believe it. Lillian Beaumont, the most ballsy woman I know, is afraid to tell her family she wants to be a painter."

The ballsy comment she took as a compliment. It was the second part she took issue with.

"I'm not afraid. Everyone in my family knows I draw and paint. Hell, I've been doing it since I could pick up a crayon. Which I used to decorate my bedroom walls with," she added with a grin. "My mother wasn't thrilled with my efforts, although I happen to think my four-year-old self showed some real aptitude for use of color and imagination."

He laughed. "Well, it's a good thing you switched to canvases, then. It's kind of tough to sell a wall."

Her smile died. "Yeah, well, as far as my parents are concerned, it's still just my little hobby. They're waiting for me to get over my immature rebellion phase"—she air quoted the hurtful words she'd heard once too often—"and start taking a genuine interest in my future."

"Why can't that be painting?"

"Because they already have the future they want for me all mapped out and waiting." That claustrophobic little knot came back, making her swallow hard. "I can't do it, though. I can't be what they want me to be." She hated how critical of her parents that sounded. "Don't get me wrong. I know they love me, and they want what's best for me. But..."

"But they don't really know you, or they'd see that if you've stuck with something for more than twenty years, it's not a hobby. It's a part of you."

It was as though someone had shined a spotlight on the point none of her friends, and no one in her family, with the possible exception of her twin, ever seemed to get. It didn't matter if she ever sold a single painting, ever had her name mentioned in *Art Review,* was ever hung in galleries in New York or L.A. She was an artist because it was a part of her, right down to her very marrow.

The fact Rafe had figured that out in a matter of minutes was mind-boggling.

And just a little bit dangerous to her heart.

"How come you can see that, and no one else can?"

Rafe shrugged as he looked around the room. "I don't know how anyone wouldn't get it the second they saw what you can do. These are...amazing."

Ignoring the giddy little twirl her stomach did at his praise, she slid her arms around his neck and gave him a quick kiss. "Thank you. That means a lot."

"It's only the truth. You're extremely talented."

"Not for the praise." Although the ego stroke was kind of nice too. "For getting it. For getting me." That didn't happen very often. People saw the outer shell. The heiress, the party girl, the rebel. Some saw several layers underneath. One or two had managed to mostly understand her and her quirky ways.

But no one had ever seen straight to the heart of her before.

The kiss started as a thank you, turned into a question, and finished as a promise that they weren't going to make it back to the bedroom this time. As Rafe slipped the shirt off over her head, he nibbled along her neck to her earlobe. "Just tell me something."

Squirming under the sensation of what he was doing to the sensitive stretch of skin, she moaned. "What?"

"My ass doesn't really look like that, does it?"

It took a few seconds for her lust-addled brain to realize he was talking about the painting on the easel. She laughed.

"That was pure imagination. But now that I have the real thing to study"—her hands slipped down his bare back and into his unfastened jeans to grab the muscular ass in question—"I'll make sure I do it justice."

Lillian's brothers were going to kill him.

Not only had he spent the better part of the afternoon defiling their sister, but they seemed to *know* he'd spent the afternoon defiling their sister. In that spooky, psychic way siblings had, they'd zeroed in on him the moment he and Lillian walked into the room. It took all of five seconds for a unified look of fury to appear in their eyes.

Not that he blamed them.

It didn't make it any easier to shake hands and wish Theo Beaumont a happy birthday, knowing he'd feel the same way about any bastard who touched one of his sisters. When the handshake turned crushing, it was all Rafe could do not to shake it out after Theo finally released him. He met the other man's blistering gaze with a small nod.

Message received. Retribution was coming.

The eldest Beaumont son, Richard, wasn't nearly as subtle. He put his hand on Rafe's arm and used some martial arts trick to add a small twist to the handshake that had him breaking out in a cold sweat as pain shot up his arm. Anyone watching would see nothing out of the ordinary. To Rafe, though, it felt like his wrist was about to be ripped from its socket.

"We need to get together real soon." Richard's voice was calm and cultured, just like the COO of a major investment firm should sound. But Rafe saw the truth in his furious eyes. He wasn't inviting him for a round of golf at the country club.

"Name the time and place." The pain flashed to excruciating before he was freed.

"Count on it."

At least Lillian seemed oblivious to her brothers' state of mind.

She buzzed like a happy little bee from person to person, gathering hugs and kisses from family and friends. Then she chattered about inconsequential things for a few minutes before zipping off to a new cluster of people to start the entire process all over again.

Rafe escaped on the pretense of getting something to drink. He claimed a spot against the wall where he could observe without the risk of being caught back up in her social whirlwind.

The woman was exhausting.

Where she got all that energy from, he didn't have a clue. Not after their earlier activities. He swallowed a groan along with a sip of scotch, his dick twitching at the memory of Lillian's very talented mouth on it when they'd realized they didn't have any condoms handy in her studio. Neither of them had wanted to stop long enough to go and get one.

They'd gotten creative instead, and *holy fuck* had his little pixie blown him away. Quite literally. He hadn't come so hard or long since before he could remember. If ever.

He'd been afraid he was too rough with his enthusiasm at the end. But the look Lillian gifted him with as she licked her lips with all the delicate greed of a lazy house cat had been pure smug satisfaction.

A look he planned on making sure he saw again later tonight.

If he made it out of the party alive.

"Rafael, I'm so glad you were able to make it."

Fuck me sideways.

Cursing the fates of bad timing, Rafe pushed away the erotic memories and turned to greet Lillian's mother. He hoped to God she didn't have the same psychic powers her sons seemed to have where his dirty thoughts were concerned.

"Patricia. Thank you for inviting me."

"No, thank *you*." Her meaning was clear when he followed her gaze to Lillian, who was laughing at something her father said even as she shook her head at him.

Guilt at the ruse they were perpetrating pinched at him. But then, after today, was it really that much of a lie? They might not be in an actual relationship like they'd told Patricia they were, but he and Lillian were...well, more than they'd been the night before, at least.

"I won't let anything happen to her."

Patricia looked surprised. "I never expected you would. But that's not what I meant." She dipped her head toward her daughter. "She's here, and she's smiling. It's like she's her old self again. So please, whatever it is you're doing, don't stop."

Nearly choking on his drink, Rafe almost missed the wicked twinkle in the light brown eyes that made her look like her imp of a daughter. He wanted to laugh, but settled for a grin.

"I'll see what I can do."

"Rafe. Buddy." An iron-clawed hand slapped down on his shoulder and squeezed. "Good to see ya."

Rafe winced but didn't try to pull away, not with Patricia watching. "Hey, Pete."

"Can I talk to you for a sec? Excuse us, Mom."

He didn't give Rafe time to answer. He used his grip to herd him away and out through the French doors onto the back terrace overlooking the pool. Lit all around with fairy lights, it was currently deserted in deference to the evening chill.

Away from any audience, Rafe shrugged himself out of Pete's grip and started to turn. "Look, I know—" The fist that slammed into his jaw almost took him off his feet.

Surprise let Pete get in a second shot before instinct and training kicked in. Rafe avoided the blow meant for his gut and went into a defensive stance, backing several feet away as he ignored the twinge his leg gave at the sudden movement. "What the *fuck*, man?"

"You sorry son of a bitch." Pete's eyes glittered in the dim light. "You *touched* my *sister*."

I did a helluva lot more than touch her. The taunt was on the tip of his tongue, but some sliver of sanity in his rattled brain kept him from voicing it.

"I asked you to watch her, to *protect* her, not—"

"Be very careful what you say, my friend." Rafe growled the warning.

"Your friend? Only scumbags take advantage of someone they're supposed to be taking care of, and I don't have scumbags as friends, asshole."

The accusation stung.

"Well, I didn't think I had idiots for friends, so it looks like we were both wrong."

Rafe watched the way the other man's shoulders tensed and knew he was going to attack. The three inches and about twenty pounds Pete had on him didn't worry him too much.

The police academy may have taught them both how to fight well, but the kids in the neighborhood Rafe had grown up in had taught him how to fight dirty. Part of him wanted the chance to get even for the sucker punch that left his jaw throbbing, but somehow, his common sense prevailed.

"I don't want to get into this with you right now, Pete. This is your mother's house, and she invited me into it. I won't disrespect her by throwing down with her dumb-ass son, no matter how much he deserves it."

Pete sneered. "Sure, hide behind my mother's skirts. That's mature."

"Hey, if you want to take this someplace else tomorrow and finish it, I'm more than willing. But you may need to get in line behind your brothers," he added with a wry grimace, remembering the unspoken promise in their eyes. By the time they each got their piece of him, he wasn't sure there would be enough left over for Pete.

"Works for me. You just keep your sorry ass out of Lil's bed in the meantime, and maybe I won't have to kick it too hard."

"That's between me and Lillian."

Pete's usually affable face twisted into frustrated rage. "You can't protect her if all you're thinking with is your dick!"

Something had been off with Pete right from that first sucker punch. Now Rafe had an inkling what it might be. "Something happened with the case, didn't it?"

"*Shit.*" Tugging at his short hair, Pete spun away and stalked to the stone balustrade.

Rafe was right behind him. "What?"

"I can't..." Pete slammed his hands onto the rail. "Shit, I hate this."

"I can't protect her if I don't know from what."

"You think I don't know that?" Letting out a long, pent-up breath, Pete turned. "We have a person of interest."

News to him. "That's good. Right?" he asked when Pete didn't agree.

"Not really." Peter gave him a searching look. "Has my sister mentioned Sean McManus to you?"

The name didn't ring any bells. "Not that I recall. Why?"

"Yeah, well, you'd remember if she did." He seemed to debate over his next words. "Short version, he was fired from the security detail here about a year and change ago, and he might blame Lil for it."

"What did he get fired for?"

"You'll have to ask Lil. It's her story," Pete said when Rafe snarled at him.

He was getting sick of all the secrecy, but worse, he was forming all kinds of horrible conclusions of his own. "Just tell me this fucker didn't touch her."

"If he had, he'd be dead, not fired."

Rafe grunted in satisfaction. "So, you think this McManus might be good for it? Have you brought him in yet?"

"We would if we could find him." He nodded as Rafe spat out a string of curses. "My sentiments exactly."

"What made him pop to the top of your list?"

Pete gave a helpless shrug. "We don't have anyone else."

Which meant they had nothing.

A year-old grudge as motive and no evidence to connect him to the current vandalism wouldn't even get them a search warrant, even if they could find this McManus character. Throwing his name into the mix was a desperate Hail Mary to keep the case from going stone cold.

"Fuck." Rafe winced as he scrubbed at his sore face, trying to think of their next step. "What about the guy from the gallery? Reynolds?"

"Nothing yet. And I mean *nothing*. Not even a parking ticket to his name."

"Nobody's that squeaky clean."

"No shit."

"What about—"

"We know how to do our job, fuckwad."

"Yeah, I can tell by how much progress you *haven't* made so far."

It was an unfair jab, and he knew it. But Rafe's frustration, not only about the stalled investigation, but at the reminder he wasn't a part of the "we" that was doing it, made his mouth work before his brain. It was sheer dumb luck he was able to dodge the fist that swung at his face.

"I warned you, mother—"

"Peter Matthias Beaumont, don't you *dare* finish that sentence!"

Chapter 11

Both men froze at the icy command. Rafe had never heard Patricia Beaumont sound anything but sweet and pleasant. Now, hearing the absolute steel in her voice, he understood how she'd been able to raise three strong-willed boys without having to kill any of them. He turned to see her standing outside the French doors, arms crossed, glaring at the two of them with disapproval.

"You're in trouble now," Rafe muttered. He'd seen that same expression on his own *mamá's* face more than once. It didn't bode well.

"So are you." Pete sounded far too amused for a man facing his angry mother. Then Rafe saw the furious little pixie dressed in green standing to her mother's right.

Oh, he wasn't just in trouble. He was *screwed*.

"I can't believe you'd act this way tonight," Patricia said, shaking her head. "To start a fight with one of our guests—"

"He's not a guest," Pete mumbled.

"—not to mention your *friend*—"

"He's not my—*oof*." Pete scowled at Rafe for the elbow into his ribs.

"Shut it," Rafe hissed. "You're just making it worse."

"—in the middle of your brother's birthday party. And then using that language!" Patricia propped her hands on her hips. "Well, what do you have to say for yourself?"

Pete drew in a breath before blurting out, "He slept with Lil."

Un-fucking-believable.

Rafe glared at him even as he heard Lillian groan "Oh my God."

"You do *not* embarrass your sister that way, dickhead. Sorry, ma'am," he added to Patricia, who leveled a narrow-eyed look of maternal disapproval on her youngest son. His gaze flicked to Lillian, but she was too busy hiding her face in her hands.

"Peter, first apologize to your sister," Patricia said.

"But..." He sighed. "Fine. I'm sorry if I embarrassed you. Even if it was the truth," he added, half under his breath.

"You are such a jerk." Lillian sounded more exasperated than upset, so Rafe decided he didn't need to pound some manners into her brother. Not right now, anyway.

Later was another story.

Patricia wasn't as forgiving. She pointed at her son. "I want to talk to you. In private."

"But, Mom—"

"Right now, mister." She turned the direction of her finger toward the house. "*Move* it."

"Yes, ma'am." Head hanging, Pete followed his mother back inside like a man headed for the gallows. When the door closed behind them, Rafe was left alone on the terrace with Lillian. He eyed her warily.

"How much of that did you—"

"Enough."

Crap.

"How did you and your mother end up out here, anyway?"

"She came and got me after Peter brought you outside and you didn't come back in right away. She didn't want the two of you to spend the whole party 'talking shop.'"

More like she'd seen the gleam in her youngest son's eyes when he all but force-marched Rafe away from her, and wanted to head off any bloodshed that might mar the evening. Patricia Beaumont was nobody's fool.

"For God's sake, Rafe," Lillian said, walking toward him. "Couldn't the two of you take one night off from...oh my God, he *hit* you!" She touched his jaw, which had faded to a dull ache until she poked at it and brought it roaring back to life. "Does it hurt?"

He hissed and jerked away. "It does *now*."

"Sorry, sorry!" She wrung her hands. "What can I do?"

"Besides not poke it again?"

"I said I was sorry," she snapped.

Despite the pain now radiating through his jaw like a throbbing toothache, he wanted to laugh at her put-upon expression. "Some ice would be good."

"Ice. Right." She looked at the house, considered for a moment, then took his hand and tugged him in the opposite direction, down the steps toward the pool. There was no lighting on this far from the house. Guests were clearly expected to stray no further than the terrace. Despite the darkness, Lillian had no trouble leading him to the pool house.

"Have a seat." Switching on a table lamp, she indicated the cluster of chairs while she headed for the kitchenette on the other side of the room. There was the sound of drawers opening and closing, then the rattle of ice cubes.

"Here." Lillian took the chair next to him and pressed the ice-filled hand towel to his jaw, making him hiss in pain again. She did the same. "Sorry." Gentling the pressure, her lips thinned into a line of displeasure. "I swear, I am so going to kill him for this. What was he *thinking*?"

"He was defending your honor." Rafe didn't know why he was bothering to throw Pete a bone after the bastard sucker punched him. But it felt important Lillian know her brother wasn't a *complete* jackass.

"He doesn't need to worry about me or my honor." She adjusted the makeshift icepack. "Seriously, just because he's my brother doesn't give him the right to stick his nose into my personal life."

Rafe happened to disagree. Brothers had a duty to look out for their sisters. That's just the way it was. He shrugged. "It's what brothers do. The other two would have done the same if they could have gotten me alone for a minute."

"Richard and Theo?" Lillian asked in surprise. "How would they even... Never mind, I don't want to know." She rolled her eyes. "Brothers."

"They love you. And they want to protect you." Especially from bastards like him.

"Yeah, well, I can take care of myself. Did I hear Pete mention Roman's name? Did they find out something about him?"

There was a note of anticipatory glee in her tone that told Rafe there was more than a little animosity going on there. His suspicions were confirmed when she looked disappointed at his reply of, "No, nothing."

"So much for killing two birds with one stone."

"Care to explain that?"

"No."

"Lillian..."

She groaned. "Okay, okay. Maybe I was kind of hoping it would turn out to be Roman who damaged my car, because then he could be arrested and Felix would maybe see what kind of a jerk the guy really is and fire his incompetent ass."

It didn't take much coaxing to get her talking about all the reasons she thought Roman was a colossal jackass. But it sounded to Rafe like a simple case of two people who just didn't like each other.

"You don't believe me either," Lillian said when her recitation of Roman's wrongdoings wound down. She sounded depressed, as though she'd expected different from him. "You think I'm being paranoid."

"I didn't say that." But he'd thought it, and that made him feel like a shit.

"Never mind. It doesn't matter." Her tone said the opposite was true.

"Hey." Rafe touched her face, bringing it back toward him when she tried to turn away. "It matters."

Yes, her suspicions about Roman going through her notes to try and sabotage her upcoming show were paper-thin at best. But sometimes thin was all you had to work with. Rafe decided he'd make a point of dropping into the gallery sometime soon so he could observe this Roman guy for himself.

Lillian shrugged, but her eyes lost a little of their disappointment. "Besides," she said, readjusting the ice pack once more, "if it's not Roman, who else could it be?"

"There is someone else they're looking at."

"Oh yeah? Who?"

"Sean McManus." Shock and shame filled her expression, and Rafe cursed first himself, then Pete, for not giving him more information so he'd know the right way to proceed. Well, fuck it. He'd already stuck his foot in it. The only way to go was forward.

"Do you remember him?"

"Remember him?" She gave a hollow laugh that made his chest hurt. "He's kinda hard to forget."

"Lillian. *Querida*." He wanted to pull her into his arms, but something in the stiff, almost brittle, way she was holding herself warned him against it. Taking the towel and putting it on the table, he clasped her hands in his. "What did he do? You can tell me."

———◆◇◆———

You can tell me.

No, she really didn't think she could.

Rafe chaffed her hands, clammy from more than the icepack, while inside her head a crazed banshee was running around screaming *No, no, no!* Her stomach twisted into knots and did a few somersaults, looking for a way out of her tense body.

You can tell me.

The only people besides her family, security, and her therapist who knew were Thea and Des. They were two of her closest friends, and it had still been almost impossible to tell *them*. But she'd been in desperate need of someone to talk her down from the ledge of hysteria she'd climbed up on right after The Incident.

Then she'd packed it all away in the back of her mind and never, ever talked to anyone about it, ever again. And now Rafe wanted her to break open that seal and tell *him*?

Setting herself on fire would be more enjoyable.

When Rafe pulled her into his lap and cradled her close, she made no protest. The heat from his body slowly seeped through the iciness encasing her. It eased her tight muscles inch by inch, and she realized she'd been on the verge of another of those damn panic attacks.

God, I am such a wussy wimp.

As he held her, he whispered to her in Spanish. She didn't understand what he was saying, but the way the words reverberated in her ear in his deep, sexy voice was as good as a Xanax. It soothed her jagged nerves and calmed her frantic thoughts until she let out a contented sigh and snuggled in closer against him as the last of the tension leaked away.

"You don't have to tell me," he murmured, stroking her back in a slow, gentle rhythm.

She sighed. "Yes, I do. It's just...God, this is humiliating." She fought the roiling in her stomach. "How much did Peter tell you?"

"Only that he worked as security for your family and he was fired. And he might blame you for that happening."

She was almost disappointed her ratfink brother hadn't spilled more of the beans. Then there would have been less of the whole sordid mess for her to have to tell.

Fickle much, Lil?

"He only worked here for about five or six months." Just long enough to throw her entire concept of privacy into chaos. "He seemed nice. Quiet. We didn't interact all that much, but he was always very polite when we did. Then one night when I was supposed to be staying over at Thea's for a girls' night, I wasn't feeling well, so I decided to come home instead.

"It was late, like maybe a little after midnight, and I really felt like crap. All I wanted was to crawl under the covers and go to sleep. I didn't realize there was anyone in the room until I turned on the light. And there he was, standing next to my bed, stroking his...himself with a pair of my panties."

An image forever burned into her brain, no matter how hard she tried to scrub it out.

Rafe snarled something under his breath, which for some reason made her smile.

"Yeah, my feelings exactly."

"Then what happened?" It sounded like he was working very hard to stay calm.

"He tried to apologize, but really, what could he say? Sorry you caught me waxing my junk in your bedroom?"

"I'm surprised your father didn't end him."

He almost had. It had taken two of their security people to hold her dad back once he realized what was going on. He might be in his fifties and spend his days behind a desk, but Rupert Beaumont still had the bulldog physique he'd acquired working Louisiana shrimping boats as a teen.

If he'd gotten his hands on Sean, he probably would have broken his neck.

"It wasn't a killing offense. Now if he'd used one of my La Perla panties, *that* would have been worth a little bloodshed." Although she'd ended up getting rid of every piece of underwear she owned after that, including the La Perla. She just couldn't stand putting it on and wondering if he'd touched it or not.

"You do that a lot, don't you?"

"Do what?"

"Try to downplay things by making a joke."

She shrugged, a little unnerved by how easily he'd seen through her bravado. "It beats bursting into tears every time I think about it."

Or admitting how violated she felt.

"So, what happened after that? I don't remember hearing anything about him being arrested."

"Which was exactly why he wasn't. There's no way the story of The Midnight Panty Wanker wouldn't have made the rounds down at the police station in like ten minutes flat after he was booked. *Everyone* would have known. It would have been humiliating. Not just for me, but for my whole family. Especially my brother." She gave him a look when he made a sound of protest. "Be honest. All of you would have ridden Peter for months over something like that, wouldn't you?"

He didn't look happy about it, but said, "Yeah, probably. We all give each other sh—crap over stuff. It doesn't mean anything, though. It's just guys having a little fun."

It would have meant a whole lot more to her brother, done in good fun or not. He was still fighting the bias of his family's financial status with some of his fellow officers. Having women's panties stuck in his locker or the glove box of his patrol car for weeks on end wouldn't have been a joke to him. And as much of a pain as her little brother sometimes was, she couldn't sabotage his career like that.

Besides, making his life miserable was *her* job.

"Panty jokes aside, according to the lawyers there wasn't much he could have been charged with, anyway. A few misdemeanors at best. He claimed it was the first time he'd done it, that he'd just broken up with someone and was depressed, and given in to a stupid urge in the middle of the night while he was on his rounds and thinking about her."

"And you believed him?"

"God, I wanted to, but...no. I'm pretty sure I was missing a few other pieces of underwear, but since I couldn't swear to it…" She shrugged, trying not to think too hard about where those missing panties might have ended up, and why.

"He swore he'd only gone into my room because I wasn't supposed to be home that night. That he'd never meant for me to see him, well, like *that*." Going to town at her bedside, eyes closed with a rapturous expression, like he was fantasizing she was there with him.

The thought still made her skin crawl.

"At the time, it seemed easier and a lot less trouble to fire him and have Hans put the fear of God into him to never showed his face in Boulder again. I'll be kicking myself if it turns out he actually has something to do with trashing my car."

"Don't beat yourself up over choices you made in the past. It doesn't change anything, and it'll just make you crazy."

She studied his face, which had gone unreadable.

"Well, that sounded a little like personal experience talking." When he didn't say anything, she made an exasperated sound. "Really? I tell you all of this embarrassing stuff, and you're going to hold back on me?"

Looking uncomfortable, Rafe said, "I'm not…look, it's not something I want to talk about right now." Or ever, judging by his tight-lipped expression. "Right now, we're trying to figure out whether or not this Sean character is the one who's been vandalizing your car."

"Fine. But don't for a second think we're not going to circle back around to this discussion later on, buster." She gave him the stink-eye to make sure he knew she meant it. What she knew about Rafael Delgado could fit inside a thimble. No way was she letting a golden opportunity to peel back one of those mysterious layers go to waste. "And no, I honestly don't think he's the one who slashed my tires."

"Why not? You're the one who came home and caught him with his hand down his pants. To his mind, you're the reason he lost his job."

"I'm also the reason he didn't get arrested. It was my decision to let it go. Plus, it's been like a year and a half, almost. Why would he suddenly do something now?"

"I don't know. That's why we need to find him and ask him."

"Find him?" The skin on the back of her neck prickled. "Does that mean you don't know where he is?"

"According to Pete, the police are still tracking down his last known location."

She didn't miss the slight hesitation that came before his answer. "Don't go all Five-Oh on me, Officer Delgado. I think I deserve to know the truth, not the party line."

"You don't have to worry about him, *querida*. Nobody's going to let him get anywhere near you."

"Who's worried? I may be embarrassed, but I'm not worried. I stopped letting what he did affect my life a long time ago. It's in the past."

"Is it?"

"Yes." Mostly.

Rafe leaned closer. "Then why can't you even say his name?"

Her mouth opened, but no words came out. She shut it.

"Why did you move out of your house?"

Because she hadn't been able to sleep in her own room anymore. Not without waking up in the middle of the night in a cold sweat, heart racing like she'd just run a marathon, sure that someone was there in the dark, watching her. Even changing to a different bedroom hadn't helped.

"Why did you refuse to let your father assign a security detail to watch over you when you moved out?"

"Because I didn't *need* anyone watching over me." Lillian tried to get up from his lap, but the arms around her held her firmly in place. She slumped back with a huff. "It doesn't mean anything."

"And now? Knowing someone might be targeting you?"

"Okay, okay, I get it. What happened with *Sean*"—she curled her lip at the nasty taste his name left in her mouth—"made me uncomfortable with having people around me, watching me, being in my space all the time, having access to my private things. I just...I couldn't handle it. So yes, I moved out of my parents' house because of him. Yes, I refused to let my father stick a security detail in the apartment across the hall. Yes, I wouldn't let a bodyguard move in with me while this whole stupid thing gets sorted out, or move back here for the duration. I'm not an idiot. I know it would have been the smart thing to do. I just *can't*."

She hated how pitiful she sounded, but it was the truth. She couldn't stand to have someone—anyone—watching her, invading her space. Logic said what happened with Sean would never happen again. But logic held no sway over her panic attacks. Those operated on pure subconscious angst.

Rafe gave a small groan as he hugged her even tighter to his body. "Ah, *mi pequeña duendecilla*, don't cry."

"I'm *not*." Oh God, she was.

Sniffling, she wiped at the wetness that had somehow appeared on her cheeks. Could the night get any more humiliating?

There was the dull rattle of ice cubes hitting the floor before Rafe pushed the cold towel into her hand. As she dabbed at the tears, she decided a little distraction was in order. "What does that mean? I know *pequeña* is little, but what's the other word?"

"There's no exact translation in English, but it's what *mi abuela* used to call the garden spirits back in Cuba. You'd probably call them pixies."

He'd called her a little pixie?

No, *his* little pixie.

Maybe she should have taken offense with the double diminutive, considering how sensitive she was to comments about her lack of height. But the sexy, possessive way he said it took all the sting out. In fact, it kind of made her a little tingly in all the right places.

Unfortunately, it was the wrong time to be having tingles, since they still needed to go inside and face her family over cake and presents.

As if her thoughts had conjured him, there was a sharp rap at the pool house door a whole two seconds before Richard shoved it open. Rafe went rigid beneath her. When he relaxed again, she realized it was more the unexpected entrance than the person making it that had made him tense up.

She especially liked that he didn't try to rush her off his lap despite the look of death Richard was shooting his way. If anything, his grip on her tightened. Like he wasn't giving her up without a fight.

"Mom sent me to get you."

Lillian snorted. "Yeah, I doubt that."

More like Richard and Theo decided to pick up being her keepers where Peter left off when their mother dragged him away to be yelled at. She was surprised it took him this long to find her.

Richard didn't bother denying her call of bullshit. "They're getting ready to light the candles."

"Fine," she sighed. "We'll be right in."

Rather than take the hint, Richard crossed his arms, his back a rigid line as he made it clear he wasn't going anywhere.

The part of her that had always rebelled against her brothers' form of silent bullying wanted to sit there and see how long it would take him to break and go away. The part of her she was beginning to recognize as her more mature self decided it wasn't worth the time to wait him out just to get her point across.

Especially not with the way he was eyeing Rafe up like he wanted to rip his spleen out through his nose.

With a roll of her eyes, she got to her feet, using Rafe's offered hands to steady herself. "Like I said. Brothers are a pain."

Rafe stood and put his arm around her shoulders. When they got to where Richard stood, she stopped and gave him The Look. The one she'd been using on all of them since she was six years old and was told she couldn't go bike riding with them because she was just a little girl and couldn't keep up.

She told him exactly what she told them then. "Just because you're bigger doesn't make you the boss of me. Try it again and you won't like what happens."

"What are you going to do, runt, punch my kneecaps?" Richard scoffed.

Lillian didn't bother to reply. She just smiled, and watched Richard's cocksure expression dissolve into one of distinct wariness. Satisfied he'd been reminded of the many, many ways she could make his life miserable as only a sister could, she gave a curt nod and snuggled in against Rafe on their walk back toward the main house.

"You know," Rafe said as they climbed the steps to the terrace, "you may look all sweet and harmless, but you're actually kind of terrifying."

She grinned. "And don't you forget it."

Chapter 12

Staring at the sleeping pixie sprawled on her stomach in the big bed next to him, listening to her dainty snores, Rafe wondered what the hell he'd gotten himself into here. And how he'd gotten in so damn deep, so damn fast.

This wasn't supposed to happen. *Feelings* weren't supposed to be a part of things between them. It was lust and attraction, period. Neither of them was looking for anything more, no matter the lies they perpetuated for the sake of Lillian's family.

And yet...

Somehow, somewhere between that first fiery kiss this afternoon and the molten sex after they'd gotten back from the party, the lines had blurred. Things weren't anywhere near as clear-cut as they'd started out being.

For him, anyway.

He had no freaking idea what was going through her nimble little mind.

Which was why this sudden shift had him wide-awake and thinking way too hard when he should have been enjoying the sleep of the well and truly sated. Had things changed for her, too? Did he *want* them to change? And if they did, what did he honestly think would ever come of it between them? Love? Marriage?

Fuck me sideways.

Feelings were a fucking pain in the ass. No wonder he avoided them like the plague.

With a sigh, he adjusted the pillow under his head and forced his thoughts onto something more constructive, but no less frustrating. Sean McManus. The man was a creep and a pervert, but as much as he wanted to pin the vandalism on his sorry ass, Rafe had a hard time making it fit. Not with the year plus that had passed.

A year, he was only now understanding, that had been a lot harder on Lillian than anyone, even her dumbass brother, had realized.

When Pete talked about Lillian's sudden decision to move into her own place, he'd made her sound like a spoiled brat having a hissy fit and wanting everything her own way. But Rafe could see now how refusing to take the penthouse condo with the doorman, concierge, and housekeeping service hadn't been about rebelling.

It had been about her not being comfortable with people monitoring her comings and goings. Or having anyone in her apartment, touching her things when she wasn't there, even if it was just to clean.

McManus was supposed to have been someone she could entrust with her life. The kind of violation she must have felt from his breach of that trust would be tough to get past.

Which was probably why her mother had been so skeptical of their story. Unlike her son, Patricia Beaumont would have understood the exact reasons Lillian all but ran away from home. It was also why she'd seemed so pleased when they convinced her their sham relationship and living arrangements were real. She would have taken it as a sign her daughter was healing from the trauma that huge betrayal had caused.

Rafe sighed. If he'd only had all of the facts from the beginning, he would have handled everything differently. Better. He sure as hell wouldn't have made a blunt declaration he was staying with her for the duration. Knowing what he did now, he was surprised she hadn't called the cops to come arrest his ass.

Of course, they'd kind of gotten distracted, what with all the hot sex they'd been having, so she probably hadn't thought of it. Yet.

Maybe if he kept her in bed for the next few days, she wouldn't have time to think of it at all.

The idea made his dick twitch with interest.

He bit back a groan. As much as he wanted to, he couldn't wake her just for the pleasure of having her again. She'd already grumped at him once about having to work in the morning and needing her sleep.

Of course, that had been followed by her licking her way down his chest, and driving him wild enough that he'd almost broken his own rule and slid into her bare. So, sleep was probably negotiable.

Giving in to temptation, he ran his fingers in a light caress down her side, over the curve of her hip, and around her delicious little ass. He loved touching her. She'd been his secret torment for so long, being in her bed still didn't seem real. He wanted to take advantage of every single second he was there.

With a small kittenish noise, her eyes fluttered open. The deep, rich brown of hot chocolate—the really good kind spiced with a bite of jalapeño—they were a little unfocused as she blinked at him.

For a split-second he worried that waking up to someone in her bed might freak her out, given what she kept referring to as The Incident. But the haziness dissipated and was replaced by a flirty half-smile.

"If you're waking me up for another round, forget it," she said, even as she snuggled closer. "I think you may have sprained my vagina with that last move."

Rafe didn't know whether to laugh or groan, so he did both. "God. I never know what's going to come out of your mouth."

She stiffened against him. "Yeah, sorry. I've been trying to work on that."

"Hey." He shifted so he could see her face. "That wasn't a complaint. I like that you can be outrageous and unpredictable. It's a part of who you are. Don't try to change."

She didn't look convinced, so he flipped her onto her back and perched over her on all fours. "I mean it. Don't change who you are. Not for me. Not for anybody."

"Easy to say now," she replied, looking up at him with a hint of vulnerability. "But just wait. I'll say something stupid and embarrass you in public, and you'll change your tune."

He grinned.

"*Querida*, I have four siblings whose sole purpose in life is to embarrass me wherever and whenever they can. I think I can take it."

Uh-oh.

From the sudden glint in her eye, Rafe had the terrible feeling she'd taken his words as a challenge. Time to distract her before that scary brain of hers came up with something to test his resolve.

"Do you know what I always wondered whenever I saw you standing in the lobby, waiting for the elevator, wearing those sexy little skirts and come-fuck-me heels?"

"No, what?"

"Whether or not your eyebrow was the only spot on this luscious body that was pierced or not." He could tell he surprised her by the way her eyes widened.

"You did?"

He nodded.

"Oh." Her tongue darted out to moisten her lips. "Well, um, I used to. In my bellybutton. But it kept getting caught on things, so I let it close up."

The news that one of his fantasies had, in fact, been a reality sent a surge of heat to his cock, bringing it from semi- to full-attention within a few strong heartbeats.

Lillian's eyes widened even further before a sly smile curled her lips. "You like that, huh?"

He looked down at his bobbing erection. The answer was pretty obvious.

"Hmm." The smile deepened as her hands came over her belly to touch the small scar at the top of her dainty little innie that marked the former site of her piercing. "Too bad."

"What's too bad?"

"That I never got around to doing the other piercing I was thinking about."

Other piercing?

"What piercing?" The words came out like a growl.

Her hands slid up her torso in a slow, erotic dance of fingers his eyes couldn't help but follow. "Oh, you know." Her fingers danced higher. "I considered, *maybe…*" Her fingertips grazed her nipples. "…getting these pierced."

The pinch she gave them made his cock jerk.

"Holy fuck." Realizing he was panting, he tried to find his usual control, but it disappeared about the same time she started to fondle herself.

"I chickened out at the time because I was worried it would hurt too much. But I've heard it can be quite the erotic sensation to have someone tug on them during sex." She tweaked her nipples again. "What do you think? Would you like that?"

Unable to look away from the hard, flushed peaks, he couldn't get the image her words had conjured out of his head. What did he think? That he was in so far over his head with this woman he might never come up for air again.

He swallowed hard.

"Sweetheart, you're killing me, you know that, right?" The smile she gave him said she did, and it sparked the devil in him when he answered her question. "What I think is that what you do to your body is your own choice. If you want to do it to make it feel good, then do it. But if all you're looking for is erotic sensations, *querida mia*, I can take care of that for you anytime you like. All you have to do is ask."

"Are you sure?" She tugged the turgid points, and he almost came right then and there. "You wouldn't get off on seeing little gold hoops hanging right here, knowing nobody else got to see them but you?"

With a snarled curse, Rafe swept her hands away and replaced them with his own, covering the generous globes with possessive greed. "You're perfect just the way you are." But he'd be lying if he said the idea didn't turn his brain to slush.

Fuck.

He'd never be able to get that image out of his head now. Which had been the little witch's intent, judging by the satisfied curl of her still kiss-swollen lips.

Determined to prove his point, and to make her pay, he covered one plump nipple with his mouth, laving his tongue over it until it was good and wet before blowing on it, raising goosebumps on her skin as she shuddered. He did the same to the other breast, earning him a tiny moan.

Good, but he could do better.

Going back to the first breast, he closed his lips around the peak and suckled. Gently at first, then adding more strength to it as Lillian's body responded with small pants of breath, her legs moving restlessly, her hands grasping at his shoulders.

With a soft pop, he released that nipple and went to pay homage to its twin. As he drew hard on the peak, Lillian gasped out a whimper.

Still not good enough.

With exquisite care, he closed his mouth once more on her turgid nipple and used his teeth to apply slowly increasing pressure, waiting until her entire body went rigid, knowing he'd reached the teetering line between pleasure and pain. Gently, he gave the nipple a tug, the exact way she'd described, and was rewarded by a long moan torn from somewhere deep inside her.

That was what he wanted.

Pleased, he eased back on the pressure, laving the nipple with tender care before moving to the other. This time Lillian knew what was coming, and the threshold to pain was pushed a little further before she tapped out and he finished her off with that gentle tug with his teeth. From the sound she made, he was pretty sure she'd just had a mini-orgasm, or at least she'd come real close.

Fuck, *he* was so close he was two seconds from humping against her leg to finish getting off. Three strokes, tops, and he'd be done. But he'd started all of this with a purpose, and he wasn't sure he'd achieved it yet.

With gritted teeth, Rafe ignored his throbbing cock and pressed his forehead to Lillian's breastbone for a few long breaths before being able to look at her and not pounce. Her eyes were glazed and at half-mast as she smiled up at him.

Oh yeah, she'd come, all right.

"That was"—she drew in a shuddery breath—"*so* good."

"Do you think getting them pierced could feel any better than that?"

"I can't imagine anything being better than that." Her words slurred a little like she was drunk. Or exhausted.

Feeling guilty because she had to get up for work in a few hours, Rafe lay back down beside her and tugged her close, pulling the sheet up over them. He'd count his blue balls as well-deserved punishment for starting something he shouldn't have. He bit back a groan when her hand accidentally brushed his erection as she settled.

Or maybe not by accident.

After the third touch, he put his hand down to cover hers and stop its wayward teasing. He felt her smile against his neck. "Go to sleep, sweetheart."

"Isn't that monster going to make it tough for you to sleep?"

Extremely. "I'll manage."

"But I could—"

"Go to sleep."

This time there was no argument, and a few seconds later, her body went boneless against his.

Thank God.

He didn't know how much longer he could have clung to his good intentions.

He closed his eyes with a sigh as he sought his own rest. It had been one damn day, and already he was wrapped so tightly in this woman's life he wasn't sure how he was going to ever get out.

He ignored the traitorous little voice that asked why he would ever want to.

***

"Well, someone's in a good mood today."

Grinning at the comment, Lillian handed Bernice the takeout cup with the logo of the coffee shop around the corner on it. "It's a beautiful morning. Why wouldn't I be?"

The receptionist blinked. "Because you hate the morning?"

Most days she did. But for some reason, this morning she was bright-eyed and full of energy despite a severe lack of sleep thanks to one insatiable sex god who'd left her a whimpering pile of goo three times over the course of the night.

Oh wait. *That* was why she was in a good mood.

"I'm turning over a new leaf." She left a disbelieving Bernice behind as she took her own coffee up to her office. She had twenty minutes before the gallery opened its doors, and she planned to use them communing with the caffeine gods and wallowing in the afterglow that seemed to be lingering far longer than it should have. Even the climb up the stairway of death couldn't make a dent in it.

Holy Kama Sutra, did that man know his way around an orgasm.

There were parts of her body that were *still* tingling. And others, she realized as she sat at her desk with a sigh, that were still a little tender, in a good, never-tried-it-but-want-to-do-it-again kind of way.

She pressed a hand to her breasts. It didn't matter that she'd worn her softest, silkiest bra. Her nipples were still so sensitive, every movement sent a whisper of remembered pleasure through her entire body.

Who knew playing on the edge of her darkest fantasies could be so arousing? Or so addictive? Because the only thing she could seem to think about this morning was when she was going to strip Rafe naked and do wicked, dirty things to his glorious body. He'd made her beg last night.

Tonight, she intended to return the favor.

Once the gallery opened, she had a lot less time to daydream about her sexy neighbor. But he was never far from her thoughts, which was a dangerous thing. What she *should* have been thinking about were the unfinished canvases waiting in her studio. *Not* how many condoms they had left and if they needed to stop and buy more on the way home.

Foot traffic was good for a weekday. More than a few people came in to ask about the painting in the window, which was both exhilarating and frustrating at the same time.

The positive feedback fed her starving artist's soul, but she hated always having to phrase her responses in such careful terms. "The artist will appreciate your praise" instead of "thank you very much, I'm glad you like my work" wore thin after a while.

Soon, she promised herself. She'd get her showing, and then she'd be able to prove to everyone she really was an artist.

Especially her father.

He'd managed to corner her during the party last night despite her best efforts to avoid it. Always the tactician, he'd waited until Rafe had gone off to get them something to drink, then sprung his latest rendition of "when are you going to stop wasting your life and come work at the real job that's waiting for you?" on her.

She knew he wasn't trying to be mean, but it hurt all the same. Even if the thought of a nine-to-five existence didn't make her break out in hives, she'd never be able to work for her father. She'd always feel like she was trying to live up to some standard she could never meet.

Refusing to let the reminder of his bull-headed attitude tarnish the wonderful day, Lillian pasted on her best smile for the customer who had just come in. He was tall, thin, late twenties, with a mop of shaggy blond hair a few weeks overdue for a haircut. Then again, given the scruff on his face and the skinny jeans, it might have been the look he was going for, somewhere between hipster and starving artist.

Starving hipster, maybe? Was that even a thing?

She hung back, waiting. Experience had taught her nothing spooked a customer more than being pounced on like a stray wildebeest the second they walked through the door. The man gave Bernice a searching look before quickly looking away again.

Lillian held back a snort of amusement. Men often had that reaction to the flirty receptionist and her bold color palette. Today she wore a violent magenta silk blouse with matching lipstick, which made her bleached teeth shine like the beacons of Gondor.

Shoving his hands into his back pockets, he slouched past her desk while carefully not looking her way again. Lillian felt a little bubble of anticipation when she realized he was walking toward *Lady Dreaming*. After letting him study it for a few moments, she made her way over, professional demeanor in place along with the smile.

"Good afternoon."

He barely looked up long enough to give her a chin tip in acknowledgement.

Dweeb.

Undeterred, she soldiered on. "I see *Dreaming* has caught your eye."

"Yeah, I wanted to see if it looked the same under true lighting as it did through the window."

"And does it?" She knew it did.

"Yeah." He straightened from his examination. "It's just as washed out and flat as I thought."

"I'm...sorry?" She had to have heard him wrong. Washed out? *Flat?*

"The colors are so muted, it's like they're an afterthought. And the lines..." He made a scoffing sound. "They look like a five-year-old finger-painted them."

Lillian blinked. Was this guy serious?

Was he even looking at the same painting?

But Shaggy wasn't done with his barbed critique yet. He cocked his head as though viewing it from a different angle might change something.

"It looks like someone started with a vague idea of what they wanted to paint and didn't know how to follow through. There's no depth, no emotion." He squinted at it for a second. "It's pretty enough, I suppose. Kind of like cotton candy. Sweet and fluffy, but with no real substance. I guess there's a market for that kind of thing."

For the first time in her life, words failed her.

Sure, she'd had people dislike paintings and sculptures she'd shown them over the years. It had always been easy to accept and move on. People had wildly varying opinions when it came to art, because it was such a subjective medium. That was part of the business. But this?

This *hurt.*

It was like each damning word was a whip that bit deep and fast into her skin.

No depth...no emotion...a five-year-old painted it...cotton candy...

The words beat at her, but somehow she kept her smile in place. "Wow. That's quite a different take than most of the people who've stopped in to see it."

It wasn't smart to call his opinion into question, since he was a customer and the customer was always right. Even when they were an idiot. She just couldn't help but point out he was the odd man out.

Really, *really* odd.

With a shrug of his thin shoulders, Shaggy replied, "That's the difference between the trained and untrained eye."

"Oh? Are you an artist, then?" That would explain a lot. Competition could be fierce and sometimes spiteful within the artistic community.

"Me? No." The sly curve of his lips said he wasn't finished. "I don't make the art. I just review it."

The sound Lillian heard reverberating in her ears was the death knell for the future of her career in art. Smiling became too hard, so she settled for a wry grimace.

"Wow. That's great. For whom?"

"*Art Regard*."

She didn't recognize the name, but it didn't matter. What did matter was putting away her wounded ego and salvaging the reputation of the gallery by making sure Shaggy left with a more positive opinion of the collection as a whole, rather than with the unpleasant taste of cotton candy in his mouth.

Ouch.

"Well, I'm sorry you didn't find this artist's work to your liking, but I think you'll be quite impressed with some of the other pieces we have on display. I'd love to show them to you." She stepped back with a sweep of her arm, expecting him to follow, but stopped when he shook his head.

"No, I think I've seen all I need to write my piece."

Lillian's stomach clenched.

"Oh, but one painting isn't a fair representation of the entire collection."

"It is when it's the one you put in the window."

The knot in her stomach bunched like a fist when he gave one last dismissive look at the painting that, up until two minutes ago, had been her pride and joy.

With another shake of his head, he didn't bother with a goodbye, just turned and slouched his way out of the gallery. There was a brief influx of street noise, cut off when the heavy door closed behind him.

Unable to move, she stood frozen in place, looking at the painting as though she'd never seen it before. What the hell had just happened?

"So, did he like it?" Bernice asked from behind her. Lillian hadn't even heard her approach. "What am I saying? Of course he did. Everyone likes it."

"No, actually. He didn't."

To her own ears, her words sounded a little hollow. But Bernice didn't seem to notice anything amiss, so it must have been her imagination. The same imagination that had her believing she had any kind of talent.

"He didn't?" Bernice scrunched her face up in disbelief.

"He thought it was flat and lacking emotion."

"Huh." Moving around Lillian to where she could see the painting better, Bernice crossed her arms and studied it. "Maybe, a little. But I still think it's nice enough." She shrugged and headed back to her desk.

Nice enough. That was almost as damning as calling a man sweet.

The time remaining till closing seemed to drag like a lead weight tied to Lillian's waist as she forced herself to give whatever customers came in her very best. Any praise they had for *Lady Dreaming* was a mere sop to her bruised ego.

Rather than bask in it, she was quick to walk them past the painting and redirect their attention to other pieces. Pieces done by real artists. Who didn't paint like a five-year-old. Or pull down the standards of the entire gallery.

Most days—even the days she had to deal with Roman—Lillian loved her job. Today, she couldn't lock the door and get out of there fast enough.

As she was setting the alarm, Bernice let out a tiny squeal from where she was waiting at the door. "Omigod, he's back!"

Lillian sucked in a breath. "He is?" Maybe he'd come up with a few more insults about her painting he wanted to share.

Just shoot me, please. I am so done.

"I'm going out to talk to him!"

If she could have, Lillian would have stayed inside the gallery until Shaggy went away. Instead, she yanked up her big girl panties and exited. If she took a few extra seconds making sure the monolithic front door was properly secured and gave it one or two more tugs than normal, well, that had nothing to do with delaying the inevitable. She was being responsible.

That was her story, and she was sticking to it.

When she finally turned, though, her entire body sagged with relief. Bernice hadn't been referring to Shaggy after all. She'd meant Rafe.

Who she had cornered against the side of his truck as she talked at him a million miles a minute, hands flying in animated flamboyance. Lillian grinned at the strained look of polite patience on his face. Poor guy probably didn't know what hit him.

Her grin slipped, though, when one of those flying hands landed on Rafe's arm. Suddenly, she didn't find the situation quite so amusing. Especially when Bernice made no effort to end the contact.

Before she thought about it, she crossed the sidewalk to where the two of them stood and gave them both a huge, tooth-baring smile. "Hey."

"Look who's here!" Bernice sounded as excited as if she'd just found Brad Pitt lurking outside the gallery. "I was telling Rafael he *has* to come dancing at Blaze tonight. It would be *so* much fun!"

Lillian's hackles flexed. *Rafael*, was it? And why the hell was Bernice's hand still sitting on his forearm like she had some right to touch him? And why was he letting her? She shot Rafe a dirty look, even though it wasn't fair. She'd apologize later. After Bernice got her grimy mitts off of her guy.

Her guy?

Rafe spoke up while Lillian stood in stunned panic at the possessive thought.

"Thanks for the invitation, Bernice, but I think we already have plans for tonight." He looked at Lillian, as though waiting for her to back him up.

"We?" Bernice's head swung in her direction, her magenta lips puckered into a frown. "As in, the two of you? Together?"

There was a moment of silence before Lillian responded, still feeling a little gobsmacked by those two words still reverberating in her head. "Um, yes, the two of us."

"But...two days ago, you said he was just your neighbor." Bernice looked perplexed.

Lillian understood the feeling.

She shrugged. "Two days ago, he was."

"Oh. *Oh*!" Understanding dawned in Bernice's expression. With a sigh, she took her hand from Rafe's bare forearm, although it looked to Lillian like more of a caress than a withdrawal. "Well, that's great for you both."

There wasn't a whole lot of enthusiasm in her words. But being deprived of a chance to get up close and personal with a man like Rafe could do that to a woman, so Lillian forgave her.

Mostly.

"You should still come to the club tonight," Bernice said. "A friend of mine is DJing, and he's like totally lit!"

"I don't know." Rafe looked at Lillian. "Didn't you have something you had to do tonight, Lil?"

Yes. She'd told him this morning when he started nibbling on her neck while she made breakfast that she needed to put in some hours in her studio before she let him distract her with sex again.

She'd also asked how he felt about modeling for her. He hadn't looked enthused, but he hadn't said no either. Then, the prospect of ogling Rafe nude for hours on end had filled her with heated eagerness and a rush of creative anticipation.

Now, it made her throat close up with panic the same way the thought of working for her father always did.

She flashed her best Queen Bee smile at them both, pumping as much enthusiasm into her voice as possible. "You know, I think dancing is *exactly* what we should do tonight."

Because if she was out losing herself in the music and crowds, she wouldn't be sitting at her easel, pretending to be something she clearly was not.

Chapter 13

Something was going on with Lillian.

For the past three days, the woman hadn't stopped moving once. When she wasn't at work—which she seemed to have developed a distinct apathy for—she was either cleaning, clubbing, or confusing the hell out of him with her manic mood swings. He was exhausted just from watching her.

Of course, that might have been from all the incendiary sex they were having, too.

While he normally wouldn't complain about having all the hot, headboard-banging sex he could ever dream of, he realized it was just another symptom of whatever was ailing his little pixie. But whenever he tried to have a serious conversation about her sudden change in demeanor, she'd insist nothing was wrong, then distract him with more sex.

Weak-willed bastard that he was, it worked every time.

Which was why this time he wasn't leaving anything up to chance. They were going to have their long-overdue conversation, and they were going to do it in a place where her usual distraction techniques wouldn't be an option. Even if Lillian might be willing to get adventurous and try for sex in a public place, having that place be his parents' restaurant would ensure there was no chance Rafe would be able to rise to the occasion.

No matter how persuasive her nimble little fingers might get.

And, to really hedge his bets, he'd called in the big guns to back him up. Lillian might kill him for it, but he was out of ideas of what else to do. Because there *was* something wrong, and he *was* getting to the bottom of it.

Sending up a prayer the evening didn't end in bloodshed—namely his—Rafe ushered Lillian through the front door of Bayamo. The familiar sounds and smells enveloped him, bringing as they always did the smallest tinge of nostalgia and regret.

This was where his entire family came together to work, and laugh, and fight, and laugh some more. Part of him wished he could be a part of that. But he'd chosen a different path. It might get a little lonely sometimes, leaving him on the outside looking in. But it was one where he could keep them all safe, and that was more important to him than anything else.

It didn't surprise him to see his sister, Brianna, standing in her usual spot behind the hostess stand. What *did* surprise him was his mother standing next to her. It was Friday night, and from the look of things, the place was booked solid, as always. For Lucia to have abandoned her kitchen in the middle of the dinner service meant she was more than a little curious about Rafe's sudden request to use the family table.

From the way she was eyeing up Lillian, who he'd tucked protectively under his arm as they maneuvered through the crowd of waiting diners, she was already picking out dates for the wedding.

Fuck me running.

Managing a smile, he leaned down and kissed his mother on the cheek. "*Mami.*" He repeated the gesture with his sister. Placing his hand on Lillian's lower back, he said, "Lillian, I'd like you to meet my younger but not youngest sister, Brianna, and my mother, Lucia, who is the culinary dynamo behind the success of Bayamo."

"It's nice to meet you both," Lillian said, smiling. "I've heard such good things about the food here. I can't wait to try it. I'm starving."

Always pleased to hear her food praised, his mother clapped her hands once. "*Bueno*! I am so glad you are not one of those women who pretend they never have to eat more than a carrot to stay alive. Come!" She slipped her arm through Lillian's. "I'll show you your table and tell you what you should try."

Not sure how Lillian would react to his mother's usual high-handedness, Rafe relaxed when she shot him a laughing grin over her shoulder as she was towed away. Before following, he looked at his sister, who nodded.

"Everything's just the way you asked."

"*Gracias, hermana*." He dropped another kiss on her cheek, ignoring the curiosity burning in her eyes, before heading after Lillian and his mother. Winding through the close-set tables, twisting aside twice to let a tray-laden waiter zip by, he had enough time before getting to the back of the dining room to start questioning what he was doing. But then he heard Lillian's excited "omigod" and it was too late to change his mind.

Joining her at the u-shaped booth in the corner nearest the kitchen, made semi-private by the wooden latticework that ran along the top of the tall banquette seating, Rafe was relieved Lillian seemed happy about the surprise he'd arranged. Inviting two of her friends to join them without telling her first had been a gamble.

But other than tying her to a chair and forcing her to tell him what was going on, he'd run out of ideas.

He was familiar in a peripheral way with the woman Lillian was clenching in an exuberant hug. Thea had been one of the tight-knit group of three that had stuck together all through high school and beyond. He'd met her at several Beaumont family functions, but couldn't say he actually knew her. He'd heard their other friend, the quiet little blonde, had moved away the previous year, so he hadn't been able to include her in tonight's ambush.

Er, surprise.

The second person waiting at the table Rafe didn't know at all, but he assumed it was Lillian's friend Desmond Finkle. Rafe pegged the man at maybe ten years his senior, although it was tough to tell. It could have been five, or fifteen. His skin tone was a shade darker than Rafe's own, with his almond-shaped dark eyes pinning his heritage somewhere in the Mediterranean region.

Eyes which watched Rafe with a level of reserve that told him this man wasn't at all sure of him and his relationship to Lillian.

Fair enough. The feeling was mutual.

Especially when Des curled his arm around Lillian's shoulders as she pulled away from their hug and tugged her down beside him. "Sit with me, kitten. We can have a nice coze and catch up on things. It's been an age."

Lillian rolled her eyes. "Des, don't be a troublemaker."

He gave her an exaggerated pout. "But I do it so well."

With a laugh, Lillian swatted his arm and got back to her feet. "Des, Thea, I'd like you to meet Rafael Delgado. Although, you probably already knew that, since he invited you here?" She gave Rafe a questioning look that went with the same tone in her voice.

The fact she slipped her arm around his waist and leaned into him while she did the introductions went a long way toward settling the hackles Des had raised.

"Thea passed along the invitation to Des for me, so we haven't technically met before." He shook the other man's hand when he stood, then gestured for Lillian to slide into the booth first followed by Thea. He slid in from the other side. Not only would that keep her boxed in and unable to leave if things went south, it also put her the furthest possible from Des, who gave him a mocking grin in acknowledgment as he slid in next to Thea.

"Thank you both for coming out tonight on such short notice."

"Anything for our Lillian," Des said. It was obvious the proprietary tone was meant to provoke. But given Lillian's comment about her friend being a troublemaker, Rafe did his best to ignore the challenge it represented.

For now.

"Speaking of short notice, I can't believe you managed to get a table," Thea said. "Doyle wanted to come here for his birthday, but even a week out they were already booked solid."

Lillian grinned and bumped Rafe's shoulder with hers. "Well, Rafe has an in with the owners."

"It's my family's place," he admitted with a shrug.

Des's lip curled. "Ah, so some poor unsuspecting diner got his reservation bumped for us."

Those recently soothed hackles twitched again.

"This table isn't on the dining room grid. It's always held for family and friends, so nobody got *bumped*." He didn't know why the other man was going out of his way to pick a fight, but Rafe wasn't about to lose his temper. Not in his parents' place, and certainly not in front of Lillian.

Later, though, he and her good friend would be having a few words.

The bubble of tension at the table broke when the waitress came by to take their drink orders. When she left, Thea and Des put their attention to their menus. Rafe knew the choices by heart, but he leaned closer to Lillian and asked why her menu was still untouched.

She grinned. "Because your mother already told me what she was making for me." She laughed at his pained groan. "It's fine. Having the chef choose your meal is a compliment."

No, it was his mother being her usual dictatorial self.

She leaned even closer and asked in a low voice, "Why did you invite my friends out to dinner?"

"Because you needed it." She needed *something*. He could only hope they'd be able to pry out of her what he couldn't.

She stared at him for a long second, her eyes misting, before she kissed him on the cheek. "Thank you."

The gratitude made him feel a little guilty. He had ulterior motives she hadn't figured out yet. But they were for her benefit, so he decided he was still on the side of the angels.

Whether Lillian would see it that way was another matter.

After their orders had been taken and an enormous platter of chips and salsa had been delivered along with their drinks, Rafe waited for Lillian's friends to begin the inquisition.

He just didn't expect them to start with him.

"So, Rafe, how do you know our sweet little Lily?"

Lillian made a gagging sound. "God, Des! You know how much I hate that nickname."

"We're neighbors."

Des raised a well manscaped eyebrow. "Very *close* neighbors, I would guess."

That was when Rafe realized he and Lillian were all but sitting on top of one another, her leg pressed in a warm line against his, their arms brushing. He also realized he'd totally wussed out on the truth, couching their relationship in the most impersonal of terms.

Kicking himself for that bit of wussery, he slipped his arm around Lillian's shoulders, grateful when she leaned into the embrace. At least he hadn't ticked her off.

"We've lived in the same building for a few months, but we've recently become...involved." He wasn't sure what other label to put on it. Dating didn't seem right. Neither did friends with benefits. And 'having hot monkey sex every chance we get' didn't seem appropriate under the circumstances.

Even if it was true.

"It must be pretty recent, since Lil didn't mention she was seeing anyone new when she came over last weekend." Thea's gaze darted between the two of them, as though only just realizing something was going on there. It seemed she wasn't as adept at reading body language as their friend Des.

"It kind of started that same day I came to dinner." Lillian tipped her head up and smiled at Rafe. "We, ah, had a moment in the elevator."

Heat prickled his skin as he remembered the teasing kiss his little pixie had blown to him as the elevator doors closed that day. Which made him remember what those luscious lips had been doing right before they left the apartment.

And that was almost his undoing.

He couldn't stop himself. He had to kiss her.

It was soft and fleeting, but loaded with promise.

"And a mere six days later, you're inviting her friends out to dinner and playing the lovesick swain." The cynicism in Des's tone was cutting, dragging Rafe from his lustful thoughts. "My, you do move fast, *Señor* Delgado."

"Des, knock it off," Lillian snapped, giving him a narrow-eyed glare.

"Just an observation, kitten," Des said, throwing his hands up in mock surrender. "No need to unsheathe your sharp little claws on my magnificent hide."

"Then don't give me a reason. Do I interfere with *your* love life?"

"All the time." His expression softened. "It's what friends do."

That deflated Lillian's annoyance with an audible sigh. "Yeah, well, you don't have to worry about me. Everything's fine."

No, it wasn't. Rafe knew it. From the expression on Des's face, he knew it too.

"So, Rafe..." Des reached for another chip. "What do you do for a living? Are you a part of the family business?"

"No, actually. I didn't get the cooking gene everyone else seems to have inherited." He was used to making light of the fact he was the outlier in his loud, close-knit family. "I'm a police officer here in Boulder."

Thea's eyes widened. "Oh! *You're* the—"

"Friend of Peter's." Lillian gave her friend a very pointed look.

"Right. Yes. That's what I was going to say."

That was *so* not what she was going to say. Rafe watched the silent communication that went on between the two women, burning with curiosity, but knew he'd never get a straight answer out of them.

He glanced at Des. At least he looked as lost as Rafe felt.

"Do they do this a lot?" Rafe asked him.

Des snorted. "Annoying, isn't it?"

For one brief moment, Rafe felt a hint of accord with Lillian's friend. But that feeling went right out the window when Des said, "Your family must have been disappointed in you when you decided not to follow tradition."

Lillian gasped. "Des!"

"No, not at all," Rafe replied, ignoring the squirming woman at his side and focusing entirely on Des. "They understood why I needed to be a cop."

"Needed?" Des repeated the word like it intrigued him. "Interesting word choice."

"Swear to God, Des," Lillian gritted out. "Shut. Up. It's none of your business."

Rafe gave her a quick squeeze. "No, it's okay, he's right. I never had any interest in being a cop until the night some slimebag pointed a gun at my father and robbed him."

"Oh, my God!" Thea gasped.

Lillian grasped his thigh in an iron vise. "Your dad was okay, right?"

Rafe nodded, thankful when her hold loosened.

For someone with such delicate little hands, she had the grip of an anaconda.

"Long story short, they never caught the guy, but I remember all the times the cops came by the restaurant to talk to my parents during the investigation, how relieved my mother always seemed to see them here. How safe she felt knowing they were keeping an eye on the place." He shrugged. "I already knew I'd never be as good as my brothers in the kitchen, and I didn't really want to be. So, I chose a career where I could make a difference."

"And protect your family," Lillian murmured.

"Yeah, maybe." Definitely.

Uncomfortable with the personal turn the conversation had taken, Rafe was grateful when the waitresses arrived with their main courses. By the time they were done transferring all the dishes onto the table, the air was thick with tantalizing and familiar aromas that had his mouth watering with anticipation.

Thea stared at the multitude of steaming bowls and platters. "This can't possibly be what we ordered. It's way too much food."

"My mother has a tendency to believe people don't know how hungry they are until she shows them," Rafe said with a laugh, reaching for one of the beef empanadas. "Dig in. I guarantee she'll be by at some point to check on our progress."

Whether it was the threat of disappointing *Señora* Delgado or the lure of the delicious food, they all dug in with gusto. At first, conversation between mouthfuls was about the dishes, which were passed around and shared family style, so everyone got a taste of everything.

Rafe made sure they knew the heat levels of each dish before they tried them, but the black bean soup still caught everyone but him by surprise, leading to a mass raid on the bread basket.

Eventually, talk branched out to other things, and as the evening wore on, Rafe saw the difference in Lillian. It was subtle at first, the faintest lessening of the tension that had kept her body strung so tight the past few days.

But as she talked and joked with her friends, he saw the impish sense of humor rising again, and breathed a sigh of relief. Whatever happened, it hadn't been bad enough to break her. It had dented her some, for sure, but his little pixie was one tough cookie.

By the time his mother came around to visit, the platters had been all but licked clean. She nodded with approval. "¡*Que bueno*! Just what I like to see. There is no greater praise than an empty plate."

"The food was amazing, *Señora* Delgado," Lillian said.

"Yes, it was." Thea shook her head as she surveyed the carnage on the table. "But I still can't believe we ate all that!"

Des rattled off a compliment to Rafe's mother in flawless Spanish, ending with a Continental flair by kissing his closed fingertips and throwing them open in the universal gesture of approval.

Rafe narrowed his eyes. The man was full of surprises, and Rafe didn't like that. He got to his feet while his mother thanked Des and bussed her cheek. She smelled the same as she had all his life, like spices and home.

"Everything was outstanding, as always."

She harrumphed even as she patted his arm. "If you liked my cooking so much, you'd visit more often."

He groaned. "*Mamá...*"

"And you would bring this woman you seem so very fond of," she continued, switching to her native Cuban Spanish. "What kind of son doesn't bring his woman home to meet his mother?"

"The kind who isn't ready to yet," he replied in the same language, shooting an annoyed look at Des, who was shamelessly eavesdropping. He lowered his voice. "I'll come by the house on Sunday. I promise."

"You'll come for church."

He wanted to argue, but decided to pick his battles. "Fine."

"And you'll bring your woman so I can talk to her."

What a terrifying thought. "We'll see."

"*Rafael...*"

"We'll see, *Mamá.*"

She harrumphed again, but she, too, knew how to pick her battles. "Fine. We'll talk about it then." She patted his cheek. Switching back to English, she said to everyone, "Coffee and dessert will be right out. It was a pleasure to meet you all. I hope you come back again. Friends of my son are always welcome."

A low groan escaped Thea after Rafe's mother was out of earshot. "Dessert? Seriously?" She offered Rafe an apologetic look as she pressed a hand to her belly. "I don't want to insult your mother, but I'm already close to popping like an overinflated balloon."

"Seconded," Lillian said, flopping back against the seat. "I'm sure it'll be delish, but I don't think I can eat another bite. Not if I ever want to move again."

Rafe's first mistake was looking at Lillian.

The second was not looking away when he saw the low burn of arousal in her eyes that seemed to always be there, simmering in the background, whenever they were near each other.

The third was not remembering what a nosy pain in the ass her friend Des had proven himself to be.

"Well, here's a thought, kittens. The night is still young, so why don't we take our no doubt *divine* desserts to-go, and head over to my place for some coffee and klatching while we wait for dinner to settle?" Des smiled at the disgruntled scowl Rafe gave him. "We wouldn't want to let the evening end too soon, would we?"

It took a few seconds for the underlying meaning of his words to sink past Rafe's annoyance. Right. The reason he'd set up this little get-together in the first place. Lillian was much more relaxed now, but he still hadn't discovered what was wrong.

And until he did, he couldn't fix it.

Which was why he found himself driving to Des's duplex for coffee he *didn't* want, instead of heading home for another round of hot sex with the woman he *did*.

Later, he promised himself.

If she was still talking to him.

"Thank you for tonight."

Rafe glanced over to where Lillian was curled up on the other end of the truck's bench seat. He could only see her face in short bursts as they passed each streetlight, but she seemed sleepy and content, like a well-fed kitten.

He scowled at the reminder of the pet name Des had used all night. "You're welcome."

"And thank you for agreeing to go to Des's. I know you really didn't want to."

"He's…"

She laughed when he couldn't come up with a single nice thing to say.

"I know, he's a troublemaker and a bitch, but only in the best way. He'd do anything for the people he loves, even when it's not what he really wants. Just like you. What?" she asked when he gave her a sharp look. "You think I couldn't figure out you weren't telling us the whole story about why you became a cop rather than work with your family?"

"I didn't lie."

"I never said you did. I just think there's something more to it, that's all."

It would have been so easy to brush off her too-keen observation. But since he was planning on prying a few secrets out of her tonight, it wouldn't hurt to give her a little *quid pro quo* ahead of time.

"My father *was* robbed by some punk. That was no lie. But it wasn't as…bloodless as I made it sound. He wasn't shot," he said when she made a sound of distress, "but the bastard pistol whipped him when he saw how little money my father was carrying. The restaurant was barely turning a profit then, and there wasn't a whole lot going to the bank every night."

"Oh, my God. How bad was he hurt?"

"Bad enough."

A concussion, twenty stitches, and a broken nose that to this day still had a slight bend to it as a permanent reminder of that hellish night. He remembered lying in bed after his parents had come home from the hospital, unable to sleep, chilled and sweating at the same time. Knowing one different choice, one pull of the trigger, and he and his siblings would have been left to finish growing up without a father.

It was the first time in his life he'd ever been truly terrified.

The second was waking up in the hospital, not knowing if he'd ever walk again.

"My mother was so afraid after that. And my sisters. Every little thing made them jump. So, my brothers and I, we all decided we'd make sure they were safe. We weren't letting anyone hurt our family again."

He grinned, remembering the very solemn oath taken by a bunch of boys who couldn't have put a whisker together between the four of them.

"We walked our sisters to and from school, escorted our mother to the market, and made a general nuisance of ourselves for the next few months. After a while, though, things got back to normal for everyone. The memory of that night was buried under life moving forward, and then just kind of got forgotten."

"But not by you."

Perceptive pixie.

"No, not by me. I decided I liked making sure my family was safe from all of the bad in the world. It made me feel like I was, I dunno, doing something worthwhile. Important." He shrugged. "I still helped out at the restaurant like always, but I started thinking maybe there was something else I was meant to do."

Something he'd done very well for the past six years.

Something he very much hoped he'd be allowed to continue doing once all the doctors got together and compared their notes at his review board.

Parking his truck at the curb not far from the duplex Lillian pointed out as being Des's, Rafe was stopped from opening his door when her hand touched his arm. They were on the outer fringes of the nearest streetlamp's halo of light, but he could see her face clearly enough to know her eyes were a little swimmy with tears.

She leaned closer and kissed him on the cheek. "You're a very good man, Rafael Delgado."

Stroking her face with his fingertips, he kissed her back, knowing her good opinion was about to be severely tested.

"Do me a favor and hold that thought."

Chapter 14

Rafael Delgado was a rat bastard.

It wasn't until she was on her second cup of very excellent French press that Lillian came to that conclusion. It took her that long to figure out what the jerk was really up to.

Nice dinner with her friends my ass.

This was an intervention. A very subtle one, no doubt arranged with the best of intentions, but it still had all the undertones of a sneak attack.

And betrayal.

Not a fair assessment, of course. Rafe didn't know the issue he was hoping her friends would help figure out was indelibly entwined to the secret she'd confided to him. But she wasn't feeling fair.

In fact, she felt like being a total bitch and giving him a real piece of her mind. And then going home to burrow under the covers to hide until she had to drag herself out for tomorrow night's showing.

One thing kept her from doing any of those things: the story he'd told her in the car.

It proved Rafe wasn't being a jerk on purpose. He just couldn't help himself.

He was a protector. Something apparently hardwired into his DNA, the same way it was Peter, and Thea's husband. They seemed to think if there was something wrong, it was up to them to fix it, whether they'd been asked to or not.

Endearing in theory.

Annoying as hell in practice.

She didn't need anybody to fix her problems. She was a big girl. Smart. Capable. A freaking warrior goddess. So what if she'd just been thinking about hiding under the covers and wallowing in disappointment and self-pity for the next twelve hours? Even warrior goddesses got to sulk once in a while, didn't they?

"Earth to Lil."

It took a second to realize from Thea's exasperated look she must have been zoned out of the conversation.

Oops.

"Sorry. I was thinking about something."

"Anything you'd care to share?" Thea asked.

The worried, expectant look on her friends' faces had her biting back the snotty retort that rose to her lips. She took a sip of coffee to buy herself a few seconds to think.

Would it really hurt to tell them at this point? It would mean sharing her ultimate humiliation, but then, these were the people she'd spilled her guts to about The Incident. Who else could she talk to if not them?

"Okay, fine." She set her cup down with a click on the glass coffee table in front of the plush sectional couch they were all seated on. Perched on the edge of the cushion, her leg bounced a crazy beat, all of the rioting emotions of the past few days rushing up and swamping her with nervous energy. "You all know about my painting. Well, I'm...I'm trying to get Felix to give me my own show."

"Well, that's fantabulous, kitten! You deserve one."

Thea was more reserved. "I thought he had strict rules against doing favors for pretty much anyone in the universe?"

"He does. Which is why I had to beg for the chance to prove I rated one on merit alone." She explained about the deal she'd struck with the painting in the window.

"Sounds pretty convoluted to me," Thea said, her lips pinched into a half-scowl.

"More than a little. But that's Felix. He's always marched to the tune of his own drummer."

"A polite way of saying the man is a wackadoodle."

There was a fair amount of truth to Thea's assessment. But Lillian was used to dealing with eccentric behavior, so it never bothered her all that much. Artists could be a rather mercurial bunch. Herself included.

They also all tended to bruise rather easily.

"Have I seen this painting?" Des asked.

Lillian shook her head. "No, it's new." She'd been afraid to show it to anyone before she brought it to the gallery, worried they might not like it as much as she did. Worried they might call her out for being a fraud.

In hindsight, that might have been better than waiting for some random art critic to do it with such casual cruelty instead.

"Here."

Lillian was shocked to see an image of *Lady Dreaming* on Rafe's phone as he passed it over to Des. She shot him a questioning look. "Where did you get that?"

"I took it through the window while I was waiting to pick you up the other night." He hesitated. "I hope that's okay."

Okay? That he liked her painting so much he'd bothered to take a picture of it?

A nugget of warmth flared in her chest. "Yeah, it's okay."

He didn't look convinced.

"This is a beautiful piece." Des passed the phone into Thea's outstretched hand. "If the rest of what you've been creating lately is anywhere near as good, your debut is going to be a smash."

"Oh, Lil." There was awe in Thea's voice. "This is...wow. Amazing. I love it!"

Stupid tears pricked at the corners of her eyes as Thea handed Rafe his phone back. God, she loved her friends. But that was the problem. They *were* her friends. Not an unbiased opinion in the bunch.

"It *is* amazing," Rafe said, staring at the screen again before shoving the phone back in his pocket. "You should see how many people stop and look at it." To Lillian he added, "You might not see it from inside the gallery, but trust me, when I'm sitting out there waiting for you, dozens of people slow down or come to a dead stop to take a better look. A couple of people even turned around and came back."

"Yeah, well, what does that prove? A picture of a two-headed cow would get the same reaction." She winced. "Okay, even I know that was snotty. Sorry."

He reached over and took her hand, lacing their fingers together. "Is that what's been going on with you? Did your boss say you wouldn't get to show your work?"

"No, not yet. But as soon as he sees that review—" She groaned and collapsed back against the cushions. "I'm so screwed."

"What review?" Rafe asked.

"There was this guy who came in. A critic." In the worst sense of the word. "Let's just say he would have liked a picture of a two-headed cow better than he did *Lady Dreaming*."

"Then he's not only blind, he's an idiot," Thea said.

She appreciated the steadfast support, but it would have meant more if she didn't know Thea would have said the same thing no matter how bad the painting was.

"Critics can leave a nasty sting when they want to," Des said. Lillian knew he had firsthand knowledge of that fact from his burgeoning clothing line.

"Oh, he wanted to, all right." The man had seemed almost giddy while delivering his scathing opinion.

Bastard.

"Who was it?"

"Um…" She frowned. Had he ever even introduced himself? The

entire conversation was a painful blur of badness in her head. "I don't remember his name, but he said he reviewed for *Art Regard*."

"Hmm." Des got up and disappeared down the hallway to the bedrooms, one of which served as his home office-slash-design studio.

"So what if this guy didn't like the painting?" Thea asked. "Is one person's opinion really such a big deal?"

"It is when he uses it to trash not just *my* work—which, of course, he didn't know it was—but the gallery as a whole."

"He didn't like *anything* he saw?" Rafe asked.

"He didn't even bother to look at anything else. He felt the quality of what we chose to put in the window would be indicative of everything we had on display."

Which was the part that made her squirm the most. She'd convinced Felix to let her put *Dreaming* in the window. Now that decision would cause a direct hit to the gallery's reputation. Any negative fallout was entirely on her shoulders.

Rafe made a noise showing disgust. "Then Thea's right, the guy's an idiot. I may not be a professional, but I know what I like. Your painting is really, really amazing, no matter what this di—dummy says." He squeezed her hand. "And remember, I thought so before I knew you were the one who painted it."

That's right. He had.

Lillian brightened before deflating again. "It doesn't matter. Once this guy's review comes out, Felix will not only yank my painting out of the window and refuse to ever give me my own show, I'll be lucky if he doesn't fire me, much less make me manager."

"He wouldn't do that, would he?" Rafe asked.

He definitely would.

Des returned to the living room, brandishing his tablet as he settled back onto the couch. "Found it."

Lillian felt her stomach try to exit her body through her toes. "It's posted online already?" She'd hoped to at least make it through tomorrow night's showing before having to deal with Felix's wrath.

"Afraid so, kitten."

"May I?" Thea reached for the tablet as Lillian groaned.

"How bad was it?" Rafe asked Des.

"Awful."

Lillian groaned again, wanting to sink through the cushions. "I told you."

"No, love, I meant the *review* was awful," Des said. "As in awful writing, awful syntax, awful thought structure. The whole thing is one long meandering hatchet job."

Wonderful.

"This guy is a moron," Thea said, shaking her head as she passed the tablet to Lillian.

She steeled herself before skimming through the review, wincing as the worst of the damning phrases all but jumped off the screen at her. "Yeah, that's pretty much what he said in the gallery. Almost verbatim."

She tried to pass the tablet back to Des, but Rafe intercepted it and tugged it out of her grasp. As much as she hated it when Des and Thea read the scathing review, it was ten times worse as she waited for Rafe to finish.

When he did, he shook his head. "I don't know what these things usually sound like, but that seemed more like a personal attack than an honest review."

"It did, didn't it?" Des gestured toward the tablet. "Anything else strike you as strange?"

She didn't want to, but Lillian leaned closer to Rafe to look at the screen again with him. "Like what?"

"Check out one of the other reviews."

Rafe shook his head, still staring at the screen. "What other reviews?"

"Exactly."

"I don't get it," Thea said. "This is his only review for them?"

"It's their only review, period."

After clicking on several links to pages that went nowhere, Rafe looked across at Des, understanding dawning on his face. "The website's a fake."

"So it would appear."

Unable to believe what she was hearing, Lillian snatched the tablet and did the same thing as Rafe, with no better results. The page holding the review was the only one that existed. "I don't understand."

"Someone's gaslighting you, sweetheart," Des said. "*Art Regard* doesn't exist. Someone made it up to try and get to you."

"But..." The words took a long time to make sense in her spinning head. Someone was gaslighting her? Purposely manipulating her into believing her work was derivative and emotionless?

"But *why*? Why go to all this trouble"—she shook the tablet—"just to give a phony review? I mean, if it's not a real review site, who's going to see it?"

"You." Rafe rescued the tablet from her grasp and put it on the coffee table. "Did you tell anyone else about this guy? What he said or who he said he worked for?"

Something in his voice made Lillian give a good, hard look. *Cop face.* She recognized it from when Peter did the same thing, switching gears and pushing everything personal under the armor of their professional persona.

But there was something else there, too. Something she might not have recognized a week ago, before she'd spent almost every free moment in Rafe's company.

He was hurt.

Damn, damn, damn.

She hadn't meant for that to happen. The blow to her ego and self-confidence had made her revert to her old habits of protecting herself. Namely, laugh, party, and surround herself with people who expected nothing more out of her than a crazy good time. She hadn't even considered she now had another option.

She had Rafe.

The realization stunned her. She *did* have Rafe. Things between them might have started out a little rocky and strange, but this past week had been incredible. And not just the sex, although that deserved a highlight reel all its own.

No, it was the comfort he brought to her life. The companionship. The fun, and understanding, and stability. All the things she'd been telling herself she *wasn't* jealous about when she saw how happy and content her friends were.

I'm falling in love with him.

Oh, boy. She was in serious trouble here.

"Lil?"

She jumped at Rafe's soft prompt. Right. He'd asked a question.

Work problems first. Earth shattering personal insights later.

"Um, no. Wait, yes. Bernice. She asked about him after he left, and I'm pretty sure I told her he'd said he was a reviewer." Or had she? She couldn't remember. "I know I told her he didn't like the painting."

The receptionist's tepid *It's nice enough* still rang clear as a bell in her head.

Nothing like being damned with faint praise when you're at your lowest to make an indelible impression.

"Did he tell you anything else other than who he said he reviewed for? Give you his card? Tell you why he was there in the first place?"

"No. I don't think so, anyway. And no card for sure. He did say he saw the painting from outside and wanted to come in and take a closer look. He made it sound like he was just walking by, like it was a fluke."

"But we know that's not the case, if he's a fake," Thea said.

"Are we sure of that, though? Really?" She was a little afraid to believe it.

"Pretty sure," Des replied. Rafe nodded in agreement.

"So, what? He just came in to give me a hard time, then? Why?"

Thea scowled. "Because people can be jerks?"

"There are some people who live to rip other people's efforts to shreds to make themselves feel good, yes," Des said. "But I think there's more to it than that, given the rather personal feel of his attack. Not to mention the fake website charade." He gave Lillian a serious look. "Who have you ticked off lately, kitten, that they'd go to so much effort to try and hurt you?"

It felt like all of the air had disappeared from the room.

No. No way.

Sucking in a deep breath, she looked at Rafe. "This can't have anything to do with that."

He didn't look convinced.

"What 'that' are we referring to, kiddies?" Des asked, sitting forward. "I'm feeling a tad out of the loop at the moment."

With great reluctance, Lillian told him about the damage done to her car—which she *still* hadn't gotten back from the police impound—and the theory it had might have been something more targeted than simple random vandalism. A theory that didn't seem to hold much water, since nothing strange or awful had happened since her tires had been slashed.

She leaned a little into Rafe and rubbed his leg. "While I appreciate all the concern, I honestly think everyone overreacted a little."

Des looked at Rafe as he raised an eyebrow. "And what do *you* think?"

"That I'd rather overreact than be caught off-guard."

He put his hand over Lillian's, which she realized was still petting his thigh. She only had a second to be embarrassed before he lifted her hand to his mouth for a kiss and put it on the cushion between them, their fingers entwined.

The kiss meant a lot, but the fact he didn't let go meant even more.

Thea made a small noise, drawing Lillian's attention to where she was grinning like a loon. "What?"

Her friend just smiled wider. "I didn't say a word."

She didn't need to. Lillian could hear the gears spinning in her head. Thea had seen her around a lot of men over the years. She would know better than anyone that Lillian was always quick to laugh off that kind of gooey, sentimental gesture. The fact she hadn't was as good as a great big alarm bell going off.

A quick look at Des showed he hadn't missed the by-play, either. His expression was full of curiosity. And a bit of the devil.

Not good.

Hoping to forestall any of his troublemaking, she said, "There's one huge problem with your theory. Whether or not this has anything to do with the other stuff going on, the fact is no one outside of this room besides Felix has any idea the painting this jerk trash-talked is mine. So, it *couldn't* have been personal."

"Damn, you're right." Rafe frowned. "Well, that's one theory shot to hell."

"Maybe not," Des said. "What if it wasn't directed at our sweet Lily specifically, but at the gallery as a whole?"

"But why?" Rafe asked. "What does he get out of it, other than upsetting Lillian? It's not a real review site. Who would see it?"

Rafe's thumb stroking over the back of her hand sent delicious shivers along her nerves and almost made her forgive Des for using that stupid name again. Deliberately, if his smirking expression was anything to go by.

Forcing her thoughts back to the discussion, she said, "He was probably just someone with a grudge. Maybe he did just walk by, like he said. And when he saw the painting in the window, it, I don't know, set him off somehow. Made him feel like he had to come inside and get his rant on."

"Maybe he's an artist who had his work rejected by the gallery," Thea suggested.

Lillian gave a slow nod. "He did have the artist vibe. I remember thinking at the time he reminded me of a starving hipster, if there was such a—oh!" It hit her then. Hipster should have been the tip-off.

How could she have been so stupid?

"Such a what?" Thea asked.

"Roman!"

"Oh, not this again," Thea groaned, flopping back against the cushion.

Lillian ignored her. She was too busy trying to keep a grip on her temper, which continued to rise as she connected the dots. And every one of them pointed right back at Roman.

"Roman put him up to it. I know he did!" She started to pop to her feet, but Rafe's hold on her hand kept her anchored to his side. She leaned into him with a huff.

"Why would he do that?" he asked in an annoyingly calm voice. "We already agreed no one else knows you're the artist."

"Because he knows I'm the one who brought the painting in and convinced Felix to feature an unknown artist for a possible show. Which is something he hasn't been able to do yet."

"But he's tried?"

"Oh, yeah. Lots of times." She made a face. "He has no eye for talent whatsoever."

"Dogs playing poker?" Rafe asked with a small, private grin.

She grinned back. "Yeah, pretty much."

Des raised that expressive brow again. "An art gallery assistant manager who doesn't know art? Interesting."

"I know, right?" Sometimes she wondered if Felix had been on heavy-duty cold medicine or something the day of Roman's interview.

"So, you're thinking Reynolds resents how much better you are at your job than he is, so he decided to, what? Give you a hard time by having some fake critic come in and tell you how horrible and trite he thought the painting was? What does that get him?"

"It might make her doubt her own eye for talent," Des said, one long finger tapping a beat on his lips. "Undermine her confidence. Maybe make her second-guess her push for the artist, if she was worried it might damage the gallery's reputation. Or her own."

"Head games." Rafe sounded disgusted.

"Precisely." Des looked at Lillian. "Does that sound like something this Roman would do?"

She pretended to think about it. "Gee, let's see. Doing something sneaky, mean, manipulative, and potentially career-damaging for a coworker to give himself a leg up? Yup, that would be Roman to a tee."

"I'm sensing there's no love lost there," Des said in a dry tone.

"That would be a great big nuh-uh."

Thea sighed. "Lil, I know I wasn't a hundred percent on-board with your idea that Roman might have been planning to sabotage the show you're putting on tomorrow night, and I'm still not sure we're right about this—"

"Who else could be behind it?" she demanded.

"—*but* to be on the safe side, maybe you should talk to Felix about it."

"Which 'it' do you mean?"

"The snooping through the files, the damage to your car, the phony critic...all of it. If there's something going on here, he needs to know. What impacts you could impact the gallery. You don't want him to get blindsided by anything."

"But I don't have any proof yet it was Roman." The frustration of that was killing her, since she knew, *knew*, deep in her bones, it was him.

"Don't say anything about Roman, then," Des said. "Just give him the facts. It'll be up to him to draw his own conclusions. But at least he'll be informed, and maybe, if he's paying attention, he'll see what you do."

Fat chance of that happening. Not while he was wearing his Roman-blinders.

"If I tell him about the review, he's going to freak."

"The *fake* review," Thea said.

"Which is posted on the *real* internet. Anyone who searches the gallery's name will be able to find it." When Felix read the way the gallery had been trash-talked, he'd lose his mind. That place was his baby. Hearing someone rip it apart, even if it wasn't on a legitimate review site, would hurt him worse than if he'd had a knife plunged into his back. And no matter how she told him, he would definitely blame her.

Still, they were right. He needed to know.

That conversation will totally suck donkey balls.

"Okay, yes. Fine. I'll tell him everything." After the show. With any luck, he'd be in such a good mood it would help soften the blow.

Maybe.

After hugging her friends goodnight, she rode home in uncomfortable silence with Rafe, wondering what he was thinking. It was obvious he was upset with her for some reason. She hadn't forgotten the hurt look he let slip earlier. If he hadn't taken very firm possession of her hand the second the truck started moving, she would have been worried.

It wasn't until they got to her apartment that he finally broke the silence. "Okay, let 'er rip. The suspense is killing me."

She blinked. "Let what rip?"

"You yelling at me for setting this up tonight."

"Oh, right. That." She went on her toes and pressed a kiss to his cheek. "Thank you." She knew she'd surprised him when he didn't immediately follow her into the bedroom. When he did, he stopped at the doorway and watched her start changing for bed.

"You're not mad?"

"Oh, don't get me wrong. I was pretty pissed once I figured out what you were up to."

Rafe scrubbed a hand over his face. "I'm sorry. You were upset, but you wouldn't tell me why, and nothing I said or did seemed to help. I didn't know what else to do."

"And I'm sorry I didn't tell you what was wrong. I just..." She sighed and sat on the edge of the bed, weighed down by all the emotions of the day. "I was embarrassed. No, more than that. I felt hollowed out. Empty. Like everything I believed about myself and my talent had been scooped out and flushed down the toilet like a bunch of stinky fish guts."

He snorted. "God, you do have a way with words."

Not when it counted.

Because she hadn't been able to find the ones to open herself up to the man looking at her with such a tender expression. The man who had become a lot more than just the sexy neighbor who currently shared her bed. Instead, she'd clammed up and left him feeling like he wasn't important enough for her to confide in.

But she could fix that.

Getting to her feet, she slowly stalked toward him, putting some extra sway in her hips. "Words aren't my best thing. I prefer actions."

His Adam's apple bobbed as he swallowed, his gaze following her like a gazelle watching a hungry tigress on the prowl.

"Actions are good."

The hoarseness of his voice had her smiling. Without her heels, she didn't have the extra height she was used to when facing a man, but with Rafe, it never seemed to matter. She slid one hand up his chest, nearly scorched by the heat blasting from him.

With deliberate slowness, she slipped the top button of his shirt free. "So, did you have a good time with my friends?"

"What? Uh, sure. Yeah. They seemed nice."

Another button came loose. "You've met Thea before, right?"

"I, uh, don't remember."

She'd be surprised if he remembered his own name at the moment with the amount of blood flowing south. The evidence of his growing arousal pressed taut against his slacks, hard and inviting. She had to bite her lip, barely resisting the urge to let her hand skip over the rest of the buttons and go right to the prize at the end of the line.

In general, her impulse control left a lot to be desired. But this was as much for Rafe as it was for her, so she held herself in check and freed another button instead.

"What did you think of Des?"

"I think he needs to stop calling you kitten."

She laughed. "He calls everyone kitten." When he narrowed his eyes, she laughed again. "You do know he's gay, right?"

It seemed he hadn't, since a subtle line of tension in his body eased at her words.

She tried not to read too much into this apparent show of jealousy. Just because she'd decided what she was feeling was more than lust didn't mean he was feeling the same way.

"Then I liked him just fine." Rafe skimmed a finger along her cheek. "Do you have any idea what I want to do to you right now?"

To hell with going slow.

She hooked her finger in the opening of his shirt and tugged him toward the bed. "Why don't you show me."

Chapter 15

"**S**top right there!"

Rafe continued to move forward, gun out and ready. "I said stop! Are you fucking deaf?"

"You need to put the knife down, Fernando, and let your wife go."

That only made the meth-head bastard grab the too-thin woman he held in front of him as a shield even tighter, squeezing a whimper from her. The rank stench of fear was so thick it almost overpowered the apartment's usual bouquet of rotting garbage and cat piss.

Fernando bared a mouthful of discolored, rotting teeth in a feral snarl. "Do I look stupid to you? Why would I do that?"

Easing his way further into the barely furnished living room, Rafe did a quick visual sweep to clear the space. "Because you're *not* stupid, and you know you don't want to hurt her." Total lie. Fernando was dumb as a rock, and he hurt Lupe on a regular basis. Usually it was with his fists, though.

The knife was an unwelcome surprise.

"*Pinche puta* tried holding out on me." The knife pricked Lupe's neck, drawing a bead of blood and making Rafe's finger twitch next to the trigger. "Said she gave me everything from her paycheck. But that was a *lie*, wasn't it, bitch?"

Tears ran over the fresh bruises that marked Lupe's face as she sobbed. "I had to pay the rent, 'nando. The landlord said—*ayi*!" She squealed as Fernando jerked her back and the knife nicked her again.

"Fuck the landlord! You're *my* woman. You do what *I* say."

"Fernando, you really need to put the knife down, man." Rafe was close enough now to see how Fernando's bloodshot eyes kept darting around the room, as if he wasn't able to focus on one thing, not even the cop with the gun trained on him.

Fuck me running.

The bastard was tweaking. He'd probably been binging for days, and now his body was reacting to its inability to reach the same state of euphoria the first hit of meth had brought. Tweakers were much more unpredictable to deal with than other addicts.

And twice as dangerous.

"No, you put the gun down, fucker, or I'ma slit this bitch's throat!"

It was difficult to ignore the terrified whimpers leaking from Lupe's throat, but Rafe couldn't allow himself to be distracted. He had an almost clear shot at Fernando's head over his wife's shoulder, but he didn't want to take it. Not unless he was left with no other choice.

Please let there be another choice.

"You know you don't want to do that, Fernando."

"Fuck I don't! Worthless bitch! Only thing she was good for was she could hold a job and bring me home decent money. But if she's not gonna do that, then what the fuck good is she, huh?"

Shit, where was his backup? Splitting his attention even for the few seconds it would take to advise dispatch of the situation and request Compton's 20 wasn't worth the risk. Rafe sent out a prayer to the universe he'd get there soon. Until that happened, he had to keep trying to talk the tweaker down from his building rage.

"Fernando, you know I can't let you hurt her. You need to put the knife down. *Now.*"

"Worthless *puta* couldn't even give me sons."

She might have, if he'd stopped using her as a punching bag for more than five minutes. But that would have made a horrible situation even more tragic. Nobody deserved to start a life with so many strikes already against them.

"What's a man without sons? Huh? He's *nothing*! Useless whore!" He shook her again, harder, eliciting another squeal. The look in his eyes had gone feral, their darting getting faster and more frantic as his body slid toward the inevitable crash, increasing his agitation and paranoia. Spittle flew from his lips as he raged.

All signs Fernando was close to losing control.

Which meant Rafe was out of time.

"Fernando, for the last time, put the knife down and step away from your wife." Rafe let out a breath and narrowed his focus on his target. It would be a close, dangerous shot, but it was the only one he had. If Fernando tried to make good on his threat, he'd have a fraction of a second to pull the trigger. "Fernando. Drop. The. Knife."

"Stupid, worthless bitch. What good are you?"

"No, please don't!" Lupe begged through her sobs.

It wasn't until his gaze flicked to her to judge the shot Rafe realized she was talking to him, begging *him*, not her husband. Unlike her meth-head spouse, she could see he wasn't bluffing. She believed he would shoot, and even with a blade to her throat, she was still asking for Rafe to spare the worthless bastard.

Unbelievable.

But he had a job to do, and that was to protect Lupe, whether she wanted him to or not. He refocused his gaze on his target, which thankfully, Fernando was too stupid to realize he was presenting like a gift.

"Please, I love him."

Fucking hell.

"Fernando. Last warning. Drop it."

Fernando bared his rotten teeth again. *"Besa me el culo, puto."* Kiss my ass, bitch.

Every instinct he had told him to take the shot. But Lupe's

pleading voice struck at his conscience, keeping him from pulling the trigger. Her asshole husband wasn't any prize, but he was hers and she wanted to keep him. God knew he'd never understand why.

Fate took the decision out of his hands.

Sirens sang through the open windows, signaling the arrival of his backup. It was a welcome relief for Rafe. For Fernando, it was the last straw.

With an angry roar, he pushed Lupe away. Whether by accident or intent, his knife scored her neck. Rafe caught her as she stumbled into him, hands grasping her bleeding neck, eyes wide like she was surprised the bastard had actually gone and done it.

Cursing himself for letting sentiment make him question what his training told him to do, Rafe slung her onto the couch and shouted to Compton, who was entering the apartment, "Call an ambulance! I'm going after the son of a bitch."

Fernando had taken advantage of Rafe's distraction with his bleeding wife to haul ass into the bedroom. Rafe followed him, then out the open window onto the fire escape. He cursed as the rickety structure bounced and swayed under his weight as he pounded down the narrow ladder after Fernando, who was already a floor and a half below and moving fast.

The metal vibrated under his feet as he hit the third-floor landing and slung himself around to the next ladder, bouncing off the railing as he made the turn, flaking rust scoring his palms. No way was the sorry son of a bitch getting away. No fucking way.

A quick glance showed Fernando already scurrying down the final ladder to the street. Fuck, the bastard was fast.

Hitting the second-floor landing, the fire escape shifted like it wasn't fully attached to the side of the building. Ignoring the danger, he slung himself around to bounce off the railing toward the next ladder, determined to be no more than five seconds behind Fernando when his boots hit the ground. Except this time when his weight hit the railing, the rusty metal gave way with a sickening screech.

There was a moment of disbelief, another of fury, and then he was falling through the air toward the ground, his own scream the only sound in his ears.

"No!" Bolting upright in the bed, Rafe had a moment of disorientation as he continued to feel the helpless sensation of free-fall.

"Rafe? Sweetie? Are you okay?"

The voice didn't belong with the dream, but it was familiar.

"Rafe? Come on, you're scaring me."

Lillian.

She shifted away from him on the bed and fumbled on the nightstand for the lamp.

"No, leave it off." His voice was hoarse. No wonder, since his heart was halfway up his throat. Which was a good thing, because otherwise he might have puked the remnants of their very nice dinner all over the bed.

"Okay." Sounding uncertain, she left them in darkness. "Are you all right? What happened?"

"Just a dream."

"Babe, that didn't sound like *just* anything. I thought someone was killing you."

How fucking close to the truth she was.

"Could we not...could we hold off on this? For a few minutes? Please?" Because he needed to pull himself back together again. Having Cris around to witness the nightmares was bad enough. This was so much fucking worse.

"Okay, sure." She moved so she was touching him and tried to urge him back down onto the bed next to her. "Take as much time as you need. I'm not going anywhere."

That was both thrilling and scary as hell.

As he tried to lie down, though, his leg spasmed, white-hot pain shooting through his thigh as the muscle locked up into a tight, angry ball. A guttural groan escaped as he grabbed it, curling onto his side as the agony threatened to consume him.

"Rafe?" Lillian sounded a little freaked out. Not that he blamed her.

"Cramp." He panted through his clenched teeth. "Bad."

"What can I do?"

He nearly bit his tongue, holding back another groan. "Heating pad."

The bed bounced as she jumped off. It seemed like hours before she was back, every one of them filled with enough misery to make him wish for death, just to make it stop. Even when the healing warmth from the pad she wrapped around his leg started to leech into the muscle, the pain kept him curled on his side in a pitiful huddle.

"Did you know it's a proven fact that cursing can help ease pain?" She stroked a hand over his sweaty forehead as he huffed out a disbelieving laugh. "It's true. They've done studies and everything."

"So?" The word exploded on a gasp of air.

"So, if you want to curse, go right ahead."

Every profanity he'd ever known rose to his lips. He swallowed every one of them back down, pressing his face into the pillow, teeth clenched, refusing to give in to the temptation.

She sighed dramatically. "For God's sake, Rafael. I'm an adult, *and* I have three brothers. Trust me, I've heard it all before."

Doubtful. Besides, there were a lot of lessons he'd let slide over the years, but the manners pounded into him by his mother and her wooden spoon weren't one of them.

"It's getting better," he gritted out.

"I call bullshit on that one." She put her hand on his back and rubbed. "I can leave the room if you want. Then you can let loose."

"Stay."

He should have wanted her gone, where she couldn't witness this pathetic weakness of his. But either the pain was screwing with his head, or her presence actually had some kind of therapeutic effect on him.

He groaned. "And please keep doing that."

She did.

As her fingers pressed and stroked his skin, the pain pulsing in his thigh like a rotten tooth receded. She worked at the knot that was holding his shoulders hostage, then moved to his neck, and finally down his back to the dip of his spine. By the time her hands were gliding over his ass, the pain in his leg was all but forgotten.

"Roll onto your back."

Rafe obeyed the soft command, anticipation making his blood race. It wasn't until she removed the heating pad and ran her hands gently over his leg he realized her intent. He was quick to press his hand over hers, stopping her.

"You don't have to do that."

Rather than being put off by his harsh tone, she asked, "Won't this help?"

Yes. "No."

She leaned over him, their noses almost touching. "Do I need to call bullshit again?"

Fucking fuck.

"You shouldn't have to touch it." The look of the scars had never really bothered him all that much. Then again, the only people who'd seen them were his doctors and physical therapists. There hadn't been any women in his life since the accident he'd cared enough about to get naked with.

Not until Lillian.

The first time he dropped his pants in front of her had been one of the most gut-wrenching moments of his life. And her reaction had been nothing like he expected. Not only hadn't she been disgusted by his scars, she'd fucking kissed them.

Kissed. Them.

Then she'd ignored them from that moment on, as if they didn't even exist. And because she'd been able to, so had he. He'd barely even given them a thought this past week whenever they'd gotten naked.

But now it was like the purple elephant in the room had stood up to sing. Her hands were on the thick, twisted flesh where the broken bone had pushed through, where the surgeons had sliced him open to screw him back together like a giant Erector set.

There was no ignoring this. No pretending.

Her expression softened. "Aw, sweetie, don't you know by now there's not a single inch of you I don't want to touch?" She kissed the tip of his nose. "Let me make you feel better. And then I'll *really* make you feel better." Her eyebrows waggled as she grinned.

Rafe both laughed and groaned. "*Mi pequeña bruja.* You're killing me."

Her lips pursed in suspicion. "Are you calling me something little again?"

"Little witch." He pressed his forehead to hers and let out a gusty sigh. "You don't have to do this."

She mimicked his sigh. "I want to do this."

It was becoming clear he wouldn't win this battle of wills.

Reluctance making his movements slow, he took his restraining hand from hers and flung his arm over his eyes instead. That way, he wouldn't have to see her expression as she touched the evidence of his biggest mistake. It wasn't her disgust which would hurt the most.

It was her pity.

The heating pad had already soothed the worst of the knot. But when Lillian's magic fingers dug into his thigh, it was all he could do to keep from moaning out loud. God, that felt good. As she pressed, kneaded, and massaged, fraction by fraction the muscle relaxed and the pain receded to its normal post-cramp level of tolerable.

That alone would have been enough to make him her slave forever. But when she continued to work on his leg, the pain eased even further, the dull ache radiating up to his hip fading, the tightness in his calf and foot disappearing entirely.

"Better?"

He gave her a groan in reply. "God, yes."

"Told ya."

He was about to address the smugness in her voice when he felt her magic fingers start to drift toward his already half-swollen cock, making him shiver. That was when he remembered the second part of her promise about making him feel good.

Dios.

As her warm mouth closed over him, he decided the next time Lillian wanted to do anything to his body, anything at all, he wouldn't be stupid enough to argue. He'd just let her have her way with him. Because fucking Christ, she wasn't just making him feel good.

She was making him feel *awesome.*

Taking his arm away from his eyes, because this he *wanted* to see, he watched in the dim light as she licked her way down his shaft like it was the best treat ever made. Her tongue dragged and swirled, tasting and teasing, drawing his entire focus to that one single point of contact.

She finally stopped teasing and took him deep into her mouth, eliciting a long, low moan of thanks. Which turned to more sounds, none of them actual words, as the new ache she created consumed his senses and drove him rushing toward nirvana. When his climax hit, he swore his eyes crossed and the heavens wept.

God, he loved this woman.

Fuck.

He loved her.

How the hell had he let it get that far? He'd known days ago he was getting in deep, but *love?* That was over-the-head-and-drowning deep.

I'm-totally-screwed deep.

What-the-fuck-do-I-do-now deep.

And yet...

He had no desire to run.

In fact, as he gathered Lillian closer when she snuggled into his side, he realized there was no place else he'd rather be than right here. With her.

She pressed a kiss to his damp chest. "How's your leg?"

It took a second to process the question. Oh, right. His leg.

"Good as new. Well, as good as it was before the cramp hit, anyway." Because new would never happen. "You need to share your secret with my physical therapist. He's never managed to do that good a job relaxing me."

"I would hope not."

The laughter in her voice had him replaying his words in his head. He cursed.

"*Bruja*. You know what I meant."

"Keep calling me a witch and I'll spike your morning omelet with some eye of newt."

Rafe laughed. "*Lo siento, mi pequeña duendecilla*. It won't happen again." He kissed her forehead, which was all he could reach with the way she was curled into his side. "Where did you learn how to do that, anyway?"

"The massage? One of my art classes was all about anatomy and musculature. I took what I learned there and sort of went with what felt right."

He picked her hand up and brought it to his mouth, kissing each fingertip in gratitude for the magic they'd worked. "Thank you."

"Does that happen often? The cramping?"

"Not as often as it used to. Usually when I push too far at PT." He grimaced. "Or if I tense up too much in my sleep." He'd known they'd eventually have to circle back around to the nightmare.

He just didn't want to.

Rubbing her hand in soft circles on his chest, Lillian snuggled closer, her nose tucked against his neck. "You can tell me anything. It will never leave this room."

"It's not like it's a big secret. It's just…" He blew out a breath and scrubbed a hand through his hair, staring up at the shadowed ceiling. "I dream about the day I fell. The call I was on. It was…"

The petting continued through the silence. Patient. Soothing. He didn't know if it was that, or the dark, or the fact Lillian had already shared one of her own most private secrets, but his tension eased enough for him to keep talking.

"It was a simple domestic call. We were at that apartment at least once a week, when the neighbors got tired of listening to them go at it. They usually broke it up as soon as they heard us coming, and the husband would take off so we couldn't arrest him for knocking his wife around. But that day, he was still there when I got to the apartment. He was holding a knife to her throat."

The expression on Lupe's face was burned into his memory. Terror. Disbelief.

Worst of all, though, had been the weary acceptance.

"My backup hadn't arrived yet, so it was up to me to get him to drop the knife and surrender."

"But he didn't?"

"Not even close. He was out of his mind, listing all the reasons she was worthless to him, like he was trying to work up the courage to kill her."

"But you were right there! What was he thinking?"

"He wasn't. He was a drug addict, and what little was left of his brain was on the fritz because he needed another fix. All he had at that moment was his rage."

"God." She shuddered against him. "So, what happened?"

"I told him if he didn't put the knife down, I'd shoot. He was using her as a shield, but I had a clear shot over her shoulder. She was smaller than him." And a lot younger. "I knew I had to take the shot, but…"

"But?"

"I didn't." A choice he'd be kicking his own ass about for the rest of his sorry life.

Lillian's fingers continued their soothing motion. "You must have had a good reason."

He snorted. "No, I didn't shoot for the stupidest reason possible. Because his wife begged me not to."

Her hand stilled. "Why would she do that if he was threatening to kill her?"

Rafe understood the confusion in her tone. "She said she loved him."

"But...you said he beat her."

"All the time."

"That makes no sense."

"Tell me about it." A few long seconds passed, during which Lillian's fingers drummed on his chest as she thought. He put his hand over hers to still it. "Don't try to figure it out, sweetheart. You'll only hurt your brain."

"So, what happened? Did he...did he kill her? Is that what the nightmare was about?"

He didn't miss the small catch in her voice. Damn, he shouldn't be telling her this. Not even as sanitized a version as he was giving her. A woman like her, sweet and sheltered and still wearing the shine of innocent naiveté, shouldn't be exposed to the ugliness of the world where he worked.

Especially not the parts that were his fault.

"You know what? I shouldn't be telling you this crap. We should—"

"Don't you dare stop talking now, buster." She poked a finger into his chest. "Not unless you want to see what kind of *bruja* I can really be."

Despite the topic, her fierce words made him grin. Something he was quick to hide. He wasn't worried about eye of newt, but there were plenty of other disgusting things his little witch could come up with to put in his breakfast if he pissed her off enough.

"Okay, okay." He patted her hand until she laid it flat again on his chest. "No, he didn't kill her that night. He did cut her throat when he pushed her into me as he ran, but my partner was able to slow the bleeding while I went after him."

"Please tell me you arrested the bastard."

"He was arrested, but not by me." He'd been too busy bleeding on the ground. "I was following him down the fire escape when part of the railing gave way."

She sucked in a harsh breath. "Oh, God. *Rafe.* You could have been killed!"

"I only fell from the second story."

"*Only!*"

"It wouldn't have been so bad if I hadn't landed on the broken railing when I hit the ground. That's what did the most damage to my leg. It acted like a fulcrum. A few inches to the left and I might have ended up with nothing more than a simple fracture or break."

Of course, a few inches in another direction might have broken his back and left him paralyzed. Or dead. So, at the end of the day, he didn't have all that much to bitch about except his own poor decisions.

Which wouldn't have been so bad if they'd affected him alone.

Lillian wrapped her arm tight around him as she burrowed deeper into his side, her breathing harsh. "I knew you were hurt in the line of duty, but I had no idea you could have been killed. *God.*"

Probably better not to point out that a freak accident like his was the *least* life-threatening thing a police officer had to face most days. Judging by how tight she was already squeezing him, she might just snap one of his ribs.

"I hope they put him away for a really long time," she said after a tense minute of silence. Rafe would have grinned at her bloodthirsty tone if the reality hadn't been so grim.

"He's dead."

"What?" She pulled back to look at him. "What happened?"

His worst nightmare.

"He crashed a stolen car."

"But...you said he was arrested."

"He was. His wife bailed him out the next day." The bastard had been back on the streets before Rafe even made it out of surgery.

Lillian gaped at him. "His *wife*? The one he beat? And threatened to kill?"

"It happens all the time." He cupped her cheek. "I told you, sweetheart, don't try to make sense of it. People sometimes do the stupidest things for the people they love."

She blew out a frustrated breath. "Well, at least he can't hurt her anymore."

Guilt made him hesitate before answering.

"She was in the car with him."

Lillian's hand flew to her mouth, eyes wide.

The sour taste of guilt flooded him further.

"It's my fault."

"What is?"

"That she's dead."

"What? Rafe, you were in the hospital. How could it be your fault?"

"They were in that car because I didn't take the shot when I should have."

"They were in that car because his wife didn't leave him behind bars where he belonged. And because he was a dirtbag criminal committing another crime." She touched his chest in that soothing circle-pat motion again. "It wasn't your fault."

If only absolution was that easy.

"It wasn't just them, though. During the chase, he crashed into some cars at an intersection. Five other people were hurt."

"Rafe—"

"If I'd done what I was supposed to, none of that would have happened." A fact that ate him up every single time he thought about the innocent lives his bad decision had ruined.

"Okay, just stop it." She swung her leg over his hips and straddled him, hands pressed to his shoulders as she stared down into his face, her expression more serious than he'd ever seen it. "Stop beating yourself up over something you can't change, because *you didn't do anything wrong.*"

It was the same thing Internal Affairs had told him. That his partner told him. That his shrink kept telling him every time they went round and round about that damn day.

Hearing Lillian say it didn't budge the boulder of guilt off of his conscience one single inch. It was a mistake he was going to have to either learn to live with, or find a way to somehow make amends for, before it drove him insane.

But for tonight, for right this moment, he was done thinking about it. He had a warm, sexy woman he adored sitting on top of the part of him that was quickly gaining interest again, and he still had some catching up to do in the orgasm-giving department.

He raised his hands to cup her breasts and rolled her nipples between his thumbs and forefingers. They instantly came erect.

She sucked in a sharp breath and bit her lower lip. "You're trying to change the subject so you don't have to talk about—*ahh*, God."

"Is it working?"

She let out a low moan as one of his hands found her clit and stroked it in time with the tugs on her nipple. When her gaze fixed on his again, her eyes were cloudy with desire. The smile she gave made his cock harden even more. She wiggled her ass against it.

"I'd say it's working just fine."

Chapter 16

"**Y**ou're looking deliciously relaxed this morning, kitten. I wonder why that is, hmm?"

Feeling deliciously relaxed, Lillian let a wide grin at Des's suggestive tone be her answer. She stepped back to let him into the apartment. "Amazing what a good night's sleep will do for you."

"A good night of something, anyway." Des leaned down to buss her cheek, careful not to crush the garment bag draped over his arm.

Since he was one hundred percent accurate, Lillian didn't bother to reply. Instead, she danced around him as they walked to the living room. "Is that my dress? Lemme see! Lemme see!"

"Patience, love."

"Did you forget who you're talking to?" Rafe entered the room from the direction of the bedrooms. His dark hair was still damp from his shower, one rebellious piece curling over his forehead. She had to fight not to reach out and brush it back into place.

"You're right." Des rolled his eyes. "Whatever was I thinking? Come on, then. Let's do some show and tell in the bedroom."

As Rafe wrapped his arm around Lillian's shoulder to follow behind Des, he whispered to her, "It's a damn good thing you told me he was gay, *querida*. He's too nice a guy for me to hit for no reason."

As they entered the bedroom, she shot a quick look around to make sure they hadn't left any pieces of clothing or stray condom wrappers lying in plain sight. When Des had buzzed from the lobby to say he was there with her dress for the showing that night, she'd only had a few frenzied minutes to straighten up.

Des hung the garment bag on the hook beside the closet. With a flourish, he opened the zipper and stepped to the side, hands extended. He didn't have to say it to hear the "ta-da!"

"Oh, Des." She walked toward the dress, awed beyond her expectations. "This is *gorgeous*."

He made a put-upon face. "She says that like it's a surprise. Of course, it's gorgeous, kitten. Would I ever put my name on anything else?"

No, he wouldn't. There wasn't a piece of clothing he'd designed yet that hadn't been amazing, or she hadn't coveted. But *this*. She touched the heavy silk, so dark a purple it was almost black. The soft material flowed like quicksilver through her fingers.

"You've totally outdone yourself."

He took the compliment as his due. "Try it on, kitten. I want to make sure it doesn't need any last-minute alterations."

He didn't have to tell her twice. She made a shooing motion at them both. "Out."

Des raised an eyebrow, but to her relief didn't argue. Rafe might have beaten back his jealous streak over Des's comments because of his sexual orientation. That didn't mean he'd be thrilled to know her friend didn't usually vacate the room while she was playing dress-up with his clothes.

The door had just thumped closed behind them when her cell phone rang. Caught between wanting to curse and whimper, she cast a longing look at the dress before she snatched it up. "Hello?"

"Lillian? This is Nancy at Top Shelf Catering."

"Nancy, hi. What can I do for you?"

"Well, not kill me, for starters."

A cold ball of dread instantly formed in her stomach. "What do you mean?"

"I'm afraid I have a bit of a situation here."

"What kind of situation? When we confirmed yesterday, everything was fine."

"Yesterday it was. Today...not so much." Nancy blew out a loud, frustrated sigh. "About an hour ago, a half-dozen inspectors from the city health department showed up and told me there had been multiple complaints lodged against us alleging all kinds of code violations."

"That's insane! Your kitchens are cleaner than most operating rooms." She should know. She'd toured them herself before she'd started hiring Top Shelf to cater gallery events last year. The place had been so well scrubbed it all but sparkled.

"Exactly what I told them," Nancy replied, sounding aggrieved. "And *showed* them. But because of the number of complaints, and the fact that several of them claimed food poisoning, they're shutting me down until they inspect every square inch and test every speck of food in the place."

"Oh, my God, that's horrible." Then the full implication hit. "Oh. Oh, no."

"Oh, yes. I'm afraid I won't be able to fulfill the contract for tonight's catering at the gallery."

Lillian sank onto the bed before her suddenly wobbly legs dumped her on her ass. "You can't be serious."

"I am *so* sorry, but it's all out of my control at this point. They've already said we won't be allowed to do any food prep until they're done, and while they can't tell me when that's going to be, they said it most likely wouldn't be today."

"But it might?" She grabbed onto that tiny sliver of hope.

Only to have Nancy snatch it away again.

"Even if they finish early, I wouldn't feel right about serving anything we have that they've gone through. There are too many people touching things for me to maintain any kind of quality control. I'm going to end up wasting out my entire perishables inventory and start from scratch. If I still have a business left when this is over."

The bitterness in her voice broke through Lillian's panic and reminded her this wasn't just about her and her show tonight. This was a professional and financial nightmare for Nancy. Even if no violations were found, the accusations alone could still destroy her company's reputation.

"You know I'll still be using you for our next function."

"Considering how badly this mess just screwed you, you don't know how much that means to me. I'm so sorry, Lillian."

"That makes two of us. Good luck."

"Thanks. You too."

Still trying to process the disaster that had just crashed over her like a late winter avalanche, Lillian hung up and sat staring at the phone clutched in her hands. The clock on the home screen seemed to mock her, ticking over from 11:22 to 11:23, marking another minute closer to the showing for which she now had no food.

There was a light knock at the door.

She barely registered it, too caught up in the thoughts spinning through her head, every ounce of enthusiasm she'd started the day with now circling the drain. Right along with her job and all her plans. How could this have happened? What was she going to do?

There was another knock.

"Lil, sweetie, if you're in there fondling the goods while you keep us menfolk standing in the hall, that's just bad form." Des paused. His tone changed when he asked, "Kitten, is everything all right?"

No, nothing is all right. Everything is a disaster.

The door opened a few seconds later and Rafe poked his head in. Spying her on the bed, his expression turned concerned. He hurried over to sit beside her. "Sweetheart, what's wrong?" His gaze landed on the phone she had in a death grip. Concern instantly morphed into hard-eyed suspicion. "Who called? What happened?"

"The caterer. They cancelled." Her stomach clenched as she said the words out loud, making them real.

Rafe muttered something growly under his breath. "They can't cancel. You have a contract."

"And they have health inspectors closing them down while they investigate a bunch of complaints about food poisoning." She gave a hollow laugh. "God, what are the odds? Today, of all days."

She stilled.

Yeah, what *were* the odds?

Teeth clenched against the scream threatening to erupt, she ground out one word.

"Roman."

"What?"

"Roman. It had to be him."

"You don't know that."

"Oh, I know, all right. And I'm going to *kill* him!" She shot to her feet and started for the door, intent on doing just that. She'd put up with a lot, but this? This was the final straw.

The bastard was going *down*.

In an act of supreme bravery in the face of her incendiary wrath, Des stepped in front of the door, blocking her way. "You may want to rethink any acts of violence and homicide, love. Especially when you've got an officer of the law as a witness."

She glanced over her shoulder at Rafe. "You wouldn't rat me out, would you?"

"Hell, I'd help you bury the body if it's true."

She gave Des a smug grin. "See?"

"But," Rafe continued, "I think you've got a much more pressing concern at the moment. You need to figure out what you're going to do about tonight."

The reminder took the starch right out of her fury. Her entire body sagged.

"Oh, God, tonight. What *am* I going to do?"

"I don't suppose you could forgo food this one time?"

It was Des who answered. "The only thing worse than subpar

food at an event like this is *no* food. It leaves the masses hungry for whatever meat they can tear off your bones instead."

Rafe laughed, but stopped when neither of them joined in. "You're serious."

"As serious as a bad review. And not the fake kind."

"This is a nightmare." Lillian walked back to the bed and dropped onto the end. "Ammar is going to lose his mind if his show is ruined. I had to all but promise him my firstborn to get him to sign with us." She flopped back onto the mattress with a groan. "I am so fired."

And for once, she wasn't just being melodramatic. Felix would need to do something to appease the histrionic artist. It went without saying she'd be the scapegoat he sacrificed to save face for the gallery.

"What kind of food are we talking about here?" Rafe asked.

"Finger foods," Des replied. "Appetizers. Think things you can poke with a toothpick. Why?"

Rafe gave him an exasperated look as he pulled out his phone and dialed. "Are you kidding? Have the two of you already forgotten what my parents do for a living?"

Lillian bolted upright as adrenaline and hope spiked through her. "Oh! Do you think—"

Rafe shushed her with his hand as he spoke in rapid Spanish into the phone. She didn't have a clue what he was saying, but by the growing grin on Des's face, it was something that might just save her butt.

A hope that proved accurate when Rafe held out his phone to her a few minutes later.

"Here. Talk to my mother about the details."

Still in a bit of a daze, she took the phone and spent the next ten minutes going over food choices, many of which she'd sampled the night before at the restaurant and knew firsthand were delicious. They talked quantity and cost, and by the time she hung up, there was a full replacement plan of food and catering staff in place which would arrive at the gallery at six o'clock sharp.

As she handed the phone back to Rafe, she almost couldn't believe things had been fixed that easily. She kept waiting for the other shoe to drop.

"Everything set?" Rafe asked.

Launching herself at him, she threw her arms around his neck and hugged him until he grunted at the excessive force. She loosened her grip and kissed his cheek.

"Thank you."

"*De nada, querida.*"

Des held up his phone. "I hope I get a little of that sugar sent my way, since I just got Sheila to come up with a few of her sinfully delicious desserts to compliment the menu."

Lillian gaped. His former roommate and very good friend made the most incredible desserts in the universe. She'd landed a full-time gig as head pastry chef for Q's and was quickly gaining the kind of reputation that was drawing people to the exclusive restaurant as much for her innovative offerings as for the rest of its excellent food.

"How could she possibly find the time? It's already"—she looked at the clock and swallowed—"almost noon."

"Leave that to Sheila, kitten. She wouldn't promise if she couldn't deliver." He held out his arms expectantly. "Well?"

With a laugh, she gave him a rib-crushing hug and a kiss on the cheek. "Thank you." She looked at Rafe. "Both of you. This would have been a freaking disaster without your help."

"I hate to debuzz your high," Des said, "but if I were you, I'd check your other vendors to make sure there aren't any more surprises in store."

That sobered her in a heartbeat. "You're right."

"You think Roman had a hand in this too?" Rafe asked Des.

"I think somebody did. As for who…" He gave a one-shouldered shrug. "That's tomorrow's mystery. Let's just focus on getting through today first."

An excellent point. Lillian headed for her tablet. "I'll check with every other vendor right now." And, if she found any more problems when she was done, God help whoever was screwing with her.

Rafe might have been kidding about burying the body, but she wasn't.

<hr>

"You totally owe me for fucking up my Saturday night off, *hermano*." Cristiano shoved a plate of mojo shrimp in Rafe's face.

Picking up one of the tangy delicacies and popping it in his mouth, Rafe struggled between responding to his brother with a smart-ass answer or an apology. Most of the catering crew had taken the last-minute job because they were available and wanted the extra money.

Family, however, was expected to fill in whenever needed without complaint.

Even he'd been dragooned into putting on a waiter's uniform from time to time. Although only in the direst of situations, since he never managed to turn his inner cop all the way off. His mother had gotten more than one complaint about him making people uncomfortable.

"*Lo siento*. We had a situation, and—"

"I know. I heard. *Mami* was very clear that you'd called in a favor for your girlfriend. So...maybe it's her who owes me."

Rafe recognized that particular tone. His brother wanted something.

"Maybe you should ask me and not think about bothering Lillian while she's busy." Which she had been, from the second they hit the door late that afternoon.

She'd always been a whirling dervish of energy. Seeing her in her element, though, gave Rafe a new appreciation of how important that kind of personality was to the extreme multi-tasking her job required. No matter how many people spoke at her at once, how many demands were made of her, she handled it with competence, calm, and a smile.

Even so, he knew under that composed surface was a crazy woman sweating every single detail to make sure the night went off without any more issues. She didn't need his brother bothering her with something stupid on top of it all.

"I'm not sure you can give me what I want."

"Try me."

"Okay. Introduce me to the blonde."

Rafe followed his brother's gaze. "Bernice? Seriously?"

The receptionist who'd checked out his ass the first time he visited the gallery hovered behind Lillian's shoulder as she spoke to several people about a pair of bold, geometric paintings on the wall. The purple stripe in her bleached hair had been toned down somehow, but she still looked like she was ready to hit the clubs, her dress just a little too short and tight for the professional setting.

Yeah, he could see *exactly* why Cris had zeroed in on her.

"I could," he said with some reluctance, "but she's a little bit, ah..."

Cris grinned. "I like them a little bit ah."

It seemed warning his brother off would be a waste of breath. Surrendering to the inevitable, Rafe shook his head and led him over for the introduction. He smiled and winked at Lillian when her gaze darted to him as he approached, letting her know she didn't need to interrupt her sales pitch for him.

When Bernice realized Rafe had come to talk to her and not Lillian, her face lit with a huge, too-white smile. "Well, hello again, you."

"Hi, Bernice." Not liking the avaricious gleam in her eye, he pushed his brother forward as he dropped back a step. "Have you met my brother, Cris?"

The length of time it took for her to even glance at his brother made it obvious she wasn't interested in talking to anyone but Rafe.

But then the fading smile started to bloom again as her gaze shifted from one to the other and back, no doubt marking the similar looks that had dogged them all their lives.

"Oh, well, *hello.*"

Expertly balancing his tray, Cris took Bernice's hand with his free one and gave a small continental bow over it. "*Que mujer hermosa.*"

"Um, what?"

Cris smiled. "What a beautiful woman."

"Oh. Oh, well." She raked Cris from head to toe with an approving look. "You're pretty nice yourself."

Giving his brother a small jostle with his shoulder, Rafe leaned in to whisper, "Don't forget you're working." After a quick head-tip to Bernice, he made a strategic retreat to the other side of the room, where Lillian joined him not long after. She put her back to the wall beside him as they gazed out over the finally thinning crowd.

"You looked bored all alone over here."

Because he was.

Not that he'd ever admit it to her.

"Just keeping an eye on things." Things being anyone who came within two feet of her. And there had been more than a few who'd come a lot closer, which pissed him the hell off. Far too many men seemed to think it was okay to get right up on top of her as they talked.

Didn't these assholes have any respect for personal space?

Lillian chuckled. "Well, you're doing a great job. Ammar wanted to know who the scary guy glaring at his guests all night was."

Meaning he hadn't been as subtle as he thought. "Great. What did you say?"

"That you were law enforcement. He assumed I meant security hired for the event, and was impressed we thought enough of him and his work to take those kinds of precautions." She grinned up at him. "I didn't have the heart to burst his bubble of self-importance."

"Think we could slip away for a few minutes to your office?"

Her humor dimmed. "Is something wrong?"

"Yeah. I haven't been able to touch you in hours, and it's making me kinda crazy."

Standing this close to her now, with that enticing spicy perfume reaching out and wrapping itself around him, it was a struggle to not pull her close and take a small taste of her lips, her boss be damned.

The smile she gave him didn't help.

At. All.

"Only another hour, baby." She slid a little closer as she turned, using her body to block the fact she gave his ass a quick squeeze. As she walked away, she threw an impish glance over her shoulder.

Oh yeah, the little witch was *so* going to pay for that.

The hour ended up being closer to two by the time they were able to lock the gallery door and head for home. Wrapped up in that purple silk dress that moved over her curves like it was water, Lillian looked exhausted, elated, and good enough to eat.

A fact that made Rafe bend a few speed limits on the short drive. The light kiss he'd stolen when he helped her into the truck only whetted his already ravenous appetite for her. If he didn't have her naked and quaking with pleasure in the next ten minutes, he might explode.

Lillian seemed oblivious to his frantic state. She was too busy riding the high of a successful evening. "I can't believe how well everything went tonight. I kept waiting for something else to go wrong."

"I guess that means you don't have to worry about losing your job?" He pulled his truck into the parking garage beneath their building.

"Are you kidding? Ammar is happy, which means Felix is happy, which means *I* am *golden*. For today, anyway," she added, scrunching her nose. "Felix can be a bit capricious."

"Sounds more like Felix can be a fucking asshole," Rafe muttered as he walked around the truck to open the door for her. He staggered slightly as she launched herself at him, arms around his neck, and kissed him until he thought she might cause them both to spontaneously combust.

When she broke the kiss on a gasp, he sucked in a much-needed breath. "What was that for?"

"Everything. Being there when I needed you. Coming up with a solution for the food." She smiled. "I have to call your mom tomorrow and thank her again. There wasn't a bite of anything left by the end of the night. Everyone loved it. That woman is a genius in the kitchen."

He tugged her by the hand toward the elevator. "My mother loves to feed people. It's her joy in life."

"Well, her joy made me look good, despite *somebody's*"—she shot him a look saying she knew who that somebody was but was restraining herself—"best efforts otherwise."

"We'll figure that out tomorrow." He pulled her close as they rode to the fourth floor. "Tonight, we celebrate your success."

Leaning into him, one hand began to wander. "Mmm, I like the sound of that. So, what's my prize?"

He sucked in a breath and caught her hand before it made it to its final destination. "You really need to remember there are cameras in here, sweetheart." He placed a kiss on her palm, laced his fingers with hers, and when the doors slid open, tugged her toward her apartment.

"Didn't you ever have the urge to be just a little naughty in public?"

"Not even a little bit." He nipped at her pouting lower lip. "You can be as naughty as you want to be, but please, for my sanity, make sure it's behind closed doors."

She pushed past him into the apartment, her delectable ass swaying like a tantalizing metronome under the silk, making his mouth water. He shot the locks and reset the alarm, struggling to keep his hands from shaking as he punched in the numbers.

Dios, what this woman did to him.

When he turned, she was still standing in the living room, watching him with an expression he couldn't quite decipher. "What?"

Moistening her lips, she tipped her chin toward the door. "It's closed. And I'm behind it." She ran her hands down her sides and over her hips until she found the slit that had played peekaboo with her gorgeous leg all night. Pulling it back, she cocked her knee and put a foot with another of those fuck-me heels on the couch, baring her stocking-clad leg all the way to the black garters holding them up. "So, how naughty do you want me to be?"

There was a moment where Rafe couldn't move, because all his blood had shot to his groin in one throbbing rush. When he broke free of his temporary paralysis, he went to her and dropped to his knees.

He laid a gentle kiss to first her ankle, her knee, and then to the very top of the stocking, which was a wispy, gossamer barrier matching the silkiness of her skin. He dragged his tongue along the edge of it, and was rewarded by the shudder that ran through her body.

"No, *mi seductora*." *My seductress.* He kissed the skin above the stocking and added a small nip, making her gasp. "The question is, how naughty do you want *me* to be?" He pushed the heavy silk further back and blew a hot breath against the barely-there panties he'd exposed.

"Oh, *Dios*," Lillian groaned, making Rafe laugh as he stood and swept her into his arms. Wrapping her arms around his neck as he strode to the bedroom, she said, "I'll make a bad boy out of you yet, Rafael Delgado."

"And I'll gladly do the penance for the pleasure of sinning in your arms, *ángel*." He set her on her feet. "Now, I suggest you take off that dress before Des puts out a contract on me for ripping it off your delicious little body."

Laughing, she stripped, tormenting him a little by taking the time to hang the dress up with great care before strutting toward him in just her bra, panties, stockings, and heels. She pushed him down on the bed and straddled his lap, making sure to squirm against the hard press of his erection. "I'm all yours."

Rafe wasn't sure how he got his clothes off or where they ended up. All he knew was that as he sank into her welcoming body, it was the sweetest feeling in the world, and he never wanted to leave it.

He never wanted to leave her.

When they finally collapsed into a sweaty, satiated pile, he held her tight, wanting to say something about how he felt but too afraid of ruining the moment to do more than whisper, "*Te adoro, mi ángel.*" He felt her smile against his chest before her entire body went lax with sleep. He kissed her head and sighed.

Tomorrow. Somehow, he'd find the courage to tell her how he felt tomorrow.

It felt like he'd been asleep for mere minutes when the piercing screech of the alarm clock startled him awake. With a groan, he rolled over to slap at the damn thing on the nightstand, only to realize that wasn't what was making all the racket. It was the smoke detector in the hallway.

It took a few seconds more for his half-awake brain to process what that meant.

The apartment was on fire.

Chapter 17

"Lillian, wake up!"

"Guh." Swatting at the annoying hands shaking her awake when her body clock said she still had plenty of time left to sleep, she buried her face deeper into the pillow. "Lemme alone."

"Lillian!"

She squawked as she was abruptly manhandled into a sitting position. "What're you doing?"

"The building's on fire. Get up!"

"The what is what?" Her sluggish brain finally engaged. The first thing she realized was the annoying sound splitting her eardrums was the smoke detector going off beyond the closed bedroom door. The second was that she could smell smoke.

Just like that, she went from comatose to wide-awake. "Oh, my God."

"Get up. Get some clothes on, quick."

Clicking on the lamp, Lillian scrambled out of bed and grabbed the first things she could lay her hands on. By the time she shoved her feet into her sneakers, Rafe had already yanked on jeans and sneakers and was heading for the door. After testing the knob for heat, he cracked it, his shirt held to his face. He ducked his head out for a fast look, then moved back and slammed the door shut, coughing.

"The fire's blocking the front door."

Lillian's heart pounded harder. "What do we do?" But she knew, since Rafe was already heading for the window. Her heart sped up even faster.

"Fire escape." Unlatching the casement window, he slid it all the way open. "Come on, let's go." He shrugged on his shirt as he waited for her.

She couldn't move.

Go down the fire escape? Four whole stories? In the dark?

"Lillian, *come on.*"

Not even the knowledge that every second she delayed put them both in more danger could get her feet moving toward the opening that beckoned like the gaping maw of hell. "I can't." It was no better than a hoarse whisper.

"Lillian..." The frustrated expression on Rafe's face as he strode over to her eroded when he took a good look at her and seemed to realize there was something more going on than stupid stubbornness. "*Querida*, are you afraid of heights?"

She gave a semi-hysterical laugh. "Afraid? No. Terrified to the point of paralysis? You bet."

He cursed in Spanish. At least it sounded like he cursed. She really had to learn to speak the language better if they were going to be staying together. If they lived through tonight, of course. Which wasn't looking all that promising at the moment.

"Sweetheart, I'll be with you every step of the way. You won't fall, I promise."

"You can't know that."

"I can. Trust me."

She did trust him. But the closer she got to the open window, the harder it was to pull oxygen into her lungs, and it had nothing to do with the smoke thickening the air. When she was only a few feet away, she dug her heels in and struggled against his hold on her arm. "I can't. I'm sorry, I can't."

To his credit, he didn't just drag her the rest of the way and toss her out. But he didn't let go of her arm, either. "You can, and you will. It's the only way out, and you know it."

It was. That didn't mean she had to use it.

"I can go into the panic room." There was an edge of hysteria to her voice now even she could hear. "Remember? I showed it to you. It's totally secure. I can wait in there until they put the fire out." It was right next door in the other bedroom.

With all of her paintings.

It felt like a knife had been plunged into her heart. "Oh, God, my paintings," she moaned.

"Lil. *Lillian*." He shook her until he had her attention again. "Is it fireproof?"

Was it? She had no idea. "Probably. Maybe." What did it matter, when all her hard work was about to go up in smoke and ash?

Rafe took hold of both her arms and forced her to look at him. "Lillian—" He broke off to cough. "I'm not risking your life on a maybe. We have to go down the fire escape, and we have to do it *now*."

He was right. She knew he was right. But...she just couldn't do it. She shook her head.

"Yes. If I can do it, so can you. So, stop being a whiny baby, pull up those freaking big girl panties of yours, and move that sweet ass *now*, before I spank it."

Her big girl panties? Move her ass?

Seriously?

Indignant fury raced through her veins, chasing away the numbing fear. She opened her mouth to tell him *exactly* where he could shove his Attila the Hun attitude, but for once her brain kicked in before her voice. "You did that on purpose."

He nodded. "Ready?"

Much as she wanted to say no, there was no real choice. She was either going out the window under her own power, or Rafe would toss her over his shoulder and carry her out, and wouldn't *that* be fun? She'd probably end up getting them both killed.

That was the thought to get her moving. Risking her own life was one thing. Risking Rafe's was unacceptable. He was in this mess because of her.

Panic seized control again as she swung her feet out into the darkness. Only Rafe's steadying hands on her shoulders kept her moving in the right direction. By the time he joined her out on the metal grate platform, her heart was hammering so hard she could feel it thudding in her ears like a Led Zeppelin drum solo.

Rafe put himself at her back, hands on her shoulders. "You okay?"

Hell to the no.

"Yeah. Are you?" Because now that they were hanging out in the middle of the air four stories up, she remembered the last time he'd been in this situation, *he'd* fallen. And almost died. *If I can do it, so can you.* God, he had to be freaking out every bit as much as she was. And yet, he was calm, cool, and one hundred percent focused on getting her to safety, without any regard for his own issues.

Was it any wonder she loved the guy?

Calling on every bit of willpower in her possession, she gave a jerky nod.

"I'm good. Let's go."

He gave her a fast kiss before he got them moving down the ladder. He went first, blocking her body with his in case she slipped. With every rung conquered, she was grateful for the darkness cloaking the very long way to the ground. If she'd seen how far there was to fall, she didn't think she'd be able to move an inch.

When they hit the next landing, there was the urge to do a little victory dance. Since they were still about twenty-plus feet in the air, she settled for a sigh of relief. But when she headed for the next ladder, Rafe shook his head and pulled her to the window that faced the landing on that floor.

"What are you doing?" she asked as he tried to open the window, then pounded on the glass with the heel of his hand when it wouldn't budge.

"This is Cris's room. *Cris!* Open up, damn it!" He pounded again, hard enough to rattle the glass.

"Why aren't we going all the way down on the fire escape?" Not that she was looking forward to it. But they'd just gotten out of the burning building. Why would he want them to climb back inside it?

"Because that's what whoever set the fire would expect us to do, and I'd rather not drop right into their hands. Cris!" He pounded again, and there was finally the sound of the latch being thrown on the window sash.

"Whoever set…" She stared at him, her world tilting. "You think—"

"I'm not taking any chances. Not with you." He kissed her hard as the window slid open. Sirens were already screaming in the distance. "Go inside. Tell Cris to knock on everyone's doors to wake them up, then get down to the ground level. Use the stairs. Stay with the crowd. Don't get separated."

When he turned away, she grabbed his arm. "Wait! Where are you going?"

"Trust me." He kissed her again. "Stay with Cris. I'll be right back."

Before she could object, he bounded back up the ladder and through her window. Back into her apartment. Where the fire was.

Her heart screamed out in protest.

"Rafe!" Was he crazy?

She almost started to follow him. Had her hand on the ladder railing, foot raised to the first step. Only the fact she'd be nothing but a hinderance to whatever insane thing he was doing—and because she wasn't sure she'd actually make it back up the ladder without freezing up again—kept her from trying it.

Instead, heart pounding, she turned for the open window and, with one last look up to say a prayer for her brave idiot, she climbed through into darkness.

"Cris?"

A lamp came on. She shielded her eyes from the sudden light, cursing as she blinked away the spots that danced across her vision. When she could see again, it wasn't Cris standing beside the nightstand. "Bernice? What are you doing here?"

Lillian had seen her following Rafe's brother around the gallery with a look that said she wanted to sample more than the food on his tray. She hadn't realized they'd actually hooked up.

The receptionist's lip curled. "What, so now I'm not even good enough for your boyfriend's brother?"

"What?" The angry tone made even less sense than the question. "Of course not. That's not...whatever, okay? You slept with Cris. Fine. Fantastic. I'm thrilled for you both. Now, can we get the hell out of here, please? In case you haven't noticed, the building is *on fire.*"

She pushed past Bernice and shook Cris where he lay sleeping on the bed, his lax face so like Rafe's it almost hurt. "Cris, wake up."

Bernice didn't move. "Not the whole building. Just *your* apartment."

"Which is connected to the rest of the building, and is, guess what? *Right over this one.*" She gave Cris another shake, but his head just lolled to the side.

This wasn't right.

"Cris?" She fought back a pinch of panic. "What's wrong with him?"

Rather than answer, Bernice looked at the open window, face pinched into an annoyed scowl. "I can't believe I forgot about the stupid fire escape."

"What? Bernice, focus. Something's wrong with Cris, and we need to get him up and all of us out of here before we turn into crispy critters. Now!" She tugged on Cris's arm, trying to get him to the edge of the bed. He moaned and mumbled incoherently. "Bernice, damn it, get over here and help me!"

"We're not at work, bitch. You can't tell me what to do."

Lillian snapped her head around to stare at her, dumbfounded.

"Seriously? You're gonna cop an attitude *now*?"

"Why couldn't you have just stayed where you were supposed to? Why do you always have to *ruin* everything for me?"

"Ruin everything?" What bizarro dimension had she fallen into? "What the ever-freakin' hell are you talking…"

Oh. Oh, no. Oh holy, holy hell. This was *not* happening.

"Bernice? What did you do?" She had to be wrong. She had to.

"What did *I* do?" She gave a crazed laugh. "No, it's what *you've* done. Which is everything you can to keep me from getting what I want. What I deserve. You cheated me!"

"Out of what?"

"How about my job, for starters. I should've been the one Felix promoted to assistant manager, not you. *I* should've been the boss."

Yep, definitely an alternate dimension.

Felix barely tolerated Bernice's borderline NSFW personality and style as their receptionist. There was no way he'd ever consider her for a sales position, much less jump her right over that job to a managerial one.

Not that she was telling that to the crazy lady who evidently *set her building on fire*.

She strove for a calm, rational tone.

It wasn't easy, with the acrid smell of smoke wafting in through the open window.

"I'm not assigning blame here, but wouldn't that make it *Felix* you should be pissed at, not me?" She gave Cris's arm a pinch. He barely reacted.

Damn, what was wrong with him? And where the hell was Rafe?

"He never should have hired you. You don't need the job. You've got buckets of money. If you weren't there, Felix would have given the job to *me*."

Pieces clicked into place with hard, angry snaps.

"So, what? You've been doing all of this crap to me to try and get me to leave?" Now *that* pissed her off. Her poor little Cooper!

Bernice ranted on without answering. "And *then*, the hottest piece of sex-on-a-stick ever walks in, and you snatched him right out from under me!"

"What?"

"You *knew* I wanted Rafe. I told you so. And you were all, 'he's just my neighbor,' blah blah, and the next thing I know, you've jumped his junk and are practically living with him before I even got my chance, just to keep him away from me! It was a totally skanky thing to do!"

"That is so not how it—"

"Then imagine my surprise when your *boyfriend* comes over to say hello to me tonight, and what does he do? Pawns his stupid little brother off on me, that's what. Like I'm some charity case or something."

More like she was some freaking nut case or something.

"I'm sure he was just being nice."

Lillian cringed at the loud crack that came from somewhere above them. The fire was eating away at the building with a voracious appetite. They needed to get out before something came down on their heads or the toxic smoke killed them.

Her watering eyes darted to the window, stomach twisting.

Rafe, please be safe.

A malevolent smile curved Bernice's lips. "But I had the last laugh on all of you. The whole time I was with his brother, I pretended it was your boyfriend who was screwing me. I even called out his name when I came."

That was just...twisted.

"Look, you can hate me, hate Rafe, hell, hate everyone in the entire world for all I care. But right now, we need to get out of this building or we're going to *die*." She tugged on Cris again. She succeeded in getting him to throw his legs over the edge of the mattress, but even that was a struggle.

She shot a furious glare at Bernice. "What did you do to him?"

"Just a little Xanax in his tequila." Bernice smirked. "Poor baby can't handle his women *or* his liquor."

"Why would you drug him?"

"How else was I supposed to sneak upstairs with his keycard and get the real party started?"

Meaning set the fire that now put all their lives at risk, along with all the other innocent tenants in the building. Her heart squeezed when she thought of Walter and Andrew in the apartment next to hers, and the other neighbors across the hall. Had they gotten out okay?

Focus, Lil.

The sirens had reached their apex and died, and firemen shouted from below as they set up to fight the fire. She had to have faith they'd be able to save everyone else. It was up to her to worry about saving the people in this room.

"What were you going to do? Leave him here to die?"

"Why not? He served his purpose, getting me in past all the stupid security this building has. And to tell you the truth, he wasn't all that good a lay."

Lillian's temper snapped. "You psychotic bitch!" She shoved past Bernice and ran to the window to stick her head out and yell to the firemen. "Hey, we're up here! We need help! Somebody—*umph*." All the breath left her lungs in a rush as she was grabbed around the waist, dragged back from the window, and slung to the floor.

"You are *not* going to ruin this for me too!" Bernice shouted, standing over her, fists clenched and shaking with rage.

Lillian was doing plenty of her own shaking. How dare this bitch put her through such hell? How dare she risk people's lives for her vainglorious delusions?

Rolling to the side to put more space between them, she popped back up to her feet and snarled. "It's over! Get it through that thick head of yours. You're done."

"No!" Bernice launched herself at Lillian with a scream.

Expecting an actual attack, Lillian was surprised when all the other woman did was slap at her and try to grab her hair. Trained by her father's security team how to take care of herself, it took all of two seconds to put Bernice on the ground.

Eyes wide with shock, Bernice touched the small trickle of blood at the corner of her mouth. "You *hit* me!"

If the situation hadn't been so serious, Lillian would have laughed. She settled for rolling her eyes. "Bitch, please." She was interrupted by a loud pounding out at the apartment door.

Yes!

She had a moment of indecision about leaving the vulnerable Cris alone with psycho-bitch to go let the firemen in. Realizing there was no better choice, she bolted out of the bedroom toward the front door, where the pounding was now accompanied by the muffled shouts of men asking if anyone was in there.

"Yes!" she shouted as she ran. "We're here! We're here!" Her adrenaline ran so high it made her fingers feel fat and useless as she fumbled at the locks. "Come on, come on, *yes!*" The deadbolt turned at the same instant a sharp prick came against the side of her neck, freezing her in place.

Chapter 18

I'm a fucking idiot.

Wiping sweat, soot, and tears from his face with the t-shirt he'd had tied around his mouth and nose, Rafe doubted he'd have very many people who'd disagree with him on that. Firemen were supposed to be the only ones crazy enough to run *into* burning buildings.

Yet here he was, hacking up enough smoke to choke an elephant, skin burning like a thousand wasp stings from the heat, eyes watering and hurting like a motherfucker. And for what? To save a stupid painting?

It was the dumbest decision he'd ever made in his life.

But he'd make the same one if he had it to do over again. The fate of the rest of Lillian's collection might be a great big question mark, but he could at least save this one piece for her. The singed skin on his hand from the hot metal doorknob just meant he'd cut it a little closer than planned.

Like he'd told Lillian about Lupe's irrational choices, sometimes people did the stupidest things for the ones they loved.

As he climbed out of her window for the second time that night, the hiss and roar of water hitting the crackling flames in the apartment behind him signaled firemen at last battling the fiery bitch which was nipping at his heels. Hopefully that meant they'd been able to clear the other three apartments on the floor, and the only thing lost tonight would be some possessions, not lives. If he hadn't woken up when he did...

Damn, it had been close.

Too fucking close.

Resolve mingled with the terror sitting like a chunk of the Rockies on his chest. He was done being reasonable. No way could he risk losing Lillian like this again. As soon as she was tucked away somewhere safe with a dozen bodyguards—preferably armed to the teeth—he was going after Roman's sorry ass.

The bastard would be lucky if he lived long enough to regret his decision to target her.

Climbing down the narrow metal ladder holding the canvas proved more awkward than he'd anticipated. But that wasn't the only thing making him clumsy. There was also the memory of the last time he'd made this kind of descent. Without Lillian's fears to focus on, his own pressed in on him, making it twice as hard.

Take your time. The railing's in perfect condition. You're not going to fall.

His leg gave a twinge as he began to tense up while trying to think his way past his building anxiety.

"Not now, damn it!"

Continuing down another two flights with the possibility of cramping up wasn't an appealing option. Or, he realized, a necessary one. He crawled through the open window to Cris's bedroom instead. Back into the burning building. Again.

What was one more stupid choice after all the ones he'd already made tonight?

"What the fuck?"

Dropping the painting, he went to the bed where his brother was doing his best to sit up but kept sliding over sideways like a drunk on a rollercoaster. "Cris, what the hell, man? What happened? Why didn't you get out with Lillian?"

And why would she leave him behind when he was so obviously

helpless?

Cris tried to form words, but the only one Rafe could understand was "burn."

He shoved his shoulder under his brother's armpit and levered him to his feet. Grunting at the pain that arrowed through his leg under Cris's dead weight, Rafe adjusted his hold and half-carried, half-dragged him out of the room.

There was pounding and yelling at the apartment door. Help was only a few yards away. With luck, his fucking gimpy leg would hold up long enough to get them there.

"Don't worry, *hermano*, I won't let you burn."

Again, Cris tried to say something, but it was worse than taking a statement in the drunk tank. What the hell was going on? He couldn't believe Lillian would abandon Cris because he was too wasted to walk on his own.

Could he have been that wrong about her? About what kind of person she was?

No. Something else was going on. He just needed to figure out what.

Which happened the minute he stepped into the dark living room and saw the two figures standing in a strange embrace near the door.

"Stop right there!"

He recognized the shrill voice immediately. Cris hadn't been saying "burn." He'd been trying to say "Bernice."

Fuck me sideways.

If this was what he thought, things had gone from bad to very, very worse.

With great care, he lowered his brother onto the couch, reaching to snap on the lamp as he stood back up. His gaze took in the situation in a heartbeat. His brain took a few seconds longer to process it.

It was as though the universe had plucked his worst nightmare out of his head and set it down to be acted out in front of him all over again. Only this time, Lillian had been cast in the lead role of about-to-get-dead.

Bernice had one arm around her, holding her in front of her body like a shield, while the other hand held a long, wickedly sharp knife to Lillian's soft, vulnerable neck. One taken from the set of professional cooking knives on a magnetic rack in his kitchen.

Cris could filet a steak in five seconds flat with it. Lillian's throat would part like melted butter under the slightest pressure.

A shiver raked down his spine.

No. Not happening. Not on his watch.

"Bernice, put the knife down."

"You ruined *everything*!"

Wincing at the screech, he moved toward them with measured steps. "You don't want to do this. You haven't killed anyone yet. Trust me, you don't want to go down that road."

"Stop right there! And stop telling me what I want. You have no idea what I want."

The hysterical edge to her voice worried him almost as much as the knife. Desperate people were unpredictable. And with him in front of her and the firemen pounding on the door at her back, Bernice was looking desperate right smack in the face.

A loud groan came from overhead. Water began to trickle from the recessed lights in the ceiling as firefighters fought the blaze above them. Bernice looked up at the sound, startled, before focusing back on Rafe.

It was quick, but the distraction was enough for him to slip his gun from the holster he'd shoved into the small of his back by habit when he'd gotten dressed. He held it down along his leg, his body angled to keep it hidden.

"The ceiling could come down on all of us at any time, Bernice. We need to get out of here. Now."

"No. No. No!" She let out a scream like a two-year-old having a tantrum. "It was all supposed to be mine. It was my turn! She already had everything. I just wanted my fair share, that's all. Is that so freaking *wrong*?"

Lillian grimaced, although whether from the words or the volume they were being yelled next to her ear, he wasn't sure. "Seems I got the job she wanted. And the guy."

The look she gave made him wonder if she'd seen him pull his weapon.

"You would have picked me if *she* didn't get in the way." Bernice jerked Lillian in her anger, who hissed as the super-sharp knife scored a fine line in her skin.

He fought every instinct to attack. The proof Bernice could slit Lillian's throat before he could stop her was right there in the bead of blood running down her throat like a ruby teardrop.

With great effort, he held himself back, waiting for an opening.

"No, I wouldn't have."

"What? Yes, you would! I'm just as pretty as she is. *I'm just like her*!"

A few things that had been nagging at him since first meeting her finally made sense.

"That's it. That's why. You don't just resent her. You want to *be* her. The short, funky hairstyle, the eyebrow piercing, the silk tops and high heels. You envied Lillian, so you tried to turn yourself into a carbon copy of her."

"That's not true."

The look on her face, though, told him he'd guessed right even as she denied it.

"But it didn't work out the way you wanted, did it? So, you went even further. Dyed part of your hair purple the way she used to. Added more piercings than she has. Wore sexier clothes. And people *still* didn't look at you the way they looked at her, did they?"

"No."

"You still weren't good enough."

"I was always good enough! They were all just too stupid to see it.

To see *me!*"

"Rafe?" There was a huge question in Lillian's voice that went along with the one on her face. Both silently asking if he knew what the hell he was doing.

Short answer: no.

He was tap dancing through a minefield here, trying to find the key to Bernice's triggers so he could disarm her. Because right now, as attractive as shooting her seemed, it wasn't an option. Not when there were firemen on the other side of the door behind her that might end up getting hit by a stray bullet.

And not when Lillian might end up as collateral damage.

Damn the fucking fates for putting him in this no-win situation.

Again.

As if the universe had been listening, a fresh round of pounding sounded on the door, this time followed by a familiar voice shouting, "Fire department! We need to evacuate this apartment immediately. Open up!"

From the way her eyes widened, Lillian recognized her brother Pete's voice too, but was smart enough not to say anything. She looked at Rafe with the utmost confidence and gave a small nod. Whatever happened, she'd follow his lead.

God, he loved this woman.

"If you don't open the door, we're taking it down!"

"No, don't." Rafe shouted to make sure they heard him. "There are two civilians standing a few feet in front of it."

"Then have them open the damn thing."

"I would, but we kind of have a situation in here."

There was a pause. "What kind of situation?"

Looking more and more panicked, Bernice said to Rafe, "Shut up."

He ignored her. "Oh, pretty much about the same kind I had the last time." Hopefully Pete would remember the details of Rafe's last "situation" and not try to come in, guns blazing.

"I said shut up!"

There was a longer pause from the hallway. "Right. Got it. We're pulling back. You're clear."

"Roger that."

"Is everyone okay in there?"

"More or less."

"Shut up, shut up, *shut up!*" Bernice kicked back at the door in frustration, making it rattle with each blow. "What are you two, best fucking girlfriends or something?"

Pete remained silent, but Rafe had no doubt he was out in the hallway, listening and waiting. Rafe looked up at the ceiling, where the trickle of water through the fixtures was increasing at an alarming rate.

"Bernice, we need to get out before the ceiling comes down on us."

She glanced up with nervous eyes. Good. At least she was worried about her own skin, not suicidal. He could work with that. But it needed to be fast, because he wasn't lying. Those thousands of gallons of water had to go somewhere, and the laws of gravity said that somewhere was down.

Right on top of their heads.

"Look, just let Lillian go, and we can all walk out of here in one piece."

"No."

"We can go someplace and talk about—"

"I said no!"

"Then let me change places with her."

Lillian's eyes flew wide. "Rafe, no."

"You can hold the knife to *my* throat. They'll let us walk right out of here with me as your hostage, no questions asked."

"They'll let me walk out with her, too." Bernice's lip curled. "She's a damn heiress. You're nobody."

"Exactly. Do you think her father will ever stop hunting you down if anything happens to her? I don't have those connections. You could make a clean getaway with me along."

Bernice licked her lips, her eyes showing too much white as her true predicament started to sink in. "It wasn't supposed to happen like this. No one was supposed to find out it was me. I had it all planned!"

"But they will find out, the second you leave this apartment. There's no other way out now except with me."

"No, I...I have to think."

"We're running out of time, Bernice."

"Stop talking so I can think!"

Thinking was the last thing he wanted her to do. He needed to keep her off-balance and confused. And most of all, focusing her anger on him.

Taking another step closer, he said, "Besides, don't you still want to punish me for what I've done? For not picking you? For ruining your sabotage with the food?"

Her mouth sagged open in shock before snapping shut. "That was *you*?"

"Yup. You thought you were so clever, didn't you? Calling in those false complaints, getting the health department to shut down the caterer. All at the last minute. It should have been too late to find anyone to take their place, right?"

"Yesss." It came out like an angry hiss.

"Bet you were pissed as hell when you saw everything was going fine, despite all your efforts." He jerked his thumb at himself. "Thanks to me."

"You bastard."

"It went better than fine, actually. The night was a tremendous success. Better than Felix could have ever imagined. I really saved the day. And you? Well, you just faded into the background. Like always."

"You. Ruined. *Everything!*"

Rafe tensed at the shrieked words, finger resting on the trigger, waiting for her attack.

Which never came.

Instead, just when it seemed like she was about to shove Lillian aside and make a rush at him as he'd hoped she would, she curled her arm even tighter around her hostage and gave him a snarling smile.

"No. I'm not that stupid. Besides, I know what will really make you hurt." She jerked Lillian, who grimaced as another thin red line appeared on her neck. "Making you watch me kill your slutty little girlfriend. That way, I get to pay you both back."

"Rafe." Lillian's eyes found his. Her gaze flicked to where the gun was still hidden at his side before locking onto his eyes again with grim intensity. "I don't love her."

"What the hell is that supposed to mean?" Bernice demanded.

Lillian didn't answer her, but Rafe knew. She was telling him to take the shot someone had once begged him not to. "Are you sure?"

Unable to nod without slicing her own throat, she put her answer into her steady gaze. "I trust you."

Yeah, no pressure there. He wet his suddenly dry lips. "Love you."

"Stop ignoring me, damn it!"

Lillian smiled. "Love you, too."

"I can shut you up!" Bernice's arm tensed, the knife shaking as she prepared to follow through on her threat.

"Don't." The gun came up and leveled on her. "Last chance, Bernice. Drop the knife."

She gave a slightly crazed laugh. "What are you going to do? Shoot m—"

The gunshot was still echoing in his ears when he grabbed Lillian into his arms and pulled her away from the screaming woman falling to the ground. Blood spilled down Lillian's neck in a red tide. Frantic to stem the flow, he yanked off his shirt and wadded it against where it seemed to be coming from. "Hold this! Tight!"

He hated to leave her for even a second, but he needed to open the door for the police who were about to break it down, no doubt with

Pete leading the charge. He didn't need them, but he did need the paramedics who would be with them.

He kicked the knife further away from Bernice as he stepped over her writhing form, undid the last lock, and yelled before opening it, "Officer Delgado opening the door, hold your fire. We're clear. Suspect is down and disarmed. We need medical in here. Now!"

He was back at Lillian's side before the first officer got through the door. "Hang on, *querida*. Help is coming."

"It's okay. I don't think most of this is mine." Her legs wobbled. Rafe caught her before she fell and eased her to a sitting position on the floor.

"Or maybe it is," she added in a weak voice.

"Jesus, Lil!" Pete knelt beside them, his face a mask of worry and disbelief. He glared at Rafe, who was applying more pressure to the makeshift bandage. "What the fuck happened?"

"Bernice must have cut her with the knife when I shot her. *Damn it*! Where's the fucking medic?"

"Right here. If you'll move so I can take a look at the patient…"

With great reluctance, Rafe relinquished his spot at Lillian's side to let the paramedic take over. Wiping his bloody hands on his jeans didn't do much, but he wasn't going even as far as the kitchen to get himself a towel to clean up.

Instead, he stood vigil watching every move the medic made. Lillian had been hurt on his watch. He wasn't trusting anyone else with her safety. Not until he stopped freaking the fuck out about how close she'd been to the bullet that had taken Bernice in the shoulder.

Or how much blood she was losing.

Or how his entire life would be nothing but a pile of smoldering shit if she didn't recover.

"What the fuck happened?" Pete demanded again.

Rafe struggled to pull his attention away from Lillian long enough to answer. "Bernice fucking happened."

Pete's brow wrinkled in confusion. "Who?"

"Exactly." Rafe gestured to her, where another medic was applying a pressure bandage to her wound. Her screams had subsided to whimpers. "The receptionist from the gallery. She's the nutjob who's been targeting your sister. She used my brother"—he glanced to the couch to reassure himself Cris was also receiving medical attention—"to get into the building, then somehow set the fire in Lillian's apartment."

"She drugged him," Lillian said. She hissed when the medic peeled back the makeshift bandage to check her wound. "Xanax, or so she said."

The medic taking Cris's vitals nodded to show he'd heard.

"Christ." Pete dragged his hand through his short hair, rumpled and molded into a severe case of bed-head. "The fire's out, by the way."

"Thank God."

"It's prelim, but the fire chief says it looked like some kind of accelerant was squirted under the apartment door."

"Paint thinner." Rolling her eyes at the twin looks of disbelief she got, she said, "I smelled it on her hands when she was..."

When she was threatening to slice her throat open like a ripe peach.

A surge of fury erupted in Rafe's gut at the reminder of how close things had come. Not that they were out of the woods yet.

"How bad is it?" he asked the medic, who was putting a series of butterfly bandages on the seam that had been opened on Lillian's tender throat. There was a lot of blood all over the place, but nothing seemed to be gushing or spurting, so he took that as a good sign.

"She'll need some stitches, but she was lucky. A little deeper..." He left the rest unsaid as he wrapped gauze to help stem the oozing going on from the other two shallower cuts Bernice had inflicted. To Lillian he said, "You might want to see about getting a plastic surgeon to do the work. They can probably make the scar next to invisible. Like it never happened."

"But it did."

Her haunted words hit Rafe like a punch in the gut.

Damn it to hell, he was supposed to protect her. To keep her safe. And instead, she'd nearly gotten killed. Not once, but *twice* in one night on his watch. How could she ever forgive something like that?

How could he?

He wanted to go to her, touch her, hold on to her and never let her go. But he got shuffled aside as the gurney was brought in and they loaded Lillian on, so he went and checked on Cris. He was still way out of it, but the medic said his vitals were stable and he didn't show any signs of being overdosed.

"So much for liking your women a little bit ah," he whispered as he gave his brother a relieved side-hug. Cris showed no hint of understanding, just gave him a loopy grin.

The constriction on his heart eased a little. At least when he called his parents, it wouldn't be to tell them he'd gotten his baby brother killed.

As the medics wheeled Lillian out of the apartment, she threw him a panicked look. "Rafe?"

"Right here, sweetheart." But as he tried to get to her side, he found his way blocked by her brother.

"You have a statement to give and a shitload of questions to answer before you go anywhere, *Officer* Delgado."

Fuck me sideways.

He hated it, but Pete was right. He'd shot a suspect. In his own apartment. In a building that had been set on fire. There would be a lot of people wanting a piece of him before the night was over, not the least of which would be IAB.

The head of Internal Affairs already had half a hard-on for him after last year's clusterfuck. Tonight just might be the icing on his dismissal cake.

And yet, as important as his career had always been, the possibility of being fired paled next to not being able to go with Lillian to the hospital. To holding her hand and reassuring her everything was going to be okay now.

Fuck the job. He wanted his woman.

Funny how imminent death could rearrange your priorities in less than a heartbeat.

Or a gunshot.

Short of punching her brother in the head, though, Rafe wouldn't get past him in time to go with her now. "I'll see you at the hospital in a little while, *querida*."

"Promise?"

He hated how small and scared her voice sounded. "I promise. Nothing could keep me from your side."

"Get her out of here," Pete ordered.

They wheeled her out, Rafe's heart clenching as her pale, blood- and tear-streaked face disappeared from sight. His body actually took an involuntary step after her. Pete's hand to his chest stopped him.

All at once, exhaustion swamped him as his adrenaline high crashed, taking all his energy—and his patience—with it.

He pushed Pete's hand aside and met his angry gaze with one of his own. "Let's get this over with. I don't want to keep her waiting a single second longer than I have to."

Chapter 19

*N**othing could keep me from your side.*

That promise, and the resolute certainty it had been spoken with, were the only things that kept Lillian from freaking out on the short ambulance ride to the hospital. Well, that, and the constant stream of silly chatter from the medic riding with her.

He'd introduced himself as Orlando, and kept her distracted with a running monologue on his family. It seemed he, his brother, and sister—Nash and Brooklyn—had recently come to the conclusion they'd all been named for the cities in which they'd been conceived, based on their parents' old vacation photos.

Which had left them wondering what might have happened if their folks had visited someplace like Boring, Oregon. Or worse, Accident, Maryland.

True or not, the absurdity of the one-sided conversation helped. It wasn't until she'd been left in a curtained-off cubicle in the emergency room in the hands of a tired-looking nurse in purple scrubs hooking her up to a bunch of equally tired-looking equipment that the reality of everything that had happened sank in.

Holy. Hell.

The shakes started then. She tried to control them, but her body seemed determined to rattle her teeth loose from her head. Not even the blanket the nurse produced helped. No, what she needed was to be held by the one man who made her feel safer than anyone or anything in this world. But he wasn't there, so she had to suffer alone.

Not fair, Lil.

She knew that. Knew he didn't have a choice in the matter. The same thing had happened when Thea's then-boyfriend-slash-bodyguard Doyle had to answer a million questions from the police and Secret Service about her stalker, forcing her to go to the hospital without him.

But logic did nothing to quell the giant shudders that wracked her body as she huddled under the thin blanket, praying for Rafe to hurry up and get there like he promised.

Then she heard the next best thing.

"My daughter was just brought in by ambulance. Can you tell me where she is?"

Her heart thumped. "Daddy?"

The curtain was yanked aside. "Lillian, sweetheart."

Tears filled her eyes. "Oh, Daddy." She held out her arms and he hurried to her, wrapping her gently in the strong arms that had rocked her to sleep hundreds of times as a child and never once failed to make her feel safe and loved.

It wasn't as good as having Rafe hold her, but it was close.

Pulling back, her father looked her over with a frantic light in his eyes. "Sweetheart, what happened? Are you okay? We got the call from the alarm company that there was a fire at the building, and when I was almost there, your brother called to say you'd been taken away in an ambulance."

"I'm okay. Really."

"They don't take you to the hospital for okay." He touched the gauze bandage on her neck, his expression darkening. "Tell me everything."

"I'm afraid that has to wait." Shouldering aside the curtain, a tan young man in worn jeans, polo shirt, and a white lab jacket stepped up to the opposite side of the hospital bed, his eyes on the chart in his hands. "I'm Doctor Antonoff. I'll be taking care of you tonight.

Well, I guess that's actually this morning, isn't it?"

This was her doctor? He looked like he wasn't much older than her.

Until he directed his smiling gaze her way and she saw the fine lines framing his deep blue eyes. He might look like a twenty-something surfer dude with his thick blond hair and 3 a.m. scruff, but there was some mileage on that good-looking face. He just wore it well.

Her father, however, wasn't looking that closely. He shook his head.

"What are you, all of about two minutes out of med school? No, I want the senior doctor handling my daughter's treatment. You get him down here right now."

"Dad!" Horrified, Lillian gave the doctor an apologetic look. "I'm sorry. He's upset. He didn't mean that."

"Of course I meant it," he growled. "You're my little girl. Do you think I want some wet-behind-the-ears intern touching you?"

"Well, then, *I'm* sorry, sir, but I *am* the senior doctor on staff at the moment. And I can assure you, my ears haven't been wet for quite a few years now."

Eyes narrowing, her father said, "Then I'll call in my personal physician."

Dr. Antonoff cocked his head. "Of course, that's your right, sir. But wouldn't you rather have the doctor who's already here treating your daughter's injuries *now* rather than have her sit there, bleeding, while you wait for your doctor to get here?"

"Daddy." She placed a hand on his tense arm. "It's fine. I have total confidence in Dr. Antonoff's abilities. Please, just let him do his job so I can get out of here."

"But—"

"Is Mom here?"

Successfully diverted, he nodded. "Of course. But they wouldn't let us both come in to see you at the same time. She's in the waiting room, losing her mind with worry." He shot the doctor a look like that was his fault, too.

"Then you should go and tell her I'm fine." She was impressed by the doctor's ability to withstand the withering glare that usually reduced lesser mortals to sweaty, twitching wrecks. "Then can you send her in here, please?" The little wobble in her voice wasn't planned, but it was enough to deflate her father's over-protective bulldog mode.

"Of course, sweetheart. If you're sure." He gave the doctor, who pretended he wasn't there as he read the charts, another doubtful look.

"I'm sure." She turned her cheek up for him to kiss, concentrating on not wincing as the motion pulled at the wounds. The second he was out of earshot, she gave the doctor an embarrassed look. "I am *so* sorry. My father can be..."

"Concerned about his little girl," he finished with a smile. "Don't even worry about it. If I had a daughter, I'd want to make sure she was getting the best possible care too. I don't take it personally."

"Thank you for understanding. But he still shouldn't have been so rude."

The doctor laughed as he reached for the gauze on her neck. "Compared to some things I've had said to me, your father was a pussycat. Now, let's take a look and see what we're dealing with."

"Okay."

Her mother came into the cubicle as the last of the gauze was being cut off. Other than a quick gasp, she didn't say anything, for which Lillian was eternally grateful. She just went right to Lillian's side and took her hand.

By the time the butterfly bandages were peeled off and the doctor had examined and cleaned all three wounds, Lillian was a little bit nauseated.

"What's the verdict?" she asked as the doctor made a few notes on her chart.

"I'll be honest, those are some of the neatest cuts I've ever seen outside of an operating room. Whatever caused them must have been precision sharp."

"Is that good or bad?" her mother asked.

"Definitely good. We've got some nice, clean edges to work with. Two of the cuts aren't deep enough to require stitches, but the third is." He looked at Lillian. "I can do them, but you may want to call in the plastic surgeon on staff, considering the highly visible location."

He was the second person to make that suggestion. Just how horrible did her neck look, anyway?

Given her already queasy state, she decided against asking for a mirror to find out. "In your opinion, would there be that much of a difference in the end result?"

A look of competitive eagerness lit Dr. Antonoff's eyes. "I think I can give her a run for her money."

"Sweetheart, your father can arrange for the top plastic surgeon in the state with one phone call. He'll send his plane for him and have him here in next to no time."

That made the doctor pause. Lillian could practically see him reevaluating just who his patient was and what kind of resources were at her disposal. "I can certainly make you comfortable until he gets here."

"No, I want you to do it." Because she didn't want to sit there in her blood-soaked clothes a second longer than necessary.

"Are you sure?"

"Yes. Absolutely."

He studied her for a long second before he gave a slow nod, the gleam back in his eyes. "Okay, then. Let me go get a suture setup and we'll get you stitched and on your way."

As he left the cubicle, Lillian caught a glimpse of a tall, dark-haired man standing outside. Her heart jumped, but she realized as the curtain fell back into place it wasn't Rafe. She looked up at her mother. "Is Rafe out in the waiting room?"

Maybe the one-visitor rule was what was keeping him away.

Stroking her daughter's hair like she had when Lillian was a small child, she shook her head. "I'm sorry, sweetheart, no. At least, he wasn't when I was there."

"Oh." She bit her lip. How long did giving a statement take, anyway? "Could you go see if he's there now? Please?"

"Of course." She kissed Lillian's forehead, another familiar childhood gesture. As she got to the curtain, Lillian stopped her with another request.

"Oh, and can you check on how his brother Cris is doing? He would have been brought in around the same time as me."

Her mother nodded and ducked out of the curtain. Left alone, Lillian closed her eyes and sank back onto the uncomfortable ER bed. With no one left to perform for and reassure she was fine, she could allow herself one small moment of unvarnished emotion.

She'd almost died.

Rafe and Cris had almost died.

Every single person in her building could have died.

God.

She swiped at a tear that leaked out from under her closed lids as the curtain whooshed aside.

"Hey, are you okay?" There was genuine concern in Dr. Antonoff's voice. "Are you in pain?"

"No, I'm okay. I'm just..." Another tear snaked down her cheek. She scrubbed at it and sniffled, determined to cork that bottle of what-ifs before it got out of control. She gave him a weak smile. "It all kind of hit me, I guess. What could have happened."

Damn. There went another of those stupid tears.

"Understandable." He went about setting up his supplies on the rolling table. The only acknowledgment he gave her tears was to hand her a tissue. "From what I'm hearing, things were a little crazy for you tonight."

Bernice's insane ranting still fresh in her head, she gave a hollow laugh. "Yeah. Crazy just about covers it."

He lowered the bed flat and got her in the position he wanted her. After draping a sterile cloth over the area, he paused. "Okay, we're ready."

Realizing he was giving her one last chance to change her mind, she summoned what she hoped was a confident smile and gave him a thumbs-up. "Go for it, Doc."

She couldn't hold back a grimace as he injected something to numb the area. It wasn't until it took effect and she didn't have the constant throbbing in her neck to think about that she realized how much the rest of her body ached.

Evidently, crawling out windows and climbing fire escapes in the middle of the night wasn't as much fun as it sounded.

Partway through the stitches, her mother came back. The good news was that Cris had been admitted for overnight observation, but was expected to be fine. The bad news was Rafe wasn't anywhere in the emergency room that she'd been able to find.

She swallowed her disappointment. It wasn't his fault. He'd come to her when he could. He'd promised, and she had complete faith in his word.

By the time the last precise stitch was set, and she was bandaged up and given after-care instructions, Lillian was more than ready to go home. Until she remembered her home was now a smoldering pile of charred, waterlogged rubble.

Which was why she overruled her father and agreed to give her statement to the detective who was waiting when she walked out of the cubicle, rather than put it off until morning. The longer she delayed the inevitable, the longer she could hang onto the lie that everything wasn't as horrible as she knew it was. And the longer Rafe had to come and find her like he promised.

But he never did.

So exhausted she was punch-drunk, Lillian was barely aware of her parents bundling her into the back of the waiting Town Car as dawn broke over the city. She thought she might have asked for one of them to call Rafe to tell him where she was going, but the strain of the past few hours finally took its toll and sucked her under into unconsciousness before she was certain the words had ever left her mouth.

⊰⊱

"Sorry, he's not here."

Curling her lip into a snarl at the insincere words, Lillian gripped the phone tighter. Otherwise, she might be tempted to throw it at the wall. "Do you know when he'll be back?"

"No. Sorry."

She gritted her teeth. "Can I leave a message, then?"

The beleaguered sigh from Rafe's sister almost made her lose the tenuous grasp she had on her temper.

"I guess."

"Please tell him that Lillian called, and I'd appreciate it if he would call me back as soon as it's convenient. I haven't replaced my cellphone yet, so this is the number he can reach me at." She rattled off her parents' unlisted landline number.

"Fine. I'll tell him. *Again.*"

"Thank y—" The dial tone made finishing unnecessary.

It was the same snotty attitude she'd gotten from not just one, but both of Rafe's sisters, *and* his older brother, every time she called his parents' house looking for him. Furious, she stabbed the Off button on the phone, then stabbed it a few more times for good measure. "Bitch."

Two days.

She'd been calling him for two whole days now, and it was always the same thing. His cell went straight to voicemail, and whenever she called the Delgado home or the restaurant, his family insisted he wasn't there. Not one of her dozen messages had been returned.

Not. One.

Lillian grimaced. Okay, his sister might have a right to sound annoyed. A dozen calls in two days was kind of excessive. Stalkerish, even. Maybe it was time for her to suck it up and face facts.

If Rafe wanted to call her back, he would have by now.

Flopping onto the chair in the pool house, her last refuge from her mother's claustrophobic hovering, she debated her options. Keep calling and making both an idiot and a nuisance of herself. Or give up and admit that no matter what he'd promised, no matter what they'd shared, there was no way he could ever forgive her for almost getting his brother killed.

And for that, she couldn't blame him.

She wanted to, since this was shredding her heart into teeny tiny bits of sad confetti. But she knew how much his family meant to him. How much protecting them from harm was a vital part of who he was.

Bernice could have just as easily killed Cris as incapacitated him with her antidepressant medication. And that didn't even take into account the fire that could have finished the job if Rafe hadn't been there to save them all.

So, okay. She got it. The message in his radio silence was loud and clear.

They were done.

It felt like the knife Bernice had used on her throat buried itself in her chest.

Being reasonable sucks donkey balls.

As she wallowed in her pain and misery, the pool house door opened and closed, letting in a hint of chlorinated air and a waft of Axe body spray. That could only mean one person.

"Hey squirt, what're you doing hiding out here?"

She gave Peter a *duh* look that made him laugh.

"Right. Mom's still shadowing your every move, huh?"

"And Dad's worse. Thank God he went back to work today."

Although since he was the boss and could do whatever he wanted, she was pretty sure it had been her mother's influence that had gotten him out the door.

For how long, however, remained to be seen.

Peter dropped into the chair beside her. "Give them a break. You scared the bejeezus out of them the other night. It's going to take a while to stop freaking out. For all of us."

The haunted look in his eyes as he added that had her squeezing his arm.

"I know, I know. I just need some breathing room. Not to mention I'm getting a little sick of my own company." Two days of nothing but sitting around brooding about Rafe was enough. She'd been too busy missing him to even be bothered by sleeping in her old bedroom. So small silver lining there.

She'd still rather have Rafe, though.

"Give Thea a call. You know she'd come over if you asked."

She totally would. Just like she showed up Sunday afternoon with a shoulder to cry on and shopping bags full of everything Lillian needed to tide her over until she could get her own stuff from her apartment.

If I still have any stuff to get.

She shoved the whiny thought away and shook her head. "She's in the middle of a big job right now. I can't ask her to ditch work just to come and keep me company."

Not that it wasn't tempting. Thea and her car would give Lillian the means to escape her family for a little while. Breathe some unsupervised air.

Which reminded her.

"Do you know when I'm ever getting my car back from the police impound?"

"Uh..." Peter's eyes darted away. "Let me look into that."

Suspicion bloomed. "Peter..."

"I can give you the next best thing," he said quickly.

She sat a little straighter. "You're breaking me out?"

"*So* melodramatic."

"*So* annoying."

"Do you want to hear what I have to say or not?"

Most days, she enjoyed trading barbs with her brother. But right now, she was much more interested in escaping than sniping.

"Sorry. Go ahead." When he hesitated long enough to make it seem he wasn't going to answer, she gave him a hard poke. "Talk, baby brother."

As always, that earned her a scowl.

"Only because you pushed your way out first," he muttered, rubbing his arm.

"*Peter.*"

He rolled his eyes. "Fine. The investigators released your apartment as of this morning, and the engineers have said it's safe."

"What does that mean, exactly?"

"That you can get into it anytime you want to start packing up whatever's, um, you know..." He gave an apologetic grimace. "Left."

The news sent her stomach into a confused tailspin. While she wanted to get back to her home and see which of her possessions might be salvageable, she also didn't. When the arson investigators made it a crime scene, the choice had been easy: she hadn't had one.

Now that she did, she wasn't sure she wanted to see the result of what had happened that night. Of how close they'd come to dying. It would make it all indelibly real.

Maybe too real.

In a moment of uncharacteristic insight, her brother put his arm around her shoulders and hugged her to his side. "You don't have to go if you don't want to. We can get it all packed up and bring your stuff here for you to go through."

It was tempting. So tempting. But the thought of people going through her things, even for the best of reasons, was worse than facing the destruction head-on.

"No. I think I need to go and see..." She cleared her throat. "See how it looks. Closure, right?"

"Are you sure?"

No. "Yeah. Let's go."

Peter still looked doubtful, but he didn't say anything else to dissuade her. When they got out to the front drive, Lillian shot a disgruntled look toward the team of bodyguards standing by one of the bland beige sedans from the security motor pool.

Her brother threw his hands in the air before she could say anything.

"Hey, it was the only way Mom and Dad would agree to this without coming themselves. Be glad Dad didn't insist on sending Hans."

So, her spontaneous bid for freedom wasn't so spontaneous after all.

She wanted to be annoyed, but she was too happy to be getting a few hours of freedom, however illusory, to care. She slid into the passenger seat of Peter's car and breathed a loud sigh of relief as they passed through the high iron gates.

When they pulled into the underground parking garage, her heart twisted at how many of the parking spots were empty. No one else had been hurt because of the fire, thank God. But all the tenants on the third and fourth floors were without homes until the fire, smoke, and water damage could be assessed and repaired.

Until then, her father had relocated them to hotels on his own dime. It was generous of him, but she couldn't help but feel guilty their lives had been so disrupted because of her.

On the elevator ride up, her heart began to pound. The last time she'd made this trip three nights ago, it had been with Rafe at her side. She'd been happy, loved, and stupidly oblivious to the danger that would upheave her entire life without warning.

This time around, she was none of those things.

And she might never be again.

The acrid smell of burnt carpet almost made her gag as the doors opened and she stepped into the hall. Her other brothers, Theo and Richard, were waiting. The sight had her tearing up even as she gave Peter another jab in the arm for not telling her they'd be there.

"Don't you two slackers have jobs?" she asked as she gave each of them a hug.

"We have an in with the boss." Theo squeezed her hard enough to pick her up off her feet before setting her back down again.

Normally, she hated when he did that. Today, she was thankful to still be around for him to pick on about her height. And that he and Richard had come to lend a hand.

She eyed the stack of cardboard moving boxes leaning against the wall, then the plywood door that replaced the one the fire destroyed. How much worse was it going to be on the other side?

Taking the Tyvek booties Richard handed her, she pushed aside her misgivings and gave a resigned sigh. "Okay, then. Let's get this show on the road."

Chapter 20

Walking into the charred remains of her living room was surreal.

Thanks to the accelerant squirted under the door, the damage to the room was so severe it was almost unrecognizable. Which actually made it easier to take in, since it no longer looked anything like the cozy loft she'd lived in for the past year.

There was nothing left to be saved there, so they moved on to the kitchen, which had also taken a lot of damage. The glass fronts to the cabinets had cracked and shattered, as had some of the colorful dishes inside. The whitewashed wood stood blackened and charred and streaked with soot.

Lillian swallowed hard and turned away. It wasn't worth looking at everything that had been destroyed to find the one or two things that hadn't been.

There was less fire damage the further into the apartment they went, but the heat, smoke, and water had created their own kind of carnage. Every step down the hall to her bedroom made a squishing sound on the carpet. The paint had crackled into an almost scale-like design under a heavy coating of dark soot.

She almost couldn't hold back a whimper. This was so much worse than she'd thought. Not the damage. That was pretty much exactly what she imagined it would be. No, it was seeing her home, her refuge, reduced to this sad state of destruction.

She'd never considered herself someone who placed much value on *things*, but so far, their little tour was proving her wrong. Even losing her silly oversized mugs and colorful plates was like a stab in the heart.

Because her brothers would tattle to their parents if she turned tail and ran, she continued into her bedroom. Peter opened the window at her request, letting a welcome breeze blow in. It helped disperse the cloying smell of smoke that was so thick in the air it felt like she was breathing in something solid.

The fact there wasn't much fire damage past the charring on the edges of the door raised her spirits. But a quick check of the clothes in the closet dashed them again. Everything was discolored and smelled heavily of smoke.

"A good dry cleaning might get the smell out."

Richard's comment went unanswered as she bent to pick up the tangle of dark purple silk from where it had slid off its hanger to the floor. A lump threatened to close off her throat.

Her beautiful, beautiful dress. Ruined. Just like everything else.

She let it fall through her fingers back to the carpet in a soggy heap.

"I just…I can't." Blinking back tears, she all but ran from the room. Standing in the hall, she took in great, gulping breaths, trying to hold back the tidal wave of emotions that threatened to swamp her.

Behind her, her brothers argued in low voices. Probably about who would get stuck driving her home. When it came to tears, they were big, fat wusses, every one of them.

Speaking of wusses…

She looked toward the door at the end of the hall. Nerves were a basket of snakes in her belly as she took one step in that direction before stopping again.

Her paintings were going to be just as smoke and water damaged as her clothes were. Worse, probably. Acrylics didn't do well in high heat. She should probably just write them all off and walk away without subjecting herself to the exquisite agony of seeing her beautiful creations looking like the portrait in Dorian Gray's attic.

On the other hand, if some of them could be salvaged and repaired, even *one* of them, it would at least keep her from restarting her collection at zero.

But was it worth the pain of seeing the ones she couldn't save?

Indecision tore at her as her brothers bickered on. It wasn't until she heard Peter grudgingly agree to take her home that she got her feet moving in the direction of her studio.

Now or never.

Like the bedroom, the fact the door had been closed limited the amount of damage wrought inside, but that wasn't what stopped her in her tracks.

"Hey, we were talking and decided..." Coming in behind her, Richard looked around the room with a confused expression. "What the hell, Lil? What's all this? Where's your bed?"

"That would be back in my *bedroom*." She hooked a thumb behind them down the hall. "I've got a better question. Where are my paintings?"

"Wait, *that* was your bedroom? I thought you were just using it for extra closet space."

She eyed the pricey distressed jeans and pristine Bill Blass shirt he'd worn to pack boxes at a fire scene. "Oh, right. Because *I'm* the clothes horse in the family."

"Hey, if the high-heel fits..."

"Children." Theo stepped between them the way he had since they were kids. "Lillian, what is all this?" He waved a hand at the empty easel and jumble of paints and blank canvases, all covered in grimy soot.

"It's her studio." Peter gave her a chiding look when she glanced at him in surprise. "You've always loved to draw and paint. You got your art degree, and you fought Dad to work at the gallery. It doesn't take a genius to figure out you're chasing your dreams."

No, not a genius. Just a twin who'd done exactly the same thing.

She gave him a grateful smile, which only widened when both

Theo and Richard scowled at him in consternation.

"How did we not know about this?" Theo asked.

Lillian shrugged, uncomfortable under his hurt gaze. "I guess because I never talked much about it."

"Because everyone was so busy trying to convince her she needed to go work for Dad instead of asking what *she* wanted to do," Peter added.

Theo cursed under his breath.

"You want to be an artist?" Richard made it sound worse than Theo's curse. "Great way to waste that expensive business degree, Lil."

"I don't *want* to be an artist. I *am* an artist." Her temper stirred. Rafe had gotten it. Why couldn't her own brothers? "I have no idea if I'll ever be able to make a living at it, but I thought I owed it to myself to at least give it a shot before giving up. And for the record, that business degree was Dad's idea, not mine. I just wanted to go to art school. He only said yes when I agreed to do both." So she'd have something "legitimate" to fall back on when she stopped playing around with her paintbrushes.

She never let him know how much that comment hurt, but she'd never forgotten it, either.

"Can we see some of your stuff?" Theo asked, verbally stepping between them again.

Lillian let out a short laugh. "I'd love to show it to you, but"—she waved a hand at the wall where almost a dozen completed canvases had been leaning, but now there was nothing but a big empty spot—"they're gone."

"Gone?" Peter looked around the room. "Gone where?"

"Maybe the fire department moved them someplace safe when they were doing their overhaul?" Theo suggested.

A worse possibility hit her like a blow. "What if Bernice did something with them?" Bad enough when she thought the fire might have ravaged them. The thought of her paintings mangled and destroyed by that bitch's hand made her want to scream.

And punch her again.

Peter clicked over to cop mode. "Do you think she was actually inside the apartment before she set the fire? How would she have gotten in?"

"I don't know." Fisting her hands, she looked around the room. "But who else could have taken them?"

"They were there?" Richard stalked over to the empty space. "Right there?"

"Yes, Richard. Right there." Like that mattered?

Evidently it mattered a whole lot to her older brother, whose face turned an unbecoming shade of red. "Right there, in front of the door to the *panic room?*"

"Um..." Oopsie. "Yeah, I guess."

"You guess." In a gesture she hadn't seen since they were teens, he clasped his hands around the back of his neck like he was trying to keep his head from popping off. Which, given the look on his face, might not have been all that far-fetched a possibility.

"So, after promising Mom and Dad you'd follow all of their safety measures when you moved in here alone, you not only switched to using the bedroom *without* the panic room that was built for you, but then you thought it would be a good idea to *stack things in front of the door to it*? Do I have that right?"

"Um..." When he put it like that, it sounded pretty bad. The panic room had been overkill, but her father insisted on it. She never once thought she'd have an occasion to need it.

Of course, she never thought she'd have someone try to set her on fire while she slept, either. Which reminded her.

"Would I have been safe from the fire if I was in there?"

Theo looked nonplussed by the question. "I don't know. Maybe."

"What would it matter, since you were in the other freaking bedroom?" Richard asked, throwing his hands in the air. She'd always been able to drive him past the brink of his considerable patience without even trying.

It was a gift.

"Well, for your information, smarty pants, I *did* remember about the room, and I was going to get into it to wait out the fire, but Rafe wasn't sure it would be fireproof, and I couldn't remember, so..." Oh. *Oh.* "No. Tell me he didn't." The words were a whisper as she stared at the empty spot where the canvases had stood.

"Huh?" Peter cocked his head. "Who didn't what?"

"Rafe." Brushing past Richard, she slid her fingers along the underside of the chair rail molding and found the button that released the hidden door.

The one she'd shown Rafe just days before the fire.

"Well, at least you remember how to open it." Richard grunted when Lillian's elbow connected with his stomach. "Brat," he wheezed.

"Grouch." Pulling the door open, her breath left her with a *whoosh.*

They were there. Crammed into the small space that resembled a long, narrow closet were her missing canvases.

Unbelievable.

How could he have been stupid enough to risk his life for a bunch of worthless paintings? "Rafe, you *idiot.*"

"Well, at least we agree on something." Richard backed up a wary step when she turned on him.

"You do *not* get to say things like that about him!"

"Why not? The bastard was supposed to keep you safe, and instead he almost got you killed."

"Are you kidding me? He's the reason I'm alive!"

"You were almost burned, stabbed, *and* shot. All in one night!"

"In case you've forgotten, Rafe saved me from the first two, and as for the third, the bullet was nowhere near close enough to hurt me." The first time in her life being short had been a blessing. "He hit exactly what he was aiming for."

Not that she hadn't had a few nightmares about what could have happened if he'd missed.

"Don't forget, it was his brother who let that woman into the building in the first place," Theo said.

She stared at him in disbelief. "You too, Theo?"

He shrugged, although he did look a little uncomfortable. "It's only the truth. She wouldn't have been able to get past the building's security to set the fire if it wasn't for him. Or had the chance to cut you up."

Just talking about it made her stitches itch. She fought off the urge to scratch at the small bandage covering them.

"Okay, first off, to get inside she could have gone after any single guy in the building the same way she did Cris, so don't blame him. And second, I *worked with her*. We hung out. Hell, I considered her a friend. Sort of. She would have eventually found a way to get close enough to me to do whatever she wanted, because she was—wait for it—a crazy psycho-bitch! None of that is Rafe's fault."

"If he hadn't been so busy getting into your pants every chance he got, he might have done his job and figured out who was responsible before it got that far."

She sucked in a sharp breath. "Line. Crossed."

At least Richard had the decency to look embarrassed. "Lil—"

"No. I don't want to hear it. What happened between me and Rafe is *our* business, not yours. You don't get any say."

"But—"

"Not. A. Word."

Richard threw his hands up. "Okay, fine. Not another word about him taking advantage of the position of trust he was in to get what he wanted, like the slimy bastard he is."

A growl erupted from her throat. "You are such an—"

"For God's sake, would you two stop?" Theo gave Lillian a look that was borderline patronizing. "Lil, you're our sister. We're allowed to worry about you. Especially when we've never seen you like this with another guy before."

Because it's never been like this with any other guy before.

Blinking back the tears threatening, she gave them the truth she'd only said out loud once before. When she'd thought she might die, and needed Rafe to know. Just in case.

"That's because I love him."

"The hell you do!"

She glared at Richard. "Don't you tell me what I feel." Oh, damn, now she sounded like Bernice. Her shoulders slumped. "It doesn't matter, anyway. He's not taking my calls, or returning any of my messages, so..." She shrugged, trying not to care that her heart felt like someone had stomped it like a vat of grapes.

The same someone who'd risked his life to go back into a burning apartment to save her stupid paintings.

It made no sense.

If she hadn't looked up at that precise moment, she would have missed the look of guilt all three of her brothers shared. Her sister-radar instantly went off. "What?"

Peter fidgeted under her stare. "What what?"

"What was that look for?"

"What look?"

"The look that says the three of you are up to something you know I won't like." Peter had always been the weakest link when it came to ferreting out her brothers' secrets, and he didn't let her down now. The panicked guilt that flashed over his face said she'd scored a direct hit.

Hands planted on her hips, she glared at all of them. "What did you do?"

"Umm..." Peter looked to the others for guidance.

"Lil, it was for your own good," Richard said.

"What. Did. You. Do?"

They exchanged another of those looks.

She pointed at Peter. "You. Talk."

He squirmed for a second before folding like a house of cards. Just like old times. "We might have told Delgado to keep his distance," he mumbled.

"You *what*?"

"He almost got you killed!" Richard shouted.

Lillian held up a finger in his face. "I'll get to you in a minute." To Peter she said, "When, exactly, did you find the time to tell him this little tidbit?"

"When he called me the morning you got out of the hospital."

"When he called..." She heard the words, but they didn't make sense.

Rafe had called? And Peter hadn't told her?

"And when he came to the house," Peter added without prompting.

Theo shot him a disbelieving look. "Really? Don't you have any filter?"

"It's a twin thing," Peter said, sounding sullen. "She's always been able to make me tell her what she wants to know."

"Rafe came to the house? To Mom and Dad's?" How had she not known this? Why hadn't anyone said something? "And you sent him away? Without telling me he was there?" She pressed her hand to her chest, which hurt so badly she wanted to throw up. "*Why*?"

"To protect you," Richard snapped.

"From *Rafe*?" Was he kidding?

"From getting hurt."

She continued to press against her aching chest. "Too late."

"Lil..."

"No. My turn." Wrapping her anger around her like a protective cloak, she gave each of her brothers The Look until they were squirming.

"You had no right to interfere. No matter what you thought you were protecting me from, or what good intentions you convinced yourselves you had. The bottom line is you stuck your noses into my personal, private life and managed to ruin the best thing that ever happened to me. Thank you all very much."

Richard let out an exasperated noise. "You've known the guy for a week, Lil. You can't fall in love in a week."

"I dare you to repeat that gem to Mom and Dad." It was a piece of family lore that their parents had fallen in love at first sight and were just as stupid for each other now as they had been thirty-six years ago.

"He was only hired to watch over you for a few days while the police handled their investigation," Richard continued.

"He wasn't *hired*. Peter played the friendship card and guilted him into doing it."

At first, anyway.

"And then he used that position of trust to get close enough to make a move on you while you were vulnerable."

"Did it ever occur to any of you boneheads it might have been *me* who made a move on *him*?" From the comical looks of shock on their faces, that would be a no. She would have laughed if she weren't so bloody furious.

"Rafe didn't use me. He didn't play on my vulnerability, or take advantage of the situation. And I'm not going to say anything more about our relationship, because I don't owe you or anyone else an explanation for who I see or how I feel. Now." She crossed her arms. "What exactly did you say to him?"

They glanced at each other again before Theo answered. "Basically, we said his job was over and you didn't need him anymore."

Her jaw tightened. "What else?"

The fingers of Peter's hand tapped on his thigh in a rapid staccato. "And, um, he should leave you alone, that you wanted to forget everything that happened in the past few weeks. Emphasis on everything."

I'm going to kill them.

"Is that it?"

Richard was unrepentant. He stuck out his jaw and said, "I told him if he was expecting any kind of payday, he could forget about it. He's not squeezing a single dime from us."

Horror washed over her at his words.

"You...that...*gah*! I don't believe you would say something like that!"

"Lil, come on, what else do you think he was looking for?"

She froze.

"Wow. Just...wow. Nice to know you think I have so little to offer a guy that my *money* is the only thing he might be interested in."

"That isn't—"

"Shut up, Richard. Just *shut up*." Seething, she looked at the brothers she'd once admired more than anyone in the world. "You three have got to be the biggest bunch of monkey butts in the freaking universe. Just stay the hell *out of my life*!"

More furious and hurt than she'd ever been before, she pushed past Theo and stormed down the hall to her bedroom, slamming the door for good measure. How could they do that? Bad enough they'd interfered, but the things they said to Rafe were inexcusable. Looking for a payday? Rafe? *Seriously?*

She needed to talk to him. She had to let him know her brothers had acted without her knowledge, and that none of what they'd said had come from her. No wonder he wasn't returning her calls. He must be thinking she was some kind of massive bitchzilla planning to give him even more grief.

Maybe she should take a page out of Rafe's own playbook. She could go to his parents' house and see if he was staying there. That way, she could talk to him in person. Look him in the eye and make him listen to the truth. Or if he wasn't there, she could at least find out where he was staying.

Yes. Perfect.

Except...she'd come with Peter, which meant she didn't have a car to get there with. And she didn't know where the Delgados lived. Or if they'd even open the door if she found out. They might turn her away, just like her brothers had done to Rafe.

"Damn it." She pinched the bridge of her nose to ease the ache growing behind her eyes. "Freaking brilliant plan there, Lil. Come on, this is supposed to be your superpower. *Think*."

Okay. She didn't know the Delgados' address, but Peter might.

Nope. She was still too pissed to talk to him. And Richard would probably keep him from telling her, anyway.

She could always go to the restaurant and try to plead her case to Mrs. Delgado. Okay, yeah. That might work. She could call an Uber and...nope, she didn't have her phone.

Oh wait, her phone!

Excited, she turned to the nightstand, but it wasn't on the charger. A quick search located it on the dresser, still in the purse she'd used the night of the art show. And it was dead.

"Of course it is."

With a sigh, she tossed it on the bed. A pang of longing and loss hit her as she stared at the rumpled sheets. On a whim, she grabbed up Rafe's pillow and hugged it to her chest, inhaling deeply to catch his familiar spicy scent.

Still holding the pillow, she leaned against the windowsill and let the fresh breeze ripple over her face, cooling the last of the fury-fueled heat still stinging her cheeks. There had to be some way to get to Bayamo. Maybe she could convince one of the bodyguards sitting down in the garage to give her a lift.

Yeah, probably not.

As she was calculating in her head how long it might take her to walk there, she caught the faint strains of music in the air coming from somewhere below her window. Her body jolted.

Rafe.

If the police had released her apartment from being a crime scene, it made sense they would have done the same to his. Which meant he was probably down there, just one floor below, right at that very minute.

Her heart did a little tap dance at the thought.

There was a soft knock on the door. "Lillian? Can we please talk?"

Damn.

If she tried to go downstairs to talk to Rafe now, her brothers would probably follow, and things could get ugly. But if she didn't go, she might miss her best chance to fix what her brothers' meddling had broken between them.

That left her with only one option.

She looked out the open window to the fire escape and swallowed against a suddenly dry mouth. Maybe she could convince her brothers to let her go down and talk to him alone without having to resort to such drastic measures. They might be rational, understanding adults about it, right?

"Lillian?" Another knock, less soft this time, indicating the baton had passed from peace-maker Theo to self-righteous Richard. "If you'd stop acting like a child and listen to reason, you'd see that we were right to do what we did." The doorknob rattled, making her glad she'd taken the extra second to lock it. "Open the door, Lil."

Or maybe they wouldn't.

Without giving herself time to think about how crazy it was, she slipped off the now black and soggy plastic booties and climbed out onto the fire escape. Her breath seized in her lungs. This was a whole lot worse in the light of day, when she could see all the way to the ground.

All the very, *very* long way to the ground.

Inching her way down the ladder, she tried and failed to keep her mind off how much like a squished bug on a windshield she'd be if she were to slip. Each time her foot left a rung, she chanted under her breath, "Don't fall. Don't fall. Don't fall."

Finally, her feet found the third-floor landing outside of Cris's open window, where the music she'd heard was drifting out of. At least she hadn't wasted the soul-sucking trip for nothing. After prying her fingers off the ladder railing, she lurched over to grab the windowsill with a sigh of pure relief.

"Never again. Ground floor apartments only from now on. Screw the view."

She climbed through the window, barely resisting the urge to kiss the carpeted floor once she was safely inside. Cris stood on the other side of the bed by the dresser with a bemused expression, a stack of sloppily folded t-shirts in his hands. On the bed was a half-full suitcase.

She waggled her fingers in an awkward greeting.

"Um, hi. Sorry to just barge in like this without knocking..."

"Yeah, well, you can barge right back out the same way." He gave a chin-tip toward the window.

Not a chance in hell. He'd have to physically pick her up and push her out.

Which, given the stormy expression he wore, wasn't out of the question.

"You look good. I'm so glad you're okay after what happened." No response. Okay, then. To hell with the niceties. "Look, I came down to see Rafe. I need to talk to him."

He snorted and tossed the shirts into the suitcase.

"And he needs to not have some rich-bitch use him and tell him pretty lies to get what she wants and then break his stupid heart when she's done slumming." He turned back to his dresser, slamming one drawer and opening the one below it. "He's not here, anyway. Just go away and leave him alone."

Slumming?

Pain twisted in her gut, and she shot a malevolent glare at the ceiling. They were *so* going to pay for this.

"Whatever you think I said or did to him, I didn't. That was my dumbass brothers. And I just found out about it, like, two minutes ago."

"Whatever." He dumped a handful of socks on top of the tees.

"Look, I get that you don't want to believe me, but it's the truth. I've been trying to get Rafe on the phone for the past two days." She groaned in frustration. "If he'd just returned one of my calls, we would have *both* known what my brothers were up to."

If she hadn't been so well versed in sneaky brothers, she might have missed the look that streaked across his face. Her eyes narrowed. "Cris?"

"What?" He refused to meet her gaze, making a show of zipping up the suitcase even though it was far from full.

"Why do I get the feeling I'm not the only one who's had brothers meddling in my business?" She thought of snotty Isabella on the phone earlier. "And sisters, maybe?"

"I don't know what you're talking about."

He was a worse liar than Peter.

"Uh-huh." She went around the bed and stood in front of him, arms crossed, wearing all of her anger and frustration on her face like a flag of war.

"Take me to Rafe. Now."

Chapter 21

Well, that didn't suck as much as it could have.

Pulling into his parents' driveway, Rafe turned off his truck but didn't get out right away. Once he went inside, he'd be swarmed by whichever of his family was home and not have a moment's peace.

Instead, he sat listening to the engine tick as he considered the way the past few hours had played out. When he left for the precinct, he'd been convinced he wouldn't still have his badge when he returned. Early morning summonses to HQ were never good.

Especially after a shooting.

While on leave and under evaluation for reinstatement.

Psych evaluation.

Yeah, he'd gone in with expectations of hearing *fuck you very much, turn in your badge, there's the door.* Instead, he'd gotten some encouraging words from the brass and an hour with Dr. Wong that, for the first time, actually felt like it helped him in sorting through the tangle of emotions he'd been dealing with for the past year.

According to her, it wasn't his near-death experience that had him all twisted up inside his head. It was whether he'd held off shooting Fernando because he didn't have it in him to pull the trigger when he needed to. That he didn't have the nerve to do his job.

Saturday night seemed to have resolved that dilemma for him.

So, rather than returning home disgraced and unemployed, he

was instead cautiously optimistic that, pending his next physical evaluation, it wouldn't be too much longer before he'd be returning to the job he loved.

Too bad he wasn't having the same kind of luck with the *woman* he loved.

Grimacing at that painful reminder, he got out and headed into the house. Larger and grander than the tiny three-bedroom ranch he and his four brothers and sisters had grown up in, it was still way too small when the entire family was home at the same time.

At least, it felt that way to him. It had only been two days, and he was already feeling the walls close in.

It was like when he'd been recuperating from his injuries all over again. Freaked out by the fire and the shooting, his mother and sisters were all hovering and fetching and helping every chance they got. Not just for him, but for Cris as well.

His brother might be eating it up for the moment, but they were going to drive Rafe right into the loony bin if they didn't give him a little breathing room.

Of course, his cranky-ass attitude had *nothing* to do with the fact the one woman he wouldn't mind doing the cooing and coddling, wasn't. Or that he hadn't talked to her since everything had gone to shit the other night.

By the time he'd gotten to the hospital after giving his statements to first the detectives, then IAB, and then the arson investigators, she'd already been sent home. And when he'd gone to her parents' house to see her later that day, he hadn't made it past the front gates.

Since neither of them had grabbed their phones on the way out of the burning apartment, he'd called Pete to ask for his parents' phone number. Nothing had shocked him more than when his so-called friend had said no.

Except maybe when Pete also refused to give Lillian *his* parents' number so she could at least call him when she was ready.

Things had only gotten nastier from there.

But no matter what shit her brothers spewed, Rafe knew none of it was coming from Lillian. He'd actually been expecting something like this since the night of Theo's party. Her brothers were closing ranks, protecting their little sister. Hell, they were doing everything but pissing in a circle around her to warn him off.

He got it.

He didn't like it, but he got it.

What he *didn't* get was why she still hadn't called. Even if she couldn't find his parents' number on her own—*thanks for shit, Pete old pal*—she could always leave a message at the restaurant.

But Sunday had come and gone without a word, then Monday. And now today was half over with the same disappointing and disturbing silence. He hated to admit it, but his confidence in those words of love she'd given him was getting a little shaky.

The smell of something delicious drew him into the kitchen where his youngest sister, Bella, was sliding a tray of cookies out of the oven. He took a deep breath. "Mmm, chocolate chip. My favorite."

Smiling, she used the spatula she was sliding the cookies onto a cooling rack with to smack his hand as he tried to take one. "*¡Espere!* They're hot."

"That's when they're the best."

He waited until she was busy scooping more dough onto the tray to snatch one up. Juggling the scalding treat hand-to-hand, he responded to his sister's exasperated eye-roll with a kiss on her cheek before taking a bite. The melting chocolate nearly blistered his tongue, but it didn't stop him from devouring the entire thing.

"And everyone says *I'm* the child." Shaking her head, Bella poured him a glass of milk, which he drank down in a few quick gulps.

"*Gracias.*" He wiped the back of his hand across his mouth, eyeing another cookie.

"Ah!" Bella swatted at him again. "If you're that hungry, I'll make you a sandwich."

He might complain about his sisters coddling him, but he'd never say no to one of them offering to make him food.

They were driving him crazy, not stupid.

Dropping another kiss on her cheek, he said, "You were always my favorite sister."

She snorted. "Sure. Until you want something from Bria." Rafe grabbed his chest and gave her a wounded look, making her laugh. "Go. Out of the kitchen and away from my cookies. I'll bring you your sandwich."

"You're too good to me."

"*Eres mi hermano y te amo,*" she replied with a shrug. "I'd do anything for you."

Suddenly, being annoyed about all the care and attention he'd been getting made him feel like an ungrateful shit. "Love you too, Bella."

As he started out of the room, his gaze fell on the telephone sitting on the counter. A big red zero taunted him from the message window. "Oh, um, I didn't get any calls while I was out, did I? Any messages, or...anything?"

She hesitated, then yanked open the refrigerator. "Nope. Sorry."

Something about that small hesitation tickled at his cop instincts, but he shrugged it aside as he went out to the large stone patio off the back of the house. Bella probably just felt bad about giving him news she knew would make him unhappy.

And he was. Very unhappy.

He hadn't realized how much he'd grown to crave Lillian, how integral a part of his life she'd become, until she'd been so abruptly yanked out of it. Leaving him with a sucking chest wound that showed no signs of healing on its own. The only thing that was going to fix it—fix him—was getting her back.

And he couldn't do that until he found a way to fucking talk to her.

Sinking into one of the chairs facing the manicured back yard, he considered his options for making that happen. He could go to the

Beaumont estate again and hope for a different result. He could also try showing up at the gallery, the one place he knew she'd eventually be.

Or he could cut his losses and admit that everything they'd shared had been just heat-of-the-moment stuff. Nothing more than powerful chemistry and good sex.

Hot, incendiary, mind-blowing sex.

So hot that just thinking about what they'd done in Lillian's bed after coming home from the art showing had him swelling to half-wood in three seconds flat. And so mind-blowing there was no way he could just chalk everything they'd shared up to great sex and walk away. Not without a fight. She was worth more than that.

They were worth more than that.

"Rafe?"

His head whipped around, wondering if he'd imagined her voice because he was thinking about her. But no, it was really Lillian, standing at the edge of the patio with an expression that said she wasn't sure of her welcome.

Fair enough. Neither was he.

But then she squared her shoulders and walked toward him. More curious than her sudden appearance was her hand wrapped around Cris's arm as she tugged him along with her.

What the fuck is that about?

"Before you say anything, like how you don't want to talk to me and I should turn my skanky ass around and leave, I need to tell you that I just found out my oh-so helpful brothers have been keeping you from getting in touch with me, not to mention telling you all kinds of shitty lies I swear to God I never once even thought, much less said, so please, *please* believe me."

"Wow. All in one breath. Impressive." He fought but couldn't control a grin as he stood up to face her. "Skanky ass?"

She threw her free hand in the air. "That's the part you heard? Seriously?"

"No, I heard the whole thing."

"And?"

"And I already figured most of that out already." Her face morphed through several expressions before settling on disgruntled. Probably that he'd stolen the impact of what she expected to be a huge bombshell.

Then her eyes narrowed. "Did you also happen to figure out that all of the noses getting stuck into our business don't belong to just *my* family?"

"The hell you say!"

She looked smug. "Guess not." She gave Cris a little push. "Go ahead. Tell him."

Cris looked about as miserable as he had when he came home from the hospital. Rafe pushed aside the guilt of that and focused on the implication of what Lillian was saying. "Cris?"

"It's not like we *did* anything," Cris muttered, refusing to meet his eyes.

"No, it was more like what they *didn't* do," Lillian said, scowling. "Like tell me the truth about whether or not you were home when I called, or give you any of the messages I left."

"You called?"

There was a flash of hurt in her eyes. "You really thought I didn't?"

"Did you think I hadn't called *you*?" He nodded when she looked away. "It's okay. We both had people we trusted lie and make us doubt ourselves, and each other. Why that is, I'm still trying to figure out," he added, giving Cris a look that made him squirm. "But believe me, I'm planning to get to the bottom of it."

His brother closed his eyes and uttered a heartfelt curse. "We wanted to stop her from making your life miserable."

"Miserable?" Lillian exchanged a confused look with Rafe. "And how was I doing that?"

"I heard what your brother said to him on the phone," Cris said, getting angry. "He was Rafe's friend, but because of you, he treated him like shit. Like he wasn't good enough for you. The precious little heiress." His lip curled on the sarcastic words.

Lillian winced and threw Rafe an apologetic look before saying to Cris, "Yeah, well, sometimes brothers can be morons."

Seeing the exact moment Cris realized she wasn't just referring to her own brothers, Rafe stepped in before things got nasty.

"*Hermano*, while I appreciate you were trying to help, you should have come to me first and found out what *I* wanted. Didn't you think the fact I was always asking if anyone called might mean that I *wanted* to talk to her?"

"Maybe," Cris muttered, staring at his feet.

The door to the kitchen opened and Bella breezed through, holding a plate with a sandwich the size of Manhattan on it. "I wasn't sure if you wanted turkey or—" She came to an abrupt halt. "What is that *puta* doing here?"

The vulgarity from his normally sweet sister took him by surprise.

But maybe it shouldn't have. That slight hesitation in answering his question before made perfect sense now. He crossed his arms, his level of pissed going up a few more notches. "Watch your mouth when you're talking about my girlfriend."

Bella gasped. "Your *girlfriend*? Rafael, you can't be—"

"Did you or did you not lie right to my face a few minutes ago when I asked if anyone had called for me?"

"But...you don't...it wasn't like that."

"No? Then how was it?"

Bella sputtered for a few seconds. "She almost got you killed. You and Cristiano both!"

"I know," Lillian said. "And I'll never be able to forgive myself for that."

"Oh, please. Poor you." Bella rolled her eyes. "If you'd cared at all, you never would have asked him to get involved in the first place."

"It was never supposed to be dangerous," Lillian said in a small voice.

"And she didn't ask," Rafe said, clarifying what Lillian hadn't. "I had to convince her to let me help."

"Yeah, I'm sure she put up a real fight about it."

"Enough." Holding onto his temper by the very edges, he gave his siblings a hard look. "I get that you both did what you did because you were under some misguided impression I needed protecting from this horrible, wicked woman who somehow managed to Svengali me into doing something entirely against my will."

He shot Lillian a quick look and caught her rolling her lips together to contain a grin. That eased the raw ache in his chest just a little. Things weren't entirely ruined between them if she could still smile.

"But don't make the mistake of thinking I either need or want your interference in my personal life. You both crossed the line. The meddling stops right here, right now. Got it?"

Cris muttered an agreement, refusing to meet his angry gaze, but Isabella tossed her head back, fire in her eyes.

"You would pick *her*? Over *family*?"

"It shouldn't have to be a choice, Bella. You're the one making it that way."

Her nostrils flared. In Spanish she said, "You're making a big mistake, Rafael. Can't you see she's using you? Do you really think she won't drop you like yesterday's garbage the second her fancy-assed parents decide it's time for her to marry one of her own kind and start the next generation of little lily-white billionaires?"

There was too deep a vein of pain in her words for them not to have some personal meaning to her. How had he missed something as important as a love affair that had failed badly enough to leave the wounds he could now see in her eyes?

The fact he'd been too absorbed in his own personal drama these past months to be there to protect his baby sister hurt. Which was why his voice was gentle when he replied.

"Not everyone sees things through those kinds of colored lenses.

Please don't judge Lillian by someone else's mistake."

Bella bit her lip. "She'll hurt you. Just wait."

"No, she won't." He switched to English again. "I love her."

Blinking back tears, Bella said, "That will only make it hurt worse." She turned and disappeared into the house, not sparing Lillian a glance.

Looking between Rafe and Lillian, Cris hooked his thumb toward the house. "Yeah, I think I'm gonna..." He escaped the same way their sister had gone.

Leaving the two of them staring at each other with far too much distance between them.

"She looked kind of upset." Lillian's fingers twisted together in anxious knots. "Shouldn't you go after her?"

He shook his head. "I think I'd make things worse if I did." But the fact she'd thought of his sister after everything Bella had said and done made him love her that much more. "I'm sorry my siblings meddled."

"Me too. I mean, I'm sorry mine did too."

And still, neither of them moved closer.

"So." More finger-twisting. "What happens now?"

"How about now you kiss me?"

She responded to the almost-dare the way he'd hoped, throwing her chin up and saying, "How about *you* kiss *me*?"

Then they were both in motion, meeting somewhere in the middle, arms wrapping around each other. Mouths seeking, devouring, conquering, until the need for air made them pull apart, gasping and hungry for more.

"God, I missed you," she groaned as he laid tiny kisses along her cheek and down to her chin before circling back to her mouth again.

"I missed you, too. I want you," he growled against her lips, "naked and wet for me."

"Well, we're already halfway there." She kissed his chin when he groaned. "Where can we go to take care of the other half?"

His pants felt two sizes too small for the erection her throaty words caused. "*Bruja*, you're killing me." He took her hand and started towing her toward the house.

Remembering his sister and brother inside, he changed course and started down the path around the house to the driveway. For what he had planned, they needed a lot more privacy than his bedroom walls could provide.

Lillian was so quiet once he got the truck moving, he had a moment of worry she was having second thoughts. But a quick glance showed she was watching him with a hungry look and barely restrained desire. The quiet was the calm before the storm that would be unleashed once they were behind closed and locked doors somewhere.

His foot pressed harder on the gas.

For that look on her face, he'd risk a ticket.

Pulling into the lot behind the all-suites hotel on the edge of town, Rafe helped Lillian out of the truck, stealing a kiss before leading her inside, savoring the feel of her hand in his. He headed straight to the elevator and up to the second floor.

It wasn't until he pulled the key card out of his wallet when they reached his room that he realized Lillian was looking at him with a question in her eyes.

"Your father booked rooms for everyone the fire displaced. I haven't gotten around to moving into it yet." Because he'd wanted to be somewhere she could find him if—when—she came looking.

And she had.

Which made dealing with all his family's smothering attention worth it.

But a sliver of awkwardness made him hesitate before opening the door.

"Is this too weird? Being here, I mean, in a room your father is paying for? We can go someplace else. There's another hotel a couple of blocks over."

In answer, she plucked the key card from his hand and inserted it in the lock. Pushing the door open, she went in first, sending him a challenging glance over her shoulder. He caught the door just before it slammed shut and followed, heart thumping like a runaway truck picking up speed on a downhill grade.

By the time he put out the Do Not Disturb sign and slid the security lock home, Lillian had managed to discard every bit of clothing she wore. Everything except the silky black panties and matching bra which did more to frame her magnificent breasts than cover them.

Dios.

She teased one bra strap off her shoulder as she wet her bottom lip. "Is this naked enough?"

The predator instinct she aroused in him with her teasing snapped its leash and had him stalking toward her in long, rangy strides.

"Not even close. Take it all off. Now."

Tucking her thumb under the other strap, she toyed with it. Just like she was toying with him. "Or what?"

"Or I'm going to spank that pretty ass of yours until you beg me to take you." He couldn't rip his gaze from the creamy delights that all but spilled out into view from the loosened garment. His voice turned raspy. "And then I will."

He loved the flush that streaked over her bare skin. His little pixie was as turned on by that idea as he was, even though she pursed her lips like she was unsure.

So, she wanted to play, did she?

He could oblige.

"One."

She put a finger to her mouth as though in deep thought.

"Two."

Her lips closed around the tip of her finger while her eyes sparkled with a challenge he couldn't ignore any more than he could the jerk of his cock.

The hell with three.

Chapter 22

S he saw the exact instant when Rafe's restraint shattered.

Not that she hadn't expected it. Or wanted it. But the sight of that magnificent wild streak he kept so tightly bottled inside breaking free was worth any effort it took to achieve. The man might be sexy as hell, but Rafe unleashed?

That was the stuff of erotic fantasies.

Hers, anyway.

Watching him stalk toward her like a panther on the prowl for its next meal, she barely had time to gasp in surprise as he scooped her up. He carried her to the bedroom, deposited her on the bed, and went down on top of her as he sealed his mouth to hers. She groaned into his mouth as he picked up right where they'd left off in his parents' backyard, driving her crazy with his wicked and oh-so talented tongue.

With other men, kissing had been something that went along with sex. With Rafe, it was a sex act all on its own. The man knew how to drive her wild, then back off just enough to have her close to weeping with want until he came back to give her more.

And that didn't even take into account all the naughty, oh-so tantalizing things he was doing with his hands.

Like unhooking her bra and sliding it along her upraised arms until it was twisted around her wrists, loosely binding them together. Her heart kicked into the next gear as moisture pooled between her legs, saturating her already soaked panties. She groaned against Rafe's mouth.

"*Querida*, you have no idea what it does to me when you make that sound." He growled when she nipped at his lower lip.

"Probably the same thing it does to me when you make that one." She knew she was playing with fire. But Rafe brought out a side of her she'd never gotten to explore before. One he seemed to enjoy as much as she did.

"You'll pay for that."

Her ass cheeks tingled in anticipation.

Her excitement must have shown on her face, because he groaned again, pressing his forehead to hers. Even through his pants, she could feel the steel-hard press of him against the V of her thighs.

She wet her lips. "Big talk from a man who still has all his clothes on."

A slow grin split his handsome face. "Was that a challenge I just heard?"

In answer, she gave him the same air-kiss she'd used to taunt him in the past. Only this time there wasn't any door closing between them. There was no escape. She was at his complete and utter mercy.

A fact that, judging by the way his already hard erection seemed to swell against her, aroused them both.

When he stood and started taking off his clothes, he did it with such slow deliberateness that by the time he was down to his stretchy black boxer briefs, Lillian was panting like a racehorse after the Kentucky Derby.

He knew exactly what he was doing too, the rat, because he never once broke eye contact. His focus was all on her and her reactions to what he was doing.

Stripping for Rafe had always felt sensual. Watching him strip for her, though, was a hundred times more erotic. When his hands eased that last barrier down his legs, his erection bouncing free and straining toward his bellybutton, all her girly bits started to party in anticipation.

At that moment, a good, stiff breeze would have sent her over the edge.

Something Rafe seemed to sense, because he ignored the part of her needing relief the most when he rejoined her on the bed. Instead, he focused on the rest of her body, starting at her bound wrists and *slowly* inching his way down. By the time he got to her feet, every nerve ending in her body was singing the halleluiah chorus despite the fact he'd avoided every obvious erogenous zone along the way.

The panting had turned to moaning as she squirmed under his unrelenting sensual assault. If she didn't get to come in the next ten seconds, swear to God she would twitch her way right out of her skin.

"Rafe, *please.*"

All it took was the touch of his tongue on her clit to send her screaming over the edge. Her entire body shook with the force of the orgasm. When she finally came back down to Earth, she saw Rafe waiting between her legs, watching her as he stroked his erection. Her gaze focused on the drop of moisture the motion squeezed from his tip.

She licked her lips. "Yes. Now."

"No. Not yet." He gave himself one last stroke before letting go. "I'm not nearly done here yet."

Her words of protest were sucked away when his mouth found her already swollen folds. If she thought his tongue knew wicked ways with her mouth, that was nothing compared to the way he played her body like a maestro, wringing another orgasm out of her in record time as he slid two long fingers deep into her and found her G spot.

Once more, she came down from her orgasmic high to find him watching.

Waiting.

Stroking.

It was too much.

Reaching out her bound arms toward him, she said, "Love me,

Rafe. Please."

Don't ever let me go.

As always, he seemed to hear what she didn't say out loud. He untangled the bra and tossed it aside, freeing her before he stroked his fingertips over her face. "You are *mi corazón*, my heart. My soul. My other half. How could I exist without you?"

Quickly sheathing himself in the condom from his wallet, he laced his fingers with hers and pressed into her with one swift thrust. Her body, already heavy with pleasure, welcomed him home. His gaze never left hers and they strained against each other in a slow tempo that drove them both wild with the need for the other to be the first to go.

Finally, they both went over.

Together.

⚬

"I have a bone to pick with you."

Still lethargic from the orgasm that had nearly ripped his spine from his body, Rafe stroked a hand over Lillian's shoulder. From where she was nestled against his side, he didn't have a clear view of her face. But her voice sounded more dreamy than pissed, so he figured he couldn't be in too much trouble.

Especially not after the past hour, and three back-to-back orgasms.

"And what would that be?"

"You went back into a burning building for a *bunch of paintings*."

With everything else that had happened, he'd forgotten about that.

"I guess that means you found them. Were they damaged at all? You weren't sure if the panic room was fireproof, so *mmph*."

Her hand over his mouth, Lillian rose up on an elbow to look down at him, her expression stern. "You risked your life. For some stupid paintings. You *idiot*."

Kissing her hand before he removed it, he replied, "It was a calculated risk. I had a few minutes before things got too dicey."

Actually, things had gotten kind of dicey long before those minutes had been up. Not that he'd ever admit it to Lillian, who was shaking her head at him, a look of disbelief etching lines beside her kiss-swollen mouth.

"Don't you ever, *ever* do something like that again, do you hear me? I couldn't stand it if...if something happened to you."

The tiny hitch in her voice nearly killed him. "I have a dangerous job, *querida*. I'll be in dangerous situations again. Risk my life again. It's part of the package that comes with me being who I am. You know that, right?"

She sniffled. "Of course, I do. But that's different. That's your job. This...this was about saving *things*. *You* are worth more than *things*."

"It was a year's worth of your hard work."

"I don't care if it was an entire lifetime of work! You're still worth more to me, dumbass."

She really meant that. The sheen of tears that darkened her melted-chocolate eyes was proof. She honestly didn't give a rat's furry butt crack about the paintings, not when compared to putting his life in jeopardy. It was a humbling feeling.

But he still would have done the same thing all over again, because it hadn't been about the paintings. It had been about Lillian and her dream. He'd put himself on the line every damn time for that.

For her.

Putting his hand on the back of her neck, he brought her down for a kiss. His thumb encountered the edge of the bandage, and his stomach roiled at the memory of that bitch holding the knife to Lillian's vulnerable throat. "This should never have happened. I should have been able to stop her sooner."

"Are you kidding? If you hadn't shown up when you did, she would have killed me. If you hadn't gotten her talking, she would have killed me. If you hadn't shot her…" She shuddered. "Trust me. If it's a choice between being killed or getting a few stitches, I'll take Option B every day of the week." She nipped his chin. "Don't let my brothers get inside your head. You saved me. Full stop. Period." Another nip came on his earlobe.

"What are you doing?"

"Thanking you." *Nip.* "Distracting you." *Nip.* "Is it working?"

He groaned as her teeth grazed his right nipple. "*Madre de Dios.*"

"I'll take that as a *yes, please, may I have some more.*"

The groan turned into a laugh. "Wicked woman." He grabbed her arms and rolled, putting her under him. He stared into her laughing eyes. "I don't care what your brothers, or my sisters, or anybody else has to say about us. I love you."

He felt her breath catch, saw her eyes turn serious. "I love you," he repeated. That was the one thing he wanted to make certain she had zero doubts about. "Nothing else matters to me. Except whether or not you feel the same."

"You know I do." As if sensing that he needed to hear the words, she said with slow deliberation, "I love you, Rafael Delgado. You came steamrolling into my life, messed up my plans, and snuck right into my heart. You're the best thing that's ever happened to me."

Dios, this woman.

Stroking her cheek with the back of his fingers, he said, "You are *everything* to me, my sweet little pixie. There isn't a single part of you I don't adore."

Lillian grinned. "Well, maybe not my pre-coffee bitch-face."

"Even that."

"Wow." She pressed her cheek into his fingers like a cat. "You must really love me, then."

"I do, *mi corazón.* I truly do."

Her eyes took on that spark of challenge he could never resist. "Prove it."

He did.

Epilogue

I t was really happening.

Standing in the middle of the gallery, Lillian still couldn't quite believe it. So many years, so many dreams, and now everything she'd ever wished for was right here at her fingertips.

Literally.

Squeezing Rafe's hand as much to keep herself anchored as for the enjoyment of touching him, she gave him a smile that had his jaguar-green eyes darkening.

"Don't you dare start something we can't finish, *mi pequeña duendecilla*," he whispered when she stroked a fingernail down the center of his palm. "This is your night. We're not disappearing into the storage room for another quickie while you've got guests who want to meet you and buy your amazing paintings."

The reminder of the intense ten minutes they'd spent in that storage room during the setup for the show sent a flash of heat through her body. Not her most professional moment, but she wouldn't have traded it for the world. Especially not the look of envy on Felicity Landis's face when they'd emerged, slightly disheveled and thoroughly relaxed.

It was a good thing she didn't work here anymore, or she would have been out of a job.

"You're right. It *is* my night." She leaned closer until her lips were against his ear. "Which means I get to have whatever I want." The tip of her tongue touched the outer shell of his ear, causing him to growl.

"Lillian…"

"Later." She pulled back and gave him a smile of promise.

Which he returned with interest. "Count on it, *bruja*."

The way he called her a witch in that gravelly baritone always sent a shiver of something wicked through her. Oh yeah, later was going to be *spectacular*. Especially when he found out about the little surprise she had for him.

Her nipples with their new piercings throbbed in anticipation.

"Lil!"

She turned and found herself engulfed in a hug from Thea that knocked the breath out of her.

"Oh my God, Lil! Your stuff. It's *amazing*!" She smacked Lillian's arm. "Why didn't you ever show me any of these? They're incredible!"

The effusive praise from her bestie was like extra whipped cream on top of her spiced hot chocolate. It made a good thing even better. "Thanks, T. That means a lot."

"She's right." Doyle leaned down to kiss Lillian's cheek before shaking Rafe's hand. "Your paintings are amazing. In fact, she's already picked out the one she wants to hang in my office."

Shock and delight had Lillian's cheeks heating. "What? Seriously? No, you don't have to do that."

"We're not talking about a pity purchase here," Thea said. "I'd want to hang it no matter who the artist was. It's not only the right hues and size for the space, it'll also make sure that even when he's at work, he'll be thinking of me." She gave her husband the kind of smile that used to make Lillian uncomfortable to witness.

Now, she understood, because she felt the same way every time she looked at Rafe.

"Wow. Okay. Which painting?" Because she'd take it off the wall and give it to them right now. No way was she taking a dime from her friends.

"*Lady Dreaming*," Doyle replied, giving Thea the same soft look of adoration.

Well, crap.

Of course, they'd have to want *that* one. It made sense, since Thea's old security name had been the Lady. But as much as she hated to deny them the painting, especially after all that praise, neither *Lady Dreaming* nor *Lady Playing*, the piece Rafe dragged down the fire escape just in case his panic room idea didn't work, were for sale.

Rafe had already claimed them both.

She'd agreed to include them in the show as "on loan" only because Felix had begged her to. An occasion she'd enjoyed a lot more than she probably should have.

As she was trying to come up with a polite way to say no to her friend, Rafe put his arm around her and said, "I'm sorry, but that piece is already spoken for."

Grateful to him for doing the dirty work, Lillian leaned into him a little more. "But I can paint you one similar, if you like."

The disappointment in Thea's expression morphed to interest. "That would be fantastic. In fact..." The interest became speculation. "What would you think about doing commissioned pieces for some of my decorating jobs?"

What did she think? The idea rocked her. She was still coming to grips with being considered a real artist. Having her first show. But to do commissioned pieces for a highly respected decorating firm?

Holy freaking awesome.

"Um, it sounds amazing." And scary. And crazy perfect.

"Good. We'll talk."

"But not tonight," Doyle said.

"No, not tonight. Tonight is about Lil and her amazing paintings." Thea hugged her again. "God, I'm so proud of you!"

"That really means a lot, T. Thanks." She had to sniffle a little to hold back the stupid rush of emotion that came from her friend's words.

"Ah, we're gonna go grab you ladies something to drink." Rafe passed her his handkerchief. "Be right back."

She mouthed "chicken" to him with a smile as she dabbed at her eyes. He grinned and didn't deny it. Even after five months together, he still hated to deal with her tears, infrequent as they might be.

The crowd parted like prairie grass for the two tall, broad-shouldered men as they cut across the gallery floor toward the bar set up in the back corner. People probably didn't even realize they were doing it. Rafe and Doyle were the lions in a room full of well-dressed sheep whose hindbrains knew who the predators were despite the suits and ties.

"God, we did good, didn't we?" Thea sighed, tucking her arm around Lillian's waist and tipping her head against hers.

"We really did." Sometimes she still couldn't believe how lucky she was.

"Is this a private lovefest or can any old body join in?"

Laughing, Lillian accepted a breath-stifling hug from Des, then watched with amusement as he did the same to Thea. The man showed affection the same way he did everything else, with super-sized enthusiasm.

She gave a huge smile to the man standing behind Des. "Doctor Antonoff. I mean, Michael. Hi." He kissed her cheek, the restrained greeting neatly balancing Des's over-the-top one. "Thank you so much for coming."

"Are you kidding? It's all Des has talked about for weeks now. No way would we miss your big night." His surfer look had been tamed with a little hair product and a recent shave. That and the suit gave him a more polished appearance than he'd worn the night he treated her in the emergency room. "We haven't had a chance to look at everything yet, but I have to say, what we've seen so far is fantastic."

"Beyond fantastic." Des made a dramatic sweep of his arm. "Lillian, darling, this is..." His arm dropped, and so did his voice, becoming the honest, personal friend rather than the flamboyant showman. "Well, it's you, kitten. Every brushstroke. Every highlight and shadow. These are all you."

She had to swallow. Hard. No one besides Rafe had ever gotten how much of herself she wove into each of her works. Standing in a room full of her paintings while strangers looked at them kind of felt like being naked.

Or at the very least, in her underwear.

"Thank you," she said to both of them, fighting back another sniffle. She was not going to get weepy again, damn it. Waterproof mascara only held up so long before raccoon-eyes became a real possibility.

Lucky for her, Des's attention was snagged by a waiter passing with a tray of something that smelled incredible even to her jittery stomach.

"Oh, please tell me Mama Delgado catered tonight, or my taste buds might never forgive you."

She laughed. "You and your taste buds will go home very happy." Seeing his attention was still fixed on the roving waiter, who had stopped to offer one of the tasty tidbits to another guest, she rolled her eyes at Michael. "Please, go feed him before he does something embarrassing, like start to drool."

Des flicked a finger over the corners of his mouth. "Too late."

As the men set off after the waiter, who had moved off in the other direction, Thea gave a happy sigh. "They are so perfect for each other."

"They really are. And I take full credit."

She'd gotten a vibe from Dr. Antonoff the night he treated her. So, when the time came to get her stitches out, she'd gone back to him rather than her own doctor, and asked Des to go with her for some metaphoric hand holding. The minute Michael entered the exam room, the interest level on both sides jumped off the charts. It had been all she could do not to give a fist-pump.

She really loved being right.

"So, how does it feel to be back here as the featured artist rather than an employee?"

"Weird. It's a good weird, but it's still..."

"Weird?" Thea finished with a wry grin.

"Yeah." And a little surreal.

After the fire, she'd only stayed at the gallery long enough to train her replacement. It was Rafe who'd given her the guts to commit to painting full time. He'd told her that until she treated it like the career it was, rather than a hobby, nobody else would either.

Like he was about so many things, he'd been right.

Even her parents had come around. Her father actually bragged about "my daughter the artist" to his friends now, which kind of blew her mind. She glanced around the room and found them in a group that included Thea's parents and Roman Reynolds, of all people.

The sight had her shaking her head. After all the horrible things she'd thought about him, it turned out the only thing Roman was guilty of was a severe case of being Felicity's nephew. Felix had broken his own anti-nepotism rule by hiring him, and it had come back to bite him in the butt when Roman—or rather, Roger—proved to be a lot less experienced in the art field than he'd led his aunt and uncle to believe.

But for as much as he sucked at being an art dealer, Roman was outstanding as the Landis Gallery's new receptionist. Go figure.

Thea hip-bumped her out of her thoughts. "What're you thinking about so hard?"

"Just...I still can't quite wrap my head around it all. This is my dream. And...it's almost perfect."

"Only almost?"

She shrugged. "I know it's tough for Mellie to get away when school's in session." Not to mention the fact Boulder held some pretty awful memories for her. Their friend had only been back to visit a handful of times in the year and change since she'd moved to South Dakota. "It just would have been the icing on my cake if she could have been here."

Thea's lips curved into a sly grin. "Would that be vanilla or chocolate icing?"

"Huh?" Confused, she turned to see what Thea was looking at behind her and squealed like a little girl. "*Mellie!*"

She hugged the woman who, like them, was wearing one of Des's original dresses. Which meant she'd been the only one in their little circle kept in the dark. "I can't believe you made it! What about school? And the ranch?"

"Like I'd miss your very first show." Amelia rolled her eyes as she pulled back from the hug to make room for her boyfriend, who gave both women a quick, uncomfortable cheek-kiss hello.

"Congratulations, Lillian."

"Thanks, Daryl. And thank you for driving Mellie all the way down here."

True to form, the tall former bodyguard gave a laconic shrug. But it was obvious from the look he gave Amelia he'd move heaven and earth if it would make her happy. Lillian felt a tug in her chest. After a lifetime of crappiness, Amelia deserved that kind of love.

Proof positive money absolutely could not buy happiness.

For any of them.

"The guys are over by the bar," Thea said.

Lillian almost laughed at the relief that crossed Daryl's face as he excused himself. Turning her attention back to Amelia, she said, "You look amazing, Mellie. Life in Hayseed looks like it agrees with you."

It was no lie. No longer dangerously thin and popping antacids like they were candy, the form-fitting dress emphasized her health and fitness. The sun had put streaks in her long blonde hair, and toasted her once-translucent complexion a healthy golden hue, complete with freckles. But it was the happiness that radiated from the inside that showed the most change in her life.

That and...

"Holy shit." Sucking in a breath, she grabbed up Amelia's left hand and stared at the diamond ring sparkling there. "You finally said yes!"

"I finally said yes." Amelia's grin was almost wider than her face as first Lillian, then Thea, hugged her.

"Why didn't you tell us?" Thea asked.

"I didn't want to take away from Lillian's big day. But I also didn't want to take it off, even for one night," she added, sounding sheepish.

"Don't be silly! I wouldn't want you to take it off for even one second. And you putting that poor man out of his misery in no way takes from my day. It only adds to it."

Amelia's smile got even wider with relief. "Thank you."

Flagging down one of the waiters, Thea grabbed them each a glass of champagne. She tipped hers forward in a toast. "To Lil and her triumphant debut."

After they drank, Lillian raised her glass. "To us. The Royal Court. The three girls no one thought would work as friends because we were so different, but look at us now. I can't imagine being closer to blood sisters than I am to the two of you. We've seen each other at our best, and our worst, and everything in between. We've followed our dreams, and our hearts, and they've led us here, to this moment."

She had to pause and clear her throat. "Despite everything we had to go through to get here, the Lady, the Princess, and the Queen have finally gotten their fairytale endings."

"And their princes," Amelia added, making them all laugh.

"And their princes," Lillian agreed. "So, here's to the fairytale." They touched glasses. "May we all get our happily-ever-afters."

And, like in all good fairytales, they did.

Author's Note

Thank you so much for coming along on Lillian and Rafe's story. Lillian was always one of the scene stealers of the series, so I couldn't wait to put her center stage and let her do her thing. And you'll be seeing more of her and that other scene stealer, Des, in future books as well. **The Boulder Beaumonts** series continues in the same world as the Bodyguards books, featuring Lillian's three meddling brothers, Richard, Theo, and Peter. Bringing them to their Armani-clad knees is going to be so much fun!

And if you missed either Thea and Doyle's story, or Amelia and Daryl's, you can catch up by reading ***What the Lady Wants*** and ***Finding Forever***. Just scan the QR code below to visit my website's book page and pick your retailer of choice to get started. While there you can also sign up for my newsletter to be sure you hear about all upcoming book news, contests, and freebies.

Lastly, if you've enjoyed reading any of my books, please consider leaving a rating and/or review. Those are the fuel that keep authors going. Thank you!

Acknowledgements

A million thanks to everyone who helped me with this series, both in its first iteration and now in its new second life. My #GooPooGirls, Lauren Rico, Patty Blount, and Jennifer Gracen, for being my sounding boards, head cheerleaders, and overall best friends a person could wish for. My family, for not making (too much) fun of me for writing "those kissing books." Special *gracias* to my late sister-in-law, Liz (you are so missed!) who helped keep me from mangling Rafe's Spanish too badly. All mistakes there are mine. And especially my husband, Danny, who saw the dream in my heart and gave me the love and encouragement to chase it. *Te adoro, mi amor.*

Also By Nika Rhone

<u>Boulder Bodyguards series</u>
What the Lady Wants
Finding Forever
Can't Help Loving You

<u>Boulder Beaumonts series</u>
Worth Any Price *(coming soon)*

About the Author

Nika Rhone spent her childhood wearing out library cards as she read her way through the extraordinary worlds far beyond her small hometown on Long Island, NY. By her teens, her imagination was taking her places all on its own, forcing her to learn how to type (badly) so she could get all the stories down on paper. After a long love affair with science fiction and fantasy, she finally discovered romance, fell head-over-heels, and now spends her days crafting happily-ever-afters for the characters who still tell their stories faster (and better) than she can type them.

You can keep up with all the latest book news, events, and giveaways by visiting her website www.nikarhone.com and joining her newsletter.

9 781961 713048